samantha christy

Catching Caden

Saint Augustine, FL 32092

This is a work of fiction. Names, characters, places and incidents are either the product of the author's imagination or are used fictitiously, and any resemblance to actual persons, living or dead, business establishments, events or locales is entirely coincidental.

Cover designed by Letitia Hasser | RBA Designs

ISBN-13: 978-1979928953

ISBN-10: 1979928959

For all the travel ball moms who tirelessly and thanklessly devote their time to their kids. Maybe this will give you something to read during practice!

Samantha Christy

Catching Caden

Samantha Christy

Chapter One

Caden

Crack!

I know that sound. I can feel it in my hands. My body. I don't even have to look up to see the ball flying out into the stands. I don't have to look up, because by the time I hit first base, the crowd is telling me everything I need to know. They are telling me I just hit my twenty-sixth home run of the season.

Back in Little League, my coach would make us do a hundred push-ups if we watched the ball instead of running our asses off. I guess that just stuck with me. And now I know that sometimes it's mere inches that make the difference between a home run and an out. Inches between glory and defeat.

As I round second base, I allow myself to glance over beyond left field. It's where I always hit my home runs. My eyes rake over the crowd, looking for the cheering fan who caught the ball. I hope it's a kid. Whenever I know a kid has caught my ball, I send an usher over to get it so I can sign it for him.

It takes a few seconds for me to realize something isn't right. A crowd is gathering. And there is a conspicuous lack of an excited fan holding up my ball in celebration. I look up at the JumboTron to get a closer look at the situation as people rush over to the area. Fans are hovering over some seats, frantically waving park officials towards them.

Shit. My ball must have hit someone. I hope it wasn't a kid.

After I touch home plate and tip my helmet to the rest of the cheering stadium, I go in the dugout and pick up the phone to call the team offices.

"Find out who it hit," I say to whoever answered the phone, shaking my head in disgust knowing how much damage can be done by a hard baseball traveling at over 100 mph.

I hang up and sit on the bench, conflicting feelings of happiness and guilt coursing through me.

Sawyer puts a supportive hand on my shoulder before he picks up his bat and makes his way out onto the field. "Remember the guy I hit last year?" he asks. "Big goose egg on his forehead. He said it was the best thing that ever happened to him because he got to meet me. Don't worry about it, Kessler. I'm sure it'll be okay."

I nod my head. "Yeah, thanks. Good luck out there."

In the next inning, when I put on my catcher's gear and head behind the plate, I look up into the left-field stands to see the commotion has cleared. Brady, who's out on the mound, raises his eyebrows at me. I know what he's asking. He wants to know if I'm focused. I am. I absolutely am.

I'm lucky. I'm able to compartmentalize when I play ball. No matter what goes on in my life, when I'm out on the field, I'm Caden Kessler, major league ball player, #8 on the New York

Nighthawks. I'm not the kid whose mom died his freshman year of college. I'm not the guy who once knocked up a girl only to have her miscarry a week later. I'm not even the man whose sister vanished without a trace his first year in the majors.

I'm all those things, yes. But not when I'm on the field. Not when I'm swinging the bat. And definitely not when I'm catching behind the plate. Out here I'm a robot. A well-oiled machine that I've fine-tuned ever since I was five years old and played in my first T-ball game. Even back then, I knew playing ball was what I was born to do. And nothing was going to stand in my way.

I give Brady a nod as the batter enters the box. Then I do my job. I do it for the remaining seven innings without giving much more thought to who I hit with my ball and what might have happened as a result.

After the game, however, while my teammates celebrate the win, I track down Melanie. Melanie is like our team's 'Girl Friday.' She knows everything about everything and is a woman who knows how to get things done.

She sees me coming and laughs. "Caden Kessler. Somehow I knew I'd be seeing you tonight." She wrinkles her nose in mock disgust. "I was hoping it would be *after* you'd showered, however."

I look down at my dirty uniform and shrug an apology. "Who'd I hit, Melanie?"

She cocks her head and smiles. "Only you Caden," she says. "Anyone else who'd just had a game like you had would have me running their numbers to see how much their stats improved."

"Please tell me I didn't hit a kid," I say, worried.

She searches through the folder she's holding. "I don't think so," she says. "Name's Murphy something-or-other." She pulls out a piece of paper. "Yeah. Murphy Cavenaugh. Doesn't sound like a kid's name to me. More like a retired dairy farmer or something."

"He hurt?"

"Taken away by ambulance," she says with a sigh.

"Shit. Does it say where he was taken?" I ask.

She tells me the name of the hospital and I smile. "Good. My brother-in-law works at that one. Can you get me some stuff to take over right away? A jersey. A ball. Some pictures. Tickets to another game, maybe?"

She glances at her watch. "Now?"

I look down at my uniform again. "Well, not *right* now, but as soon as I get cleaned up. Once he gets cleared to leave the hospital, I might never be able to find him."

"You don't have to do that, you know," she says. "There are warning signs all over the park to watch for flying balls. It's not like you can get sued or anything."

I give Melanie a distasteful look. "I don't care what the damn signs say. *My* ball hit someone and he could be badly injured."

She studies me. "How is it that some nice girl hasn't snagged you yet?"

I laugh. "Because nobody gets past my three-strikes rule."

"Three-strikes rule?" she asks curiously.

"Yeah. You know, three strikes and you're out. I never go out with a girl more than three times."

"Never?"

I shake my head. "Not since I've been a Hawk. You never can tell who to trust."

Concern brings out the wrinkles in Melanie's forehead. "Someone must have really done a number on you."

"I'm just being careful. That's all."

"Careful with what, Caden?" she asks in a motherly tone. "Your johnson or your heart?"

I shrug. "I've got everything I need, Melanie," I say, looking at our surroundings.

"How old are you? You can't be a day over twenty-four."

"I'm twenty-five."

She nods. "You've got time. It's good you're not in a hurry to fall in love. Those who go seeking it, rarely find it anyway."

"Love?" I say, cringing at the word. "Love is overrated. Besides, I've got all the love I need. I love my sister. My nieces. My friends. And baseball—I love baseball. What more could I need?"

She looks down at her wedding ring and then smiles as if she has a secret I'm not privy to. Then she turns me around and gives me a shove in the direction of the clubhouse. "Come find me after you've cleaned up. I'll send you to the hospital with a care package."

Chapter Two

Murphy

Pain. I can't think about anything else but how horrible I feel. My head is throbbing. Everything hurts. And I can't see very well out of my left eye. I feel like I've been hit by a truck, not a tiny baseball.

Tony has been by my side since I was brought to the hospital. He and Kirsten, one of my roommates, rode in the ambulance with me. They are the ones who dragged me to the game. Said it was all part of the celebration they had planned for me landing my first big modeling job.

As my pain meds start to kick in, I begin wondering why they chose to take me there. I don't even like baseball. Kirsten—*she's* the baseball fan. She and Tony. Why didn't they take me to SoHo or something?

Oh, my God! My job! My hand comes up to touch my tender face that feels about twice its normal size. I look around the room and then at Tony. "I need a mirror," I say.

He winces and shakes his head. "Babe, you don't want to see it. It'll only upset you."

Tears escape my eyes, burning the left side of my face where I got stitches. I guess the numbing medication is wearing off. "Is it that bad?" I ask.

Tony stares at me for a second and then looks away. He doesn't have to answer me, I can tell by the look on his face that it's bad.

There's a knock on the door and then the door opens. "Miss Cavenaugh," says a tall man in a white lab coat. "I'm Dr. Benson. I have the results of your CT scan. Shall I go over them with you now?" He looks from me to Tony with raised eyebrows.

"Yes. It's okay, he's my boyfriend."

"Alright then," Dr. Benson says, walking around my bed. "You have a zygomaxillary fracture. That's a fancy way of saying you broke your cheekbone."

I sigh. "It's broken?"

"Yes. There are two kinds of breaks. Displaced and non-displaced. With non-displaced breaks, they heal on their own. But…"

I can hear in his voice that I don't have that kind of fracture. "But that's not the one I have, is it?"

"Unfortunately, no."

"What does that mean?" I ask. "I can't wear a cast on my face. How do you fix it?"

"Surgery."

"Surgery?" I gasp. "On my *face?* But I'm a model. I—I can't … this can't be happening."

I look over at Tony to see him shaking his head. He looks as upset as I am. "What does the surgery entail?" he asks the doctor. "And how long before she can go back to work?"

Dr. Benson flashes a weak smile. "I'll do an open reduction and internal fixation with a titanium plate and screws."

"Oh, my God!" My hand comes up to muffle my cry.

"How big a scar will she have?" Tony asks, now pacing the small hospital room.

"It looks a lot worse than it is. There's a lot of swelling, and it will get worse for the next twenty-four hours before it starts to get better. That's why we'll wait at least a week to do the surgery."

"A week? But I'm supposed to start my job next Thursday." I look up at the doctor, hoping this is all some sick joke. A prank. A twisted dream.

"I'm sorry, Miss Cavenaugh, but I'm afraid if you're a model, you won't be able to work for some time."

Tony kicks the side of a chair and then curses under his breath. Then he repeats his question. "How big a scar, Dr. Benson?"

"The scar from the surgery itself won't be very noticeable. I'll go in through an incision on your hairline, back by your ear. It's probably the scar from your laceration that will cause you the most concern. But if you use sunscreen and take vitamin E, your scar should fade to a pale pink line after a few months or so. Then you will likely be able to cover it with makeup."

"Months?" I cry.

"What if she doesn't have the surgery?" Tony asks. "I mean, maybe it will just heal on its own."

The doctor shakes his head. "A displaced fracture means the bone fragments have shifted. With that comes the risk of impingement of the lower muscles of the eye."

"As in her face will droop or something?" Tony asks in horror.

"Possibly. That and a lot of other painful things she won't want to deal with." Dr. Benson turns back to me. "You need the surgery, Miss Cavenaugh. There really is no other option."

Months. The word floats around in my head as I try to wrap my mind around it. In the matter of one day, my life has changed exponentially. It went from nothing special, to phenomenal, to a pile of crap—all within the last twelve hours. It was just this morning when I got the call that I'd been given my first big modeling job. I was going to be the fresh new face of a high-end clothing line.

And now, this. My face is anything but fresh and new. I'll lose my job. They won't wait for me to heal. Nobody will hire a girl with a scar when there are so many other beautiful women with perfect complexions.

What will I do? How will I pay the rent?

I look up at Tony. "Do you think Joe will hire me back?"

I quit my waitressing job the minute I found out I got the modeling gig. Actually, I didn't really quit as much as I just didn't show up for work today. Then I stupidly let one of my roommates answer Joe's text with some snarky remarks about how I was going to be rich and famous, and that working at a—what was it she said—hole-in-the-wall diner, was beneath me.

Tony raises a sorrowful eyebrow at me. He read the text.

I blow out a long breath. Maybe my roommates will help me out for a while. Surely they will understand that I can't work like this. Then again, most of them are living paycheck-to-paycheck just as I am.

Who am I kidding? I wouldn't be surprised if one of them ended up with the job I am about to lose. My roommates are all self-centered witches. They wouldn't raise a finger to help a sister out if she were drowning.

I only live with them because I have no choice. Coming from Iowa six months ago, I didn't know anyone. It only made sense to connect with others who were also trying to make it in modeling. And at twenty-three, I'm the oldest of the five girls who share the small two-bedroom apartment in the Lower East Side.

They all acted excited when I got the call this morning. But they are terrible actresses. They weren't excited for me at all. In fact, I heard Kirsten, Tori, and Pauline talking in the bathroom. They were wondering how an 'old lady' like me could get a job like that. One of them, I think it was Tori, said I must have slept with someone to get it, which makes her a hypocrite seeing as she's slept with half of New York City. Jamie was the only one who seemed genuinely happy for me. But maybe that's because she got a great contract of her own last week.

"Do you have any other questions for me?" Dr. Benson asks.

"You said I can't have the surgery until next week? Do I have to stay here until then?"

"We need to wait for the swelling to go down before we do surgery. You'll stay here for a night or two and then I'll see you on an outpatient basis until the surgery. Then after the surgery, you'll stay another couple of nights."

"That sounds expensive," I say.

He looks at my chart. "You have insurance, so it shouldn't be too bad."

I'm still on my mom's policy. She's going to freak when she finds out about this. She'll insist I come back to Iowa. It's not going to happen. I refuse to go back a failure. And besides, there is nothing for me there. Not anymore.

I decide not to tell her. I figure she won't get the bills for a month or so. By then, maybe I can get another job.

"I'll check on you tomorrow," Dr. Benson says. He starts to walk out of the room, but then turns around, looking very fatherly. "I know it seems like the end of the world now, Murphy, but it's not. Bones will heal. Scars will fade. It's what you take away from this experience that will help define you as a person. Don't let it break you."

I nod as tears roll down my face, wishing I still had my own dad to give me words of wisdom.

Tony checks his phone and heads toward the door. "I have some things I need to take care of. You get some sleep and I'll catch you later, 'kay?"

I look at the clock on the wall above the door. It's not even eight o'clock. But he's been here for hours. A lot has happened and he must be exhausted. It's not until after he leaves that I realize he didn't kiss me goodbye. I guess he didn't want to risk hurting me.

I wonder if they'll give me more pain meds so I can sleep. So I don't have to think about what I will do when I wake up in the morning with a face as big as a watermelon. So I don't lie here and feel so broken.

Chapter Three

Caden

With a bag full of Hawks stuff in one hand, I duck into the hospital cafeteria to get a quick bite to eat. I never eat before a game. I'm always too nervous. And I was so eager to get here, I plain forgot to grab some food along the way. Hospital food will have to do.

Standing in line, there is a guy in front of me talking on his phone.

"Just ask Kirsten," he says. "She'll tell you I'm not exaggerating. There is no way she'll ever model again. She looks fucking hideous. It's sad really. I mean the *day* she got the call. Her career was over before it even started. I guess I should wait a few days before I toss her to the curb."

"Tony!" I hear a woman call from across the cafeteria.

He quickly ends his phone conversation. "Gotta go, man." He puts his phone in his pocket and draws the girl into his arms, juggling his coffee and candy bar in one hand.

"Hey, babe," he says, planting a kiss on her cherry-red lips.

"Next," the cashier says, beckoning the guy forward. He pays the lady before leading little Miss Red Lips out the cafeteria door.

I take my food with me, scarfing down my sandwich on the way to Murphy Cavenaugh's room. Earlier, I texted my brother-in-law, Kyle, to see if he could tell me where I could find Murphy. As an ER doc, Kyle wasn't on duty when Murphy was brought in a few hours ago, but he's on-call tonight and texted me Murphy's room number on the third floor. Damn. Apparently, the guy was hurt badly enough to get admitted which makes me feel even worse.

The door to room 315 is open, so I stand in the doorway for a second before entering. I look down at my phone to double check the room number, because I'm pretty sure I have the wrong room. Sculpted, tan legs peek out from beneath the bed sheets and I can see waves of long blonde hair cascading down the front of the patient's hospital gown. I can't see the patient's face from behind her magazine, but my guess is that I definitely have the wrong room. This is no old dairy farmer.

The magazine gets flung across the room and the woman on the bed, who I can now see has a terribly injured face, screams before breaking down in sobs.

I try to make my escape, knowing I'm in the wrong place, but the handles of the bag I'm holding choose this very second to break, and the bag falls down, spilling the contents at my feet.

I look over at her in apology for invading her privacy as she tries to wipe tears from the side of her face that isn't damaged.

"Oh, sorry," she says, looking horrified. "I wasn't screaming at you."

"No, it's me who's sorry. I'll just pick up my things and leave you alone. I must have the wrong room. I was looking for a Mr. Cavenaugh."

Her one good eye narrows, and she winces as if it hurts like a mother to make that small facial movement. "Um, I'm obviously not a 'mister,' but my name is Cavenaugh," she says. "Are you one of my doctors?"

I laugh as I clean up my mess and pack everything back into the bag as best I can. "No. Definitely not a doctor, for which you should be grateful seeing as I just spilled everything on the floor."

She attempts to smile, and even behind the damage on her face, I can tell she has a beautiful smile.

"I'm looking for a guy named Murphy," I say.

She points to her chest. "I'm Murphy. But I'm not a guy."

I look to where her fingers are pointing. No. She is definitely not a guy.

"*You're* Murphy?" I ask. "Murphy Cavenaugh?"

"The one and only," she says. "At least I think so, but I haven't Googled my name in a while so I can't be sure."

I take in her face and it all makes sense now. *Oh, God.* The entire left side of her face is battered. There is a deep reddish-purple bruise in the exact shape of a goddamn baseball, and there are fresh stitches right below her swollen-shut eye. *Shit.*

I walk into her room. "Then I'm afraid I owe you a big apology," I say.

"Apology for what?"

"I'm Caden Kessler," I tell her.

She stares at me blankly. "I'm sorry. You say your name as if I should know who you are. But you'll have to forgive me, because I don't. Are you from my agency?" Her face falls into a frown. "Oh no, please tell me you haven't been sent here to fire me."

"Agency?"

"My modeling agency."

Double shit. This girl is a fucking model? Of course she is. I can tell that she's gorgeous, even with a swollen and bruised face.

"I'm sorry. Maybe I should start over," I say. I walk up and hold my hand out to her. "I'm Caden Kessler from the New York Nighthawks. It's my home run ball that did this to you."

Her jaw drops as she shakes my hand. "Really? You, uh, why … no, it was my own stupidity that did this," she says, motioning to her face. "I was on my phone and not paying attention to the game. I was only there because my boyfriend and roommate made me go. Baseball isn't really my thing."

My hand comes up to cover my chest as I feign abhorrence. "What? You don't like baseball? Who doesn't like baseball?"

The right side of her face pinks up in embarrassment. "I'm sorry. I probably shouldn't have said that to you."

"No, no, it's fine." I look down at the bag. "But now I feel kind of silly bringing you all this stuff."

She peeks down at what I'm holding. "You brought me something?" she asks, like a curious schoolgirl.

I look around her bare room. "I did. But if I'd known you were a woman, I'd have come with an armful of flowers, too."

She looks at her empty side table and then her eyes fall. "I'm sure my boyfriend will bring some tomorrow. He was here with me until just a little while ago."

"Of course he will," I say, putting the torn bag on the bed next to her. "Maybe your boyfriend will like this stuff. Go ahead." I motion for her to open it.

I watch her as she pretends to be impressed when she pulls out a replica of my #8 jersey, a signed baseball, some autographed photos, a hat, and VIP tickets to one of our last home games at the end of this month.

"Thank you," she says politely. "Tony will be over the moon to get all this."

My eyes snap to hers. "Tony?" I ask. "Your boyfriend's name is Tony?"

"Yeah. Why?"

Tony—the asshole from the cafeteria who said she looked hideous? The guy who said he was going to break up with her? The prick who kissed another woman while his girlfriend lies in a hospital bed as the result of an injury from a game *he* dragged her to?

"Uh, I just thought maybe I could personalize some of this stuff with his name."

"Sure. He'd like that."

What I'd really like to do is personalize the douchebag's face with my fist.

Should I tell her what I heard? What I saw? I mean, she doesn't know me from Adam, so maybe she wouldn't even believe me. But damn, he's going to cut her loose like a dead fish. It's a low blow considering what she's going through.

"What did the doctors say about your injury?"

She explains what the doctor told her. The more she tells me, the worse I feel. Surgery. Titanium plate. Scars. She's a goddamn model for Christ's sake. What is she going to do?

A nurse comes in the room, bringing an ice pack that Murphy needs to put on her face for twenty minutes. My cue to leave.

"Would it be okay if I visit you again tomorrow?" I ask.

"Why would you want to do that?"

The nurse laughs and then scolds her, saying something about when a handsome man wants to come calling, let him.

"Because this is all my fault and the least I can do is come sit with you for a while. It probably gets pretty boring around here."

She shrugs. "I suppose you can if you want to, but please don't feel obligated. I'm sure Tony will keep me company all day."

"It won't be out of obligation, Murphy. I'm coming because I want to." I get up to leave, but turn around before walking out. "What's your favorite flower, by the way?"

"I love all of them, but I'd have to say orchids, lilies and roses are my favorites."

"Duly noted. See you tomorrow, Murphy Cavenaugh."

"See you then, Caden Kessler."

I walk out of her room and go find Kyle. Because I have to know if things are as bad as she said.

Chapter Four

Murphy

Tony was right. I shouldn't have done it. I even went so far as to not turn on the bathroom light up until now. But I forgot this time. And when I see a flash of my face in the mirror, I can't help but stop and look. Kind of like when you see a train wreck. Which is what my face looks like—a train wreck.

So here I stand, stunned, looking at someone in the mirror who isn't me. Well, I look like me if you cover the left side of my face. It's worse than I thought. I know Dr. Benson said the swelling would get worse before it gets better. But as I stand here and look at my destroyed face, my hope of modeling paying the rent drains out of me as fast as my tears do.

I turn off the light, vowing not to turn it on again. I shuffle my feet back over to bed and pick up my phone.

"Hi, honey," Mom says cheerfully, after only half a ring.

"Hi, Mom."

She sighs into the phone. "What is it, Murph? What's wrong?"

How do moms always know when something is wrong from just a few words? For a second, I contemplate telling her. I mean, what would be the big deal if she begs me to come home? I might not ever be able to model again anyway. Maybe Iowa is where I should be. Maybe it's where I belong.

No. I remember Dr. Benson's words from last night. I won't let this break me.

"I'm fine, Mom. Just feeling a little down, I guess."

"Well, you can always—"

"—move back home," I say. "I know, Mom. Thanks for reminding me. Again. And moving back home will not make me happy. Everyone I care about is gone."

I realize what I said and instantly try to backpedal. "I mean, except for you."

"I know what you mean, honey. And I'm sorry you are feeling low. You know what your father would say?"

I laugh. "Yeah. I know. He would probably say he's my biggest fan and he wants everything for me that I want for myself."

"Sounds about right," she says. "He's still your biggest fan, you know. Only now he's got a lot more clout behind him."

"Thanks, Mom. But what if I don't know what I want for myself?"

I hear her sigh into the phone. I'm waiting for her to beckon me home again when someone knocks on the door. I don't want Mom to hear any doctors or nurses talking, so I tell her, "Mom, I have to go, someone's at the door. I'll call you tomorrow."

A teenage girl walks in with a huge bouquet of flowers. They are beautiful. All my favorites. I can't help the painful smile that creeps up my face. I knew Tony would get me some. Even if he wasn't the one to bring them.

He must have gotten called into work today. He doesn't normally work on Saturdays, so it's just my luck someone must have had an emergency today. He works in computer technology and is climbing his way up the company ladder, so when they call—he goes.

"Thank you," I tell the girl.

"Someone must really like you," she says.

"My boyfriend."

"You're lucky," she says on her way out.

I take a moment to smell the flowers before I open the card. When I open it, I don't know if I should laugh or cry.

> Get well soon, Old Man Murphy. And if you're bored, I hear channel 31 is pretty good for entertainment.
>
> - Caden Kessler

After I get over the disappointment of the flowers not being from Tony, I turn on channel 31 and can't help but chuckle at what I see.

It's a Nighthawks game.

~ ~ ~

I look at the clock. It's after six. Why hasn't he stopped by yet? Why hasn't he texted me?

I pull my phone out and my fingers hover over Tony's name. But then I remember what my mom keeps telling me. *Always make sure the man you love needs you more than you need him. It's the secret to a great relationship*. I drop the phone on the bed next to me, refusing to be the needy girlfriend.

At seven o'clock, I'm on the brink of tears. Other than the nurse coming in to ice my face every few hours, and the doctor checking my stitches and my swelling, nobody has come to visit me. Not Tony. Not any one of my roommates. Nobody.

I've been so bored I actually watched the baseball game. I didn't understand it, but I watched it.

"Hey, you," I hear from the doorway.

I turn around in excitement. Then my face falls when I see it's only Caden.

He laughs at me. "That might just be the worst reception I've ever gotten, Old Man Murphy."

"I don't want your ego getting too big," I say. "And what's with the *Old Man Murphy* thing?" I nod to the flowers. "Thank you so much for the flowers. They are beautiful."

He looks around the room. I know what he's noticing. He sees that his flowers are the only ones here. I wonder if he thinks I was lying to him about my boyfriend.

"You're welcome. I'm glad you like them." He walks over to take a sniff. "When I came last night, I was convinced I was looking for an old man. Someone at work said Murphy Cavenaugh sounded like a retired dairy farmer or something, and I guess I just pictured that in my head."

"That explains it then."

"Explains what?" he asks.

"How surprised you were to see me in this hospital bed when you were standing in my doorway last night."

He shakes his head. "No. I was just grateful I wasn't the magazine you were throwing across the room and screaming at."

"Sorry about that," I say.

I remember the moment I did it. I had just come across an advertisement for the very same clothing line I was hired to model for.

"So, tell me about your name. Is Murphy a family name?" he asks.

I shake my head. "You've heard of Murphy's Law, haven't you?"

"Yeah." He furrows his brow. "Whatever can go wrong, will go wrong."

I laugh. "That's what most people think. But one of the earliest versions of it is a little different. It states, '*whatever can happen, will happen*'."

"Isn't that the same thing?" he asks.

"Nope. Think about it. Whatever *can* happen doesn't necessarily have to be a bad thing, whereas whatever can go *wrong*, assumes that an outcome will not be a positive one."

"Okay." He ponders my statement. "You make a good point. And now I know you're a glass-half-full person. So, tell me, why were you named after Murphy's Law?"

"My parents tried to have a baby for ten years before they gave up. They tried everything including fertility treatments and implantation. Nothing worked. Then two years later, after they'd stopped trying and accepted a life without children, my mom got pregnant."

A brilliant smile creeps up his face and I see what I hadn't noticed before. Caden Kessler is hot. Like, freakishly hot. He's tall, but not excessively so. Built, but not crazy buff. He has dark hair and the most amazing eyelashes. They are so long. Every model I know would kill for eyelashes like that.

"What a great story," he says.

"Maybe, but I'm starting to think the other version of it is the right one." I gesture to my swollen face. "Case in point. Everything went wrong."

"Or maybe everything happens for a reason," he says. "That should be a law, too."

"Kessler's Law," I say.

He nods proudly. "I like the sound of that."

I laugh and then my hand comes up to cradle the left side of my face.

"Hurts when you laugh, huh?"

"When I laugh. When I smile. When I talk. Pretty much when I do anything except watch TV."

He gives me a look and then picks up the remote control and points it at the TV, turning it on. When he sees what channel it was turned to, a triumphant smile overtakes his face. He winks at me. "I'll make a baseball lover out of you yet."

"I don't know," I tell him. "It seems kind of pointless. Most of the time when someone hits the ball, it gets caught. And sometimes a guy can swing a bunch of times before anything happens. I'm sorry, but it's kind of boring."

"Boring?" He grabs his chest like he's having a heart attack as he backs up and falls into the chair in the corner. "You just invalidated my entire existence."

I wince from the guilt. "I'm really sorry. But obviously tons of other people like it. The stands were full."

"Yeah. Saturday games always get a great turn out."

My phone vibrates next to me. I look to see it's my agency calling. I check the time. Why are they calling me on a Saturday night?

"I'm sorry," I tell Caden. "It's my agency, I need to take this."

My shaky finger swipes across the screen before I say, "Hello?"

Chapter Five

Caden

When she answers the phone, I take a moment to look around her room. Other than the flowers I sent, there isn't any evidence that anyone else has been here. No well-wishing balloons. No get-well cards. No teddy bears. Nothing.

One thing's for sure. Tony is a deadbeat asshole.

"It's really not that bad," Murphy says to whoever is on the phone.

"Well, yes, it's broken, but—"

The person on the phone cuts her off, but I'm not close enough to hear what they are saying.

"Yes, that's right," Murphy says. "I will need to have surgery. But how do you know all this? Did you call the hospital? I didn't think they were allowed to give information."

"Who? One of my roommates?"

At this point in her conversation, the one beautiful blue eye I can see wells up with tears.

"Eight weeks, maybe less, but the doctor swears I will be able to cover the scar with makeup."

Her tears spill over and stream down her cheeks. She's trying to hold it together, but I can hear her voice cracking.

"Are you sure? Maybe if I—"

Apparently, she was cut off again. She nods as she listens, then she wipes her nose with her sleeve. "Okay. I'll call you then. Thank—" She pulls the phone away from her ear and looks at it. Then she throws it across the room, shattering the screen.

While she sobs on the bed, I walk over to the phone and pick it up, shoving it in my pocket. I go into the bathroom and let her have a few moments to herself.

When I return, she's sniffing and wiping her eye. "They're horrible. Every one of them. Why did I think any of them even cared about me?"

"Who?"

"My agent. My roommates." She shakes her head in disgust. "My agent wouldn't come right out and say it, but I know it was one of my roommates who called her. How else would she know I was injured? It was probably Tori. She's always had it out for me. But to be honest, I think any one of them would have called my agent if it meant they would have a shot at stealing my job."

"Your roommates sound wonderful."

"They are anything but," she says. "But I had no choice. I didn't know anyone when I moved here six months ago. There was an internet site that put aspiring models in touch with each other and that's how I found them."

"Where did you move from?"

"Iowa."

"That's a long way," I tell her. "You must miss home."

She shrugs. "Not really. I mean, I miss my mom. But most of my friends got married and moved away. And when Kelly … well, there's just nothing left for me there. It was always a dream of mine to live in New York City and I did some modeling in high school and really liked it, so I thought, what the heck."

"Going after your dreams. I like that. Most people would never have the courage to take that big a chance."

She looks around the room. "Yeah, well, look where it got me."

I feel like shit knowing I'm the cause of her misfortune. And she doesn't even know about Tony yet.

As if reading my mind, she says, "And Tony still hasn't shown up today." She looks sadly at the clock. "He hasn't even called. And now my phone is broken so I won't be able to talk to him when he does."

I hate to hit a girl when she's down, but she needs to know. I sure as hell am not going to be the one to tell her, however. I pull out my phone and tap the screen a few times. "Here, look at this," I say. "I got someone at the office to send me this video. You might not be ready to watch it, but it's footage of my ball hitting you."

She looks up in surprise. "It is? And you can see it?"

I nod. "Yes. The cameras always follow home run balls to see what the crowd does. It might be hard to watch, so don't feel like you have to."

"No. I want to," she says, tapping the screen to play it. She watches the close-up of the ball hitting her face and knocking her out of her seat. "Oh, my gosh, it happened so quickly, it was hard to really see it."

I tap on the screen to replay the video. "Here, you can slow it down if you want." I show her how to do it.

She watches it in slow motion. She watches it several times. When her jaw drops and she says, "What the …" I know she saw it. She watches it a few more times. Then I snatch the phone away from her.

"Sorry," I say. "I don't want you throwing *my* phone across the room."

"That fucking bastard!" she yells.

I go over and shut the door to her room, knowing it might not be the last curse word she yells. I know this, because I know what she saw on the video. I know she saw herself looking at her phone before the ball hit her. I also know she saw Tony run his hand down another girl's cheek as the girl looked at him and touched him back in a way you don't touch a guy if he has a girlfriend.

"That cheating bastard!" she yells. "And Kirsten. My own goddamn roommate. How dare she do that to me. What a slut." She covers her head with her hands. "How could I have been so gullible? He said he loved me."

"I'm sorry," I tell her, pouring and offering her a cup of water. "Did you love him?"

"Yes. No." She shrugs noncommittally. "I don't know. I thought I did. He was always so nice to me. How was I with him for almost four months without seeing what a bastard he was?"

"Guys are good at hiding that sort of thing. Trust me, I know. There are plenty of guys on my team who have wives or girlfriends, yet they hook up with random girls when we travel. Hell, some even have a girlfriend in every city we visit."

"Do you?" she asks. "Have a girlfriend in every city?"

I shake my head. "I don't do girlfriends."

"Oh, so you're a player," she says in disgust. Who can blame her given what she just discovered about her boyfriend.

I laugh. "No, Murphy. I'm not. I'm not saying I'm celibate either, but I'm also not looking for a girlfriend. In fact, quite the opposite. I rarely ever date the same woman more than a few times."

"Sounds like the definition of a player," she says.

"It might be if I went on a lot of dates. I don't. I think I've only been on a dozen or so this year."

She cocks her head to the side, studying me. "You've only been on twelve dates this entire year?"

"Or *so*," I tell her. "I guess I'm picky." I don't tell her the real reason. I don't tell her I'm afraid of being trapped. Of being played for *what* I am instead of being loved for *who* I am.

"I guess I should start being a little pickier myself." She lets her head fall back against the pillow as she sighs deeply. "What am I going to do? I have to go home tomorrow and face them. Face *Kirsten.* I just lost my job so I won't be able to pay the rent. I stupidly quit my waitressing job, so Joe will never hire me back. I've made a mess of things."

"Murphy, none of this is your fault. Tony is a douchebag and better you found that out now. Your roommates are back-stabbing sluts who you shouldn't be living with. You have a few choices here. You could go back to Iowa, which you already said isn't an option. Or you can make the best of the situation. You need to find a job and maybe another place to live."

"Nobody is going to hire me looking like this." She points to her face as if to add emphasis.

"Maybe not today, but my brother-in-law, Kyle—he's a doctor here in the hospital—he said that after surgery, your appearance will rapidly improve, but you'll have some restrictions about lifting things and leaning over. That may mean being a waitress is off the table for a while, but maybe there is something else we can come up with."

"We?" she asks, skeptically.

"This is my fault, Murph. If there is any way I can help you, you can bet I'm going to do it."

She looks at me sideways.

"What?" I ask.

"You called me *Murph*," she says.

"Is that bad?"

"It's just, nobody calls me that anymore. Only my mom and some of my childhood friends."

"Oh. Sorry."

She smiles. "No, it's okay. I kind of like it. It reminds me of some good times in my life."

"Well then, Murph," I say with a teasing smile. "Tell me all about your job qualifications and we'll see if we can come up with a plan."

Chapter Six

Murphy

There are some advantages to not having a phone. Such as not being able to call my douche of an ex and scream at him. And not being able to text Kirsten and tell her what a slut she is. And not stupidly calling my agent, begging for any scrap of a job they would throw my way, even after she told me not to call until I was completely healed. In all those cases, I'm sure I would have said things I would later regret.

I still can't wrap my head around what has happened to my life in a matter of two days.

I still can't believe in a few hours, I have to go home and face my roommates. Maybe even face *him*—the douchebag ex.

Dr. Benson said I'm free to go today. He wants to see me again on Thursday to see how much the swelling has gone down, then he'll decide on when to do my surgery. So, I'm pretty much out of commission for the next two weeks. What little savings I have will be quickly eaten up.

I was sure to keep enough money on hand for a plane ticket back to Iowa if I ever needed it. It was a crutch. A safety net. And, ironically, if I ever needed a crutch, a safety net, or a plane ticket out of here, it would be right now.

But something Caden said last night reminded me of what Kelly used to say. He said most people would never have the courage to go after their dreams. Kelly was the one who was always encouraging me to move to New York. She told me to not wait, because you never know what might happen in life. And in some sick, twisted, prophetic way, she was proven right.

Maybe this is my test. The hurdle I have to overcome to get what I want out of life. Maybe I need to give up the crutch and commit myself one hundred percent to making it on my own in the city I've always dreamed of.

A phone rings, plucking me from my thoughts, and I turn towards the sound to see Caden standing in my doorway. He looks at his phone and says, "Your mom is calling."

He hands me the phone and I look down at it to see my mother's face on the screen. I look up at him, confused. "What?"

He nods to the phone. "Aren't you going to answer it?"

"Uh, no," I say, looking at him like he's crazy. "And why is my mom calling your phone. And why do you have her listed as 'Mom'?"

"She's not calling my phone. She's calling *your* phone."

"*My* phone?" I look over to the corner of the room where I threw my phone last night and see that it's missing. "I don't understand."

"I took your broken phone in and had it replaced. Luckily, they were able to transfer all your contacts and data."

My jaw drops. "You got me a new phone?"

"It was the least I could do, Murph."

I try not to smile at his use of my nickname. "But I can't possibly pay you back right away. Those things are expensive."

"It's my treat, considering I'm the reason you broke it in the first place."

I scold him with my stare. "Caden, I wish you'd quit saying that. It wasn't your fault."

He shrugs off my words. "I hope you don't mind, I added a new contact."

I look down and scroll through my short list of contacts to see one labeled '#8.'

"What's number eight?" I ask.

He walks over to the pile of gifts he brought me on Friday and pulls out the jersey, turning it around. On the back, it has Caden's last name and under it, the number 8.

"Oh," I say, embarrassed that I didn't even pay enough attention to realize that was *his* jersey, and number eight was *his* number.

He chuckles. "You really do hate baseball, don't you?"

"I don't hate it, I just don't understand it. It's like physics—another subject I don't know anything about but also seems complicated and useless."

"Are you calling baseball complicated and useless? I think Mickey Mantle and Jackie Robinson just rolled over in their graves."

"Who are Mickey Mantle and Jackie Robinson?"

A rich, throaty laugh bellows out of him. "Oh, Lord. I guess I have a lot to teach you." He walks over to put the jersey down and pick up the tickets. "And I'm going to start teaching you on the 29th. That's when you'll come to a game."

He hands me the tickets and I look at them as if they will bite me. I vehemently shake my head back and forth until my face protests in angry pain.

He must see the horror in my expression. He puts a hand on my arm to calm me. "Don't worry, Murph. These are VIP tickets. You'll be in a suite. Behind glass walls."

I breathe out an audible sigh. "Oh, okay." I shrug. "I'll have to see."

"What's there to see?" he asks. "There will be free food, free booze, and no possible chance of getting hit by my home run ball."

My lips turn up into a small smile. "You sound pretty confident. Do you hit one every game?"

"Ha! I wish. Let's see, we play about one hundred and sixty-two games a season. This season is almost over and I just hit my twenty-sixth home run. That's far from hitting one every game. Even the best home-run hitters don't usually hit more than forty to fifty a season." He smiles proudly. "And there you go, your first baseball lesson."

"Lesson?" I ask.

He nods. "I've made it my mission to make you a fan. And to do that, you need to learn the game."

"Isn't that what Google is for?" I ask.

He furrows his brows. "Learning baseball from the internet? No way, you have to do it in person." He points to the tickets in my hand. "And you can start in three weeks."

I study the tickets. The game will be a couple weeks after my surgery. Dr. Benson said my face will be much better by then. And I'll probably need the free food considering I'll be living on ramen noodles until I can find a job. But then I realize there are two tickets. I don't have someone I can take with me. Not anymore.

There is not a single person in New York City that I can call my friend.

I am so pathetic.

I hand the tickets back to him. "It would be too awkward. I don't have anybody to bring with me."

He gets out his phone and taps on the screen a few times. Then he pours me a cup of water. Then his phone vibrates and he reads his text and smiles.

"I have a sister, Lexi. She's two years older than me and she loves baseball. She'll go with you."

"Your sister? What? No, I couldn't possibly—"

He shoves his phone at me and makes me read the text. "It says right here she would love to. Trust me, you don't want to disappoint my sister. She's married to a doctor and has two little kids, so you can believe it when I tell you she needs a night out."

"I … I guess. If you really think it wouldn't be a bother."

"There's not a doubt in my mind. You'll love her. Lexi is great."

"Lexi is a beautiful name. How old is she?"

He gives me a cocky smile. "It's short for Alexa. And is that your way of asking me how old *I* am, Murphy Brown?"

"Uh, no," I say, sure a blush is creeping up my face.

Maybe.

Okay, yes.

But only because he's the only MLB player I've ever met and I'm curious.

"And who's Murphy Brown?"

"You don't watch many reruns, do you?" He laughs. "Anyway, Lexi is twenty-seven and that makes me twenty-five. And now that you know my age, you have to tell me yours."

"I'm twenty-three."

"Good to know," he says. He points to my new phone. "I want you to text me and let me know when you get scheduled for surgery. I'm heading out of town this afternoon and won't be back for almost a week."

"You want me to text you?" I stare at him like he's crazy. Even though I don't like baseball, I understand that he must be somewhat of a celebrity. I mean, after he left the past few times, the nurses were going crazy over the fact that he was here. Why would he want me to text him? Doesn't he get texts from hundreds of people every day?

"Yes. I do." He taps his pocket where his phone resides. "If you don't, I'll just have to call you. Or get my brother-in-law to break the rules and look at your records for your home address."

I blow out a sigh. "Fine. I'll text you."

He shakes his head in wonder.

"What?" I ask.

"You're different," he says, studying me.

"What do you mean?"

"Normally, girls are begging for my phone number, and here I am handing it to you on a silver platter and you don't want to use it."

I nod in understanding. "Maybe that's because I don't want to sleep with you, Kessler. I've had my fill of narcissistic pigs, thank you very much."

"Ouch," he says, looking melodramatically dejected. "For what it's worth, I'm not a narcissistic pig. And further, I don't want to sleep with you either, Murph."

"Good. Friends then?" I ask.

"Absolutely," he says.

I smile. I smile so big my face hurts.

"What is it?" he asks.

"Nothing. It's just that you have the unfortunate distinction of being my *only* friend in New York at the moment."

"Not unfortunate," he says. "Lucky. And when you meet Lexi, the number of friends you have here will double."

He looks at the clock on the wall like he has to be somewhere and I remember he said he's going out of town.

"Don't you have a plane to catch or something?"

"Actually, yes. We're playing in Phoenix and San Diego this week." He looks like he's about to turn to leave. "Oh, hell, I almost forgot." He reaches into his back pocket and pulls out a brochure to give me.

It's a gym brochure. I open it up and stare at it, confused. "Uh, Caden, the doctor said I can't lift anything for a while. Not only that, I have no job and no money. This place looks expensive."

He points to the number on the back of the brochure. "Call Jayden, she's the gym manager, tell her Mason Lawrence offered you a job and that you'll start a few weeks after your surgery."

"Who's Mason Lawrence?"

He laughs. "You don't watch football either, do you?"

I shake my head.

"Mason is one of the owners of the gym and a personal friend. When you told me you worked at a gym for a few years back in high school, I decided to call him. There's a position coming open. It's not anything special, just a front desk job. But I thought maybe during your recovery, that would be just what you need."

"Are you for real?" I ask him.

He shrugs.

"Are you repenting for something, Caden? Did you need a charity case this week? Why are you being so nice to me?"

"Because all of this is—"

"Your fault," I complete his ridiculous thought. "For the last time, it's *not.* Now, go or you'll miss your flight."

He winks at me and turns to walk away.

"And Caden?"

He spins around in the doorway.

"Thank you." I hold up the phone and the brochure. "For everything."

"No. Thank you," he says.

"For what?"

"I don't know. For not hating me for what I did. For being so darn nice. For not wanting to sleep with me." He gives me a wave before walking out the door. "Later, Murphy Brown," I hear him say as he strides down the hall.

And for the first time since Friday night, I feel like maybe my life isn't so pathetic after all.

Chapter Seven

Caden

"Sue is hot," Brady says when the girls get up to use the bathroom.

I look in their direction. "I guess."

"Dude. What is wrong with you? You've been acting strange all night. Wait, is this date number three? Are you trying to figure out how you're going to cut bait?"

I take a sip of my beer. "No, this is number two, but I'm not sure she's going to make it to three."

"No good in the sack?" he asks, raising his brows at me.

I love Brady like a brother, but he can be a lot to take sometimes. What I was telling Murphy about some of the guys on my team having a girl in every city—that's Brady. It's not like he's a bad person, I mean they all know the score. He doesn't have a wife. He doesn't have a girlfriend. He just has *friends* in every place we play.

Murphy.

I look at my phone again, wondering why she hasn't texted me. It's Thursday. Surely she knows by now when she's going to have surgery. Maybe she just decided to go back to Iowa after all.

Murphy. That's an unusual name. An intriguing name. It's not boring like, say, Sue.

"Kess?" Brady asks, prodding me to give him an answer.

"Uh, no. I don't know. Haven't slept with her."

"Shit, really?" He gives me a cocky smile. "Then would you mind if I do?"

I dunk my fingers in my water glass and flick them at him.

Sue and Abby return to the table, giggling. "I just got asked for my autograph," Sue says.

"Is that so?" I ask.

"Yes. Some girl in the bathroom wanted to get the signature of Caden Kessler's girlfriend."

I roll my eyes at her.

"What?" she asks. "Like, I'm a celebrity now."

Brady turns to Abby. "What about you, did you get asked for your autograph, too?"

Abby turns up her nose in disgust. "No, she was just obsessed with Caden."

Brady raises his eyebrows. "This tool? But he's *just* a catcher. I'm the pitcher. Everybody loves pitchers."

I know he's only teasing. It's a long-standing joke between pitchers and catchers about who is the most important. Pitchers couldn't do their job without us. We make them look good. We save their asses when their pitching sucks. And they get all the glory.

I peek at my phone again and scroll through some texts. None of them are ones I care to answer.

"You girls coming to the game tomorrow?" Brady asks.

"Of course," they say in tandem.

"Thank you for the great seats, Brady," Abby says. "We'll be close enough to see your gorgeous eyes."

"Yeah," Sue says to me. "Like maybe you could give me a signal that lets me know you see me. You know, scratch your nose or click your heels or something."

Brady and I share a look. "Uh, no," I tell her in no uncertain terms.

"Aw, come on. I'll make it worth your while," she says with a sultry wink.

I take a long drink and stare her down. "Sue, you need to understand one thing. When I play, the only *signals* I'm sending are to my pitcher. I don't care if the fucking President of the United States is in the stands, I'm not acknowledging *anyone*."

She looks hurt. "Oh, okay." She turns to Abby. "It's just a silly little game. I don't get what the big deal is."

I blow out a long breath and down the rest of my one and only beer. "We should head back. Curfew, you know."

"You have a curfew?" Sue asks.

"It's more of a guideline than a rule," Abby says. Then I think Brady must kick her under the table or something. "What? That's what you always tell me, Brady."

Brady and I throw some bills on the table and get up to leave. "Where can we drop you, Sue?"

Sue looks dejected. But at this point, I couldn't give a shit. Any girl who thinks I will jeopardize my job to send her stupid fucking signals during a game is not worth my time. Especially when that girl gets off on being my *celebrity* girlfriend.

I should have gone with my gut and stayed home tonight.

I check my phone once more on the way out.

~ ~ ~

I've always been pretty good at tuning out the crowd. I get in the zone when I'm behind the plate, whether I've got a bat in my hand, or a glove on it. But today, thanks to Brady, Abby and Sue are sitting in seats right on the third-base line, feet from our dugout. And Sue keeps shouting things out when the crowd noise dies down. Things like how much fun she had last night. And how she loves me. Things like how I should give her my secret signal.

Man, that girl is needy. We had two dates and you'd think she already has a damn ring on her finger.

No way in hell will I give her my phone number. She'd probably blow up my phone with voicemails and texts. I learned that a long time ago. I had to change my number several times early in my career when I stupidly gave it out to someone who then stalked me, or publicized my number after I stopped dating them. I've been called a stupid prick more than once for not giving it out anymore. But my standard answer is, if they really need to reach me, they can do it through the organization.

Melanie stopped giving me messages last year. She basically screens my calls, and after eighteen months of my throwing the little pink slips of paper in the trash, she got the hint that if a woman was trying to reach me through the office, it wasn't a woman I wanted to speak with.

When I come back in the dugout after a three-up-three-down inning, Sawyer nods to the stands. "Dude, who the hell is the lunatic?"

I take my chest protector off and throw it in the corner. "That would be Sue," I say in disgust.

"Want me to send an usher over to shut her up?"

I shake my head. "It's fine. You didn't see it mess me up out there, did you?"

"Hell no. That was a great save you had on third strike."

"Thanks."

Conner steps up to the plate and hits a home run. His second of the San Diego series. *Showoff.* Sawyer and I watch the JumboTron to see where it lands. Like me, he always hopes a kid catches it, but they rarely do. Most of the time, a pushy adult will all but trample over a kid to catch a ball. It's sad. And I've seen more than a few overzealous fans get booed out of the park for robbing a kid of the experience.

This time, however, Sawyer and I smile when the large screen shows us that it was in fact a kid who caught it.

"Hey, that reminds me, what happened to the guy you hit last week. He okay?"

I smile sadly. "The guy was actually a woman, and no, she's not."

"Shit, really?"

I nod, resting my forearms on the railing as we watch Hayden at bat. "It messed her up pretty bad, Sawyer. I feel terrible. She's a model and is just starting her career. I was with her in the hospital when her agency called to drop her like a goddamn hot potato. Then her boyfriend dumped her. The girl is new to the city. She seriously has no one."

"That's fucked up," he says. "It was nice of you to go see her in the hospital."

"Every day until we left for Phoenix."

"That explains why you skipped out on us Friday and Saturday night."

"Yeah. And get this, she doesn't even like baseball. She was only at the game to make her boyfriend happy. The same boyfriend who was cheating on her."

"Wait." He takes a step back from the railing. "She doesn't fucking like baseball? What kind of chick is she?"

I laugh. "Exactly. I think I've made it my mission in life to bring her around."

"She hot?"

I give him a sideways look. "I don't know, man. I guess so. I mean she *is* a model and all. But she's so genuine. Real. I kind of find it hard to believe she was trying to break into that business with all the cut-throat shit that goes on. It's not for her, I can tell."

He pulls his eyes away from the game and studies me. "Oh, you can *tell*, can you?"

"Yeah. I can. And I gave her my phone number but she hasn't called or texted once. What's up with that? That's never happened. Not one time. And I don't even want to sleep with her. I really just want to help her out when she's down, you know?"

"Maybe she's playing you," he says.

"What, like she got hit by my home run ball on purpose and now she's playing hard to get so that I'll go after her and she can trap me?"

He shrugs.

"Murphy isn't like that," I say. "Plus, that is such a stupid theory."

"You're the one who said it, not me. Wait. Her name is Murphy?"

"Yes." I laugh. "Isn't it great?"

"If you like old man names," he says. "You gonna date her?"

"No, I told you, it's not like that. I think we might be friends."

"Friends with the hot model with the messed-up face," he says, reaching over to put on his batting helmet. "Let me know how that goes."

I watch him walk out on the field, then I go over to retrieve my own helmet. And although I never bring my phone with me into the dugout, I can't help but wish I had so I could see if she's tried to contact me.

Chapter Eight

Murphy

My skin crawls as I watch Kirsten drape herself over Tony for the hundredth time this week. Why must they always hang out *here*, in our tiny apartment that is overcrowded as it is?

I'm over him. I think I got over him the second I arrived home to find them cuddled up on the couch together. Tony belatedly made an effort to move away from her after it was obvious that I saw them together.

He never came back to the hospital after that first night. He never called either. When I saw them on the couch, I told him he could fuck whoever he wanted, including himself. And then I sarcastically thanked my roommates for coming to visit.

I make a sandwich and take it to my room—the room I share with my ex's current girlfriend. The one who calls out after me before I shut the door, "Since when did you start eating carbs?"

I may have slammed the door a bit too hard after hearing her words.

A minute later, there is a knock on the door. Then Jamie walks in. She plops down on the bed next to me. "He's a bottom-dwelling scum-sucker, I hope you know that."

Jamie is the closest thing I have to a friend in New York, but even she didn't visit me in the hospital, so I think that precludes her from earning the designation. But at least she's nice to me.

"I know. And I'm glad to be rid of him, really I am. But do they have to flaunt it in front of me?"

She sighs and puts a hand on my arm. "Murphy, Tony has had something going with everyone in this apartment except me. And that's only because I shot him down."

My eyes bug out and I drop my sandwich. "What?"

"It's true. You don't know how badly I wanted to tell you. Everyone else here grew up in places like L.A. or Miami. But you came from Iowa. You were the innocent Midwestern girl who wouldn't understand how the world really works. I guess we were all trying to protect you."

"Protect me from what—a cheating, lying boyfriend?"

"What Tony is doing is nothing new," she says. "He wants to date a model. Be on the arm of a beautiful woman when she makes her rise to fame. He doesn't have the ego or the bank account to date a successful model, so he finds up-and-coming ones."

My jaw practically hits my lap. "Are you kidding me? So, all this time …"

She nods. "He just wants to go along for the ride. He doesn't care with whom."

I look towards the door. "And they are okay with that? So, what, is Kirsten the new me, and if she doesn't work out, he'll go on to Tori or Pauline?"

"Pretty much. You should be flattered, you know. At least he thought he had the best shot with you."

I laugh, but it's not genuine, it's a bitter, cold laugh. "The best shot with me?" I ask, incredulously. "As in, if I hadn't been hit by that ball, he'd still be pretending he was in love with me so he could use me and my potential celebrity status to benefit himself? Yeah, Jamie, I'm really freaking flattered."

She holds up her hands. "Geez. Sorry I even said anything."

I sigh, and put a hand on possibly my only chance at a friend. "No, *I'm* sorry. I'm glad you told me. But it's kind of strange, Tony dumping me was one of two good things that came out of my accident."

She looks at my face, studying my now-yellow bruise that isn't quite so swollen. "Good things?"

"I thought I was in love with him, Jamie. I never would have known he wasn't in it for who I am instead of what I was. Or what I *almost* was."

"Yeah, but he's really hot," she says. "I mean, does it really matter?"

"Yes, it matters. And if he's that hot, why don't *you* just sleep with him like all of our other roommates?"

She raises an eyebrow at me. "Because I'm a lesbian, Murphy."

I cover my mouth in shock. "Oh, my gosh. Really?"

She nods, laughing. "Like I said, innocent Midwestern girl." She gets up to leave. "Hey, what was the second good thing?"

"Second good thing?" I say, realizing my slip. "Oh, nothing."

My phone chirps with a text, saving me from having to acknowledge Jamie's curious stare. She leaves the room as I pull out my phone and smile.

It's my second good thing.

#8: Are you still in NYC, or did you go back to Iowa?

My smile widens when I think that maybe I just might have someone else I can call a friend.

Me: Still in NYC, why?

#8: You haven't texted me. I figured that meant you went home.

Me: Nope. Still here and still watching my ex drape himself across my roommate every chance he gets.

#8: He's a stupid prick, Murph.

Me: You don't even know the half of it.

#8: Oh, really?

Me: Never mind.

#8: I'm not dropping this, but I want to find out about your surgery. What did the doctor say?

Me: He scheduled the surgery for Monday.

#8: Good. I'll be back in town. What time Monday?

Good? Why does he think that is good?

Me: 3:00

#8: Perfect. You'll probably be coming out of it by the time I get there. That is unless your mom will be sitting with you in recovery.

Me: I haven't told my mom yet. And you don't have to come, Caden. I'm a big girl.

#8: Are you crazy, Old Man Murphy?

I laugh out loud. It's the first time I've done that in over a week. It feels good. It feels very good.

#8: And you not wanting me to come is exactly why I will.

Me: What?

#8: Never mind. Did you call Jayden?

Me: Actually, I did. And she said the job is mine whenever I feel up to it. I can't thank you enough. You are a lifesaver.

#8: Glad to hear it. How's the living situation? I mean, other than the bastard boyfriend and the back-stabbing roommate?

Me: Torturous. As soon as I can afford it, I'm out of here.

#8: That will be our next project then. Finding you a new place.

Me: Caden, you've done enough. And DON'T YOU DARE SAY IT!

#8: Lol. I wouldn't dream of it after you shouted at me. Goodnight. See you Monday. Good luck with the surgery.

Me: Thanks.

Me: Wait! I'm so selfish. I didn't even ask you how your games were this week. Did you get another home run?

#8: No more home runs. But we did win most of our games. Thanks for asking. And, Murph, you are anything but selfish.

Me: Glad you won. Have a good weekend.

#8: You, too. Don't throw anything across the room when I'm not there ;-)

I finish my sandwich and go to bed, counting my lucky stars that I didn't end up with a loser like Tony. Things are starting to look up. After all, I have a job to look forward to.

And just maybe, a friend.

Chapter Nine

Caden

Kyle is able to get me back into the surgical recovery area. They allow one family member to sit with patients as they come around. I'm far from family, but knowing she has no one, I didn't want her to wake up alone.

"Thanks, bro," I say, after he escorts me back.

He pulls up a rolling stool and puts it next to her bed. There are a lot of beds all in a row back here. Nobody has a private room. Kyle says it's because people coming from surgery need constant monitoring. I look around and see patients in different stages of consciousness. Some are still sleeping, some are speaking incoherently, some look to be in pain.

I hope Murphy isn't in any pain.

I look down at her still body. She has wires coming out from under her hospital gown that are attached to a machine by her head. She has something clipped onto the finger of her right hand.

And there are what look to be inflatable boot things on each of her lower legs that deflate every now and then.

"She may be out of it for a few minutes after she comes around. Most patients are disoriented at first." He leans down to whisper in my ear. "And since she doesn't know you very well, she might not even remember you for a while."

I look up at him with concern.

He puts a hand on my shoulder. "Don't worry about it. It looks like the surgery went well. She should recover nicely."

I nod and mumble more thanks as he walks away.

When I look at her face, it's nothing like what I expected. My only frame of reference is how she looked last weekend. I had never seen her uninjured face. I'm not exactly sure what I thought she would look like now, but it's not this. Her face, the very place they just performed surgery, looks much better than when I saw her last. It's a bit puffy, but it's not very swollen. The stitches she got the night of the injury have been removed, and she has a long, thin bandage that runs along her hairline.

I take in a deep breath and blow it out thinking about the surgery. I looked it up online. I hope Murphy didn't. Because from what I read, to do the repair, they basically had to pull the skin off her face from a long incision they made by her ear.

They pulled the fucking skin off her face.

Because of *me*.

It's unreal they just did that today, only a short while ago, and yet she looks so … pretty.

I reach out and put my hand on top of hers. I lean over and whisper in her ear, "You did great, old man."

A nurse comes over and fiddles with something. "Looks like she's waking up," she says.

I look down at Murphy and don't see anything. I look back at the nurse for clarification.

The nurse nods to the machine. "Her pulse just went up. Usually means they are coming out of the anesthesia."

I pull my hand away, wondering if I caused it.

The nurse smiles. "It's okay, you can touch her."

Relieved I hadn't caused anything bad to happen, I put my hand back on her. Then she moves. She doesn't open her eyes, but she winces and her mouth opens and closes as her tongue presses against her teeth.

"Her throat is probably raw from the airway tube," the nurse says. "Once she can take some liquid, that will get better."

A faint noise comes from Murphy. It's a soft groan, like when you wake up with a hangover after a long night of drinking.

"Talk to her," the nurse says, encouragingly. "It'll help her wake up."

"Okay, uh …" All of a sudden I'm at a loss for words. I barely know this girl. Why did I think it would be good for me to come sit with her when she's so vulnerable? The nurse probably thinks I'm her husband or brother. "Murph, it's me. Kyle said the surgery went well. He said you will recover in no time. And you have that job waiting for you. Everything will get better now. I promise."

Hey eyes flutter open. She stares at the fluorescent lights on the ceiling for a while. Then her eyes dart around. Then her head turns towards me.

"Hey, you," I say.

She looks at me, but her eyes don't seem to focus.

"Ton …" Her words trail off and she winces.

"It's okay," I tell her. "The nurse said your throat will be sore for a little bit. You can have a sip of water when you feel up to it."

Her eyes close again and she threads her fingers through mine, squeezing them. With her eyes closed, she clears her throat and speaks again. "Love you," I think she says.

Oh, shit. She thinks I'm him. The lying, cheating bastard. Did she really love him? Does she still?

She's in and out of it for the next ten minutes. The nurse brings a cup of water and raises the head of her bed a little more. "She can have a few sips when she's ready."

"Murphy? Did you hear that? Would you like a drink?" I ask.

Her eyes open again, this time they are clearer than before. She looks at me in confusion.

"Caden. It's Caden," I say. "Are you okay? Do you remember me?"

A small smile curves her lips. "You came."

"Of course I did. I told you I'd be here."

She looks around and then back at me. "Where's Tony?"

I don't know what to say. Did she forget? I just give her a sad smile.

I see it when realization dawns on her. Her eyes close and she blows out a long sigh. "Right," she says. "I'm not with the bastard anymore."

I pick up her water cup and put the straw to her lips. "Try to take a drink."

She takes a few sips and then makes an appreciative moan.

"How do you feel?" I ask.

"Better than when your ball hit me," she says.

I laugh. "Darn. I was hoping you'd forgotten that part."

A doctor comes by to assess her. He tells me she'll be moved back to her room in half an hour.

"How long will she have to stay?" I ask.

"Probably just one night," the doctor tells me. "It went very well. Her bandages will be removed tomorrow assuming there is no drainage. The steri-strips will probably wash off in a week and she'll come back to get the sutures removed in seven to ten days."

"Just one night? Really?"

He nods. "Her recovery will be rapid," he says. "And with you there to help her, I'm sure she'll be up and around in no time."

But I'm not *there to help her.*

"Thank you," I tell him.

When Murphy falls back to sleep, I get on my phone and make some arrangements.

Sometime after she's moved to her room, she wakes up and catches me watching ESPN.

"What's a balk?" she asks, motioning to the television.

"Wait … you were listening? Little Miss I-hate-baseball was listening closely enough to hear that?"

"Well, there's nothing better to do." She shrugs.

I smile. "A balk is an illegal motion from the pitcher. It's when he pretends to pitch, but doesn't."

"Why would he do that?"

"To deceive the hitter or runner."

"I don't get it," she says.

"Okay, say there's a guy on first base. He's going to get a lead, a jump on the pitch, so he can try to make it to second. He'll take off right when he thinks the pitcher is winding up to throw the pitch. The pitcher wants him to think he's about to pitch the ball to the batter so the guy on first will start to run, but then the pitcher will throw him out at second, or at the very least, get him caught in a pickle."

She looks at me with eyes glazed over. "Pickle?"

I laugh. "Maybe *balk* is not the best place to start when you're learning baseball. I guess it can seem kind of complicated."

"You think?" She shakes her head gingerly. "I don't believe I'll ever get it," she says. "I'm a kinesthetic learner."

"What the heck is that?"

"I'm one of those people who has to *do* something to learn it. You know, use my body—touch, feel, experience things. You can talk your head off, but I'll never get it. That's why I wasn't very good in school. My teachers got sick of having to teach me *my* way."

I get a brilliant idea and I feel my face splitting with a smile.

"Oh, hell no." Murphy narrows her eyes at me and then holds up her hand to squelch my enthusiasm. "I know you don't think I'm going to *play* baseball," she says. "Did you not hear a word the doctor said? I can't do any activity that could re-injure my face."

"When did he say you'd be okay to resume normal activity?" I ask.

"Baseball is *not* normal activity, Caden. And he said I could go back to work within a week, but I still can't lift anything over ten pounds. Why?"

"What are you doing Saturday night?" I ask.

"Not going on a date with you, Caden Kessler." She gives me a hard stare.

Geez. Is the thought that daunting?

I roll my eyes at her. "No, Murphy Brown, not a date. The last thing I need is a girlfriend and the last thing you want is another failed relationship."

"What did you have in mind then?"

"It's a surprise," I say.

"A surprise?" she asks with raised brows. "A surprise that doesn't include me playing baseball or the shedding of clothing?"

I hold up my fingers in a Boy Scout salute. "Scout's honor, I will not try to get in your pants, and I won't make you play ball."

She shrugs one smug shoulder. "I'll have to check my calendar and get back with you."

I laugh. "You do that, Murph."

Chapter Ten

Murphy

I thought this week was going to be torture at my apartment. Turns out, it wasn't as bad as I feared. Mainly due to the visiting nurse who came to check on me for the first three days and the catered meals that were delivered every evening. I thought I was going to be eating ramen noodles for weeks. Instead, I ate like a queen. And flowers. I can't forget the flowers. Wednesday it was orchids, Thursday was lilies, and roses came on Friday.

My roommates were starting to get suspicious so I told them everything was from my mom and my friends back home. It was a lie. Nobody back home even knows I got hurt. And even though none of the flowers came with a card and the nurse said the hospital sent her, I knew better. This was all Caden and the guilt he feels over what happened.

However, as much as I enjoyed being the beneficiary of his kindness, I'm going to tell him tonight that it has to stop. I'm fine.

My face is healing quickly. I feel pretty good, even. I've accepted the fact that I'll have scars for the rest of my life. And strangely enough, I'm not throwing any temper tantrums over it. Because I've had a lot of time over the past weeks to sit back and watch. To listen. And if being a model means acting like my roommates, I think I chose the wrong profession.

But that doesn't mean I'm giving up my dream to live in New York. That's always been my passion. I can pinpoint the moment it happened. My girlfriends and I had a sleepover and Tami made us watch a marathon of *Sex and the City* reruns. That was it. That was all it took for me to fall in love. From that moment, I researched New York City. By the time I moved here, I could tell you which train goes where and how long it would take to get there.

New York City was the opposite of Okoboji, Iowa in every way. No county curfews. No miles of cornfields. No endless dirt roads. New York was the city that never slept. And I knew from the minute I saw that TV show, it was where I needed to be. Modeling just seemed the obvious way for me to make it here. I mean, it's expensive. A good cup of coffee here can cost as much as a meal at The Pit Stop back home.

My phone pings with a text.

#8: You ready?

I look in the mirror and pull my hair forward on the left side of my face until it hides the stitches by my ear. I'm not quite healed enough to use makeup to cover my scars, but I realize it doesn't really matter. There's nobody to impress. Not Tony, not my agent, not the other girls I used to be in competition with.

Me: Yes.

#8: Bring a jacket. It might get chilly. I'm waiting on the sidewalk in front of your building.

He never did tell me where we were going. We didn't even talk all week long. I knew everything was from him, but since he didn't put his name on anything, I figured he didn't care to be thanked. I knew I'd do it tonight anyway.

Me: Okay. See you in a sec.

I grab a hoodie and tie it around my waist. Since he didn't tell me where we are going, he's going to have to live with the fact that I'm wearing jeans and an old concert t-shirt. If he takes me to dinner at a nice place, he'll think twice the next time he wants to surprise someone.

I walk out into the living room, past Kirsten and Tori, who are doing each other's makeup.

"Where are *you* going?" Tori asks, as if I'm not allowed to have a life outside of my roommates.

"Out," I say.

"With who?" Kirsten says, straightening her back with alarm.

I find it comical that she suspects I might be going out with Tony. That maybe he could be cheating on her with me. How ironic. And why would she even care? According to Jamie, he's sleeping with everyone anyway. But out of spite, I decide to milk it for all it's worth.

"Um …" I try to look as guilty as I possibly can. "You don't know him … I mean her. You don't know her. Uh, I have to go."

I walk out the door and muffle my laughter as I dance down the hall.

~ ~ ~

"Uh … what are we doing here?" I ask, looking around at our desolate surroundings.

The cab dropped us off in front of Hawks Stadium and we are literally the only people in the massive parking lot. I give Caden an accusing look.

"We are definitely not here to *play* baseball," he says with a laugh, grabbing my arm to pull me towards the dark entrance.

"Then why are we here?"

"For your first lesson, of course."

"Are you serious? I thought you were joking about getting me to like baseball."

He stops our progress and looks me right in the eyes. "I never joke about baseball, Murphy."

I take a step back and hold up my hands in surrender. "Duly noted."

We start walking again when I see a man come out of the shadows near the entrance.

"Harold," Caden says, walking over to shake his hand. "I really appreciate this."

"It's my pleasure, Mr. Kessler," Harold says. "Everything is set up like you asked."

"Thank you. Harold, I'd like you to meet the lovely Murphy Cavenaugh."

Harold extends his hand to me as a large smile creeps up his face like he has a secret. "It's a great pleasure to meet you, Ms. Cavenaugh."

"It's just Murphy," I tell him, shaking his old and weathered hand. "It's very nice to meet you, Harold."

Harold opens the gate for us and Caden escorts me into a dark tunnel. Normally, I'd be scared. This Midwestern girl knows better than to walk into dark places in New York City. Hell, my mother even made me take self-defense classes before moving here. But with Caden at my side, I feel safe. Still, I think Caden senses my hesitation.

"Come on, Murph," he says, grabbing my hand and leading me out of the tunnel and onto what I'm fairly sure is the baseball field. But the sun is down now, and I can just barely see where we are going.

Caden keeps a grip on me so I don't trip and fall on my still-healing face. When we stop walking, he yells, "Now, Harold!"

I hear a series of pops and electrical noises and then, slowly, lights above and all around us illuminate the massive stadium. It takes almost a full minute for the lights to turn on and shine brightly, but when they do, baseball lover or not, anyone would be in awe of what I'm seeing.

I turn around, looking at the empty stands that must hold tens of thousands of fans. I look at the grass, that appears freshly mowed. I look at Caden, who looks like a kid in a candy store.

"Wow, this is … this is spectacular," I say.

He nods, turning around and taking it all in as if he doesn't do it every day.

"How did you … I mean, this is crazy."

He shrugs. "Harold likes me. He's got eight grandkids who love baseball. I showed up at one of their birthday parties and played in a sandlot game with them. It pays to know people in high places."

I cock my head at him. Harold looked like he might be the groundskeeper, not the owner of the stadium. "High places, huh?"

"Or maybe just the guy with the key who owes me a favor."

I laugh, and something to my right catches my eye. "What's that?" I ask, motioning to a picnic basket in the middle of the field.

He rolls his eyes at me as if it's obvious and then he talks to me like I'm a two-year-old. "That is the pitcher's mound, Murph. It's where a guy called a pitcher throws a little white ball with red stitching to another guy called a batter who tries to hit the ball out there." He turns around and points to the center field stands.

I playfully hit him on the arm. I shake my head and chuckle at his dramatics. "Not that," I say, walking over to the picnic basket. "This."

He gives me crazy eyes. "Did the surgery mess with your brain or something? *That* is a picnic basket."

"Oh, my God, would you quit it?" I squeal at him.

He bends over laughing. "Oh, but it's so much fun." He opens the lid of the basket to show me a variety of breads and cheeses and wine. "It's dinner."

Caden pulls out a blanket and spreads it next to the pitcher's mound. Then he spends the entirety of our dinner trying to explain to me how exciting baseball is. It's kind of hard not to get caught up in it. He talks about it with such enthusiasm. It's obvious baseball is his life.

I still don't quite understand all of it, but he's made me curious enough to come back and watch another game. Behind a glass wall, that is.

He pours the last of the wine into our glasses. "So, what do you miss most about Iowa?"

"Besides my mom?"

"Yeah."

"I'd like to say my friends, but they're pretty much all gone. So, I guess I'd have to say I miss the stars." I look up at the bright lights of the stadium.

"You know we have those here, too, right?"

"Obviously. But you can't ever see them, not like you can in Iowa. There's too much light pollution. Back in Iowa, if you looked hard enough, you could see a falling star just about every night."

"Falling stars, huh?"

"Ever seen one?" I ask.

"I don't believe I have."

"You're missing out then."

He pulls out his phone and taps on the screen with a devious smile. I give him a sideways look. "What are you doing now?"

"Looking for falling stars," he says, right before all the lights go out and the stadium falls into complete darkness.

Chapter Eleven

Caden

She reaches out and grabs my arm. The lights going out must have scared her. "Oh, my gosh," she says, lying back on the grass and looking up at the sky. "This is fabulous."

The stadium is on the outskirts of the city and the walls go up high enough to block out the light from any nearby buildings. There is still some ambient light, but not enough to spoil our view of the stars. And as our eyes adjust to the darkness, we attempt to pick out constellations. I'm not much of a star-gazer, so I can pretty much only identify the Big Dipper.

"See? Just like Iowa," I say, patting her hand.

"Thank you," she says, shifting her gaze from the stars to me.

"It was Harold. I didn't do anything."

"No, I mean it. Thank you." She sits up and looks down on me. "You've done so much for me these last two weeks. I know you feel like you have to, but you don't. If you had anything to make up for, you've done it in spades, Caden. Thanks to you, I start my new job soon. I'm going to be fine. I appreciate everything you've done, but you can stop the meals on wheels and everything."

I laugh. "Meals on wheels?"

"You know what I mean."

"What did your roommates think about all of it?" I ask cautiously.

She lies back down and sighs. "Um … I didn't exactly tell my roommates who sent them."

I look at her, surprised. "Really?"

"Well, there were no cards, no evidence of who had done all those things for me, so I figured you didn't want them to know it was you."

I smile. She's right, I didn't. But I guessed she'd tell them anyway. "Who do they think sent everything?"

"My mom."

"A missed opportunity," I say, shaking my head.

"Opportunity for what?"

"To get back at the lying, cheating bastard. You could have said they were from a secret admirer. Someone you met at the hospital perhaps. A hot doctor maybe."

She laughs and proceeds to tell me how she managed to make her roommate jealous tonight.

This girl. This *woman.* She's different from anyone I've ever met. I'm her only friend in New York and she chooses to keep that fact to herself. Most girls would have shouted to everyone who would listen that I was sending them food and flowers. Not her. Not Murphy.

Tony is a stupid motherfucker. Does he even know what he lost?

We lie in silence for a few minutes, enjoying the stars and the comfortable quietness between us. When she breaks the silence, her insightful words surprise me.

"Are you scared of anything, Caden? I mean, not like getting mugged or having your identity stolen, but are you really and truly afraid of something?"

I turn on my side and rise up on an elbow. I don't know why I'm inclined to tell this girl all my secrets, all my deepest thoughts and fears, but I am. "I'm afraid I'm living on borrowed time."

She puts a gentle hand on my arm. "Please don't tell me you're sick, Caden."

"No. It's nothing like that." I look around the dark stadium with a longing that has lived inside me for as far back as I can remember. "The average career of an MLB player is about five years. This is my third season. That means I could be more than halfway done. Sometimes I keep waiting for the other shoe to drop, you know? What if this is it? What if this is as far as I go? Who will I be if I'm not on this field, wearing this uniform, doing this job? It's all I've ever dreamed of. I never thought about what would come next. But *next* isn't going to be too far off. And it scares the hell out of me." I try to laugh away the thoughts. "Sorry, I didn't mean to get all existential on you."

"I was the one who asked the existential question," she says.

"What about you, Murph? What are *you* afraid of?" I poke her in the ribs. "Except for fly balls."

"There's really only one thing," she says.

In my mind, I try to guess what she's going to say. Not making it as a model? Not putting her mark on the world? Not getting her big break? "Well, don't keep the crowd guessing," I prod.

"I'm afraid of not being happy," she says with a sigh.

Wow. Okay, I was not expecting that. "You're not happy?" I ask.

"I'm not *unhappy*," she says. "And on a day-to-day basis, I do think I'm enjoying life. But I see so many people who get up every day and just go through the motions. They complain about burning their toast at breakfast. Then they whine about traffic, after which they get to work and grumble about their terrible bosses. Then they come home and complain there is nothing for dinner, but when they go out, they roll their eyes at the bad service. Nobody takes the time to appreciate things and be truly happy. It's a disease that has afflicted our generation. So, yeah, I'm afraid of growing old and not being able to look back on my happy life."

"So, Murphy Brown, what would make you happy? Another modeling contract?"

"You know, I've been thinking a lot about that over the past few weeks. Yes, it would make me happy, but only for a short while. Only until I have to go to work with narcissistic models, bitchy agents and pushy photographers. And being a model is so disingenuous. You have to be someone you're not. I really don't think *any* job would make a huge difference in my happiness. It's more about my life as a whole. The people in it, the places I go, the experiences I have."

I sniff and pretend to wipe tears under my eyes. She sees my gesture in the moonlight and swats my chest. I have the urge to trap her hand and keep it there. Then I remember this isn't a date. Nor do I want it to be. Murphy isn't the woman I want to date. She's more like the person I want to be best friends with.

"Tell me about 'never mind'," I say.

"What do you mean?" she asks with a wrinkle of her nose.

"When I texted you from San Diego, you said something about your ex and about me not knowing the half of it. What happened?"

"Oh, that." She huffs in frustration. "It seems Tony was fucking *all* of my roommates, well except the gay one."

I break out in laughter.

"You find that funny, do you?" she asks.

"Sorry," I say. "It's just that you're so cute when you curse."

She rolls her eyes at me.

"We've already determined the guy is a prick, Murph. Try not to let what he did bother you. It wasn't your fault."

"I know, but it hurts to find out I was being used. Jamie told me he wanted to ride to the top alongside an up-and-coming model. She said he would pick anyone. It wasn't *me* he wanted. Guys are dicks."

I elbow her. "Good thing I'm not a guy then," I joke.

She has no idea how her words have affected me. Does she have any clue how similar our lives are?

"Well, *you're* not a dick," she says. "But I think you might just be the one exception."

"Look!" I shout, pointing up. "I see one."

"That's an airplane, Caden."

I know it's an airplane. But I wanted her to see a shooting star. I hoped she'd pretend with me.

"But thanks," she says. "I know what you were trying to do." She sits up and crisscrosses her legs, resting her elbows on her knees. "How is it that you aren't married? I mean, this is the most romantic non-date I've ever been on. I can't imagine what your *real* dates must be like. And you definitely shouldn't be wasting all this on a friend."

"I'm not wasting anything, Murph. And don't go getting any crazy ideas of romance." I point my finger between us. "You might just be the best *girl* friend I've ever had. I'm not about to screw that up. And, married? No freaking way. I don't think I could ever trust anyone enough."

"Trust anyone?"

"Yeah, you know, to marry me for who I am. You, if anyone, should be able to understand that now."

She nods, giving me a sad smile. "Yeah, I guess I can."

I get my phone out and text Harold. A minute later, the lights start to come back on again. I lean over and offer Murphy my hand. She takes it, allowing me to pull her up while shielding her eyes from the bright lights.

"Come on," I say, pulling her over to home plate. "Your first lesson is about to begin."

Chapter Twelve

Murphy

I pull my hand out of his grip. "No way," I tell him, backing away. "You promised we wouldn't play baseball."

He grabs my hand again and drags me behind him. "We're not *playing* baseball," he tells me. "We're miming it."

"Miming it?"

"Yes. No actual bats. No cheekbone-shattering balls. Just us and the ball field."

Caden positions me on one side of the plate, then he cocks his head. "You're not left-handed, are you?"

"No."

"Okay, so stand here and pretend there is a bat in your hands. Here—hold your hands like this." He forms my hands into fists and puts one on top of the other and then puts them up near my right shoulder.

I glare at him. "It's not like I've never played before, you know. We did have to play softball in gym class in middle school. I'm not completely clueless."

He looks me over from head to toe. "Something's missing," he says.

"A bat maybe?" I say sarcastically.

"Funny. No, not a bat." He takes the Nighthawks cap off his head and puts it onto mine, being careful not to disturb my stitches. "There, now you're ready."

He spends the next half hour teaching me about balls, strikes, line-drives, and pop-flies. My brain is on overload from all the information. But at least I feel like I might understand it a little more when I come to his game next weekend.

I follow him into the dugout and we sit on the bench. I take off his hat and hand it to him.

"Keep it," he says, winking. "I have a few more where that came from."

I put it back on my head, knowing I'll add it to the collection of other Hawks stuff he's given me. "Thanks."

"It looks good on you," he says. "Some girls don't look good in hats but it suits you. The sign of a real tomboy."

I smile when he calls me that. Then I decide to tell him why. "When I was a kid, my dad used to call me a tomboy. I was always building forts and riding skateboards with the neighborhood boys."

"But he doesn't anymore?" he asks.

I shake my head. "No. He died when I was twelve." I look down at the concert t-shirt I'm wearing that reminds me of him. "This was my first concert. My dad took me. It was only weeks before he died."

"I'm sorry," he says, looking sad. "The shirt must mean a lot to you."

"It's my favorite article of clothing."

"We have another thing in common, you know. My dad isn't around either."

"I'm sorry you lost him," I say, knowing how terrible it is to lose a parent at a young age.

He shrugs. "No, he's not dead. At least not that I know of. Who knows, maybe he is. He was a drug addict who left us just after I was born."

"Oh, Caden, that's awful."

"No." He touches the hem of my shirt. "What *you* went through is awful, losing a dad you grew up with. A dad you loved. I never even knew mine. Big difference."

He stands up. "I'd better get you home before you turn into a pumpkin."

I laugh. "I think you're off by a few hours. But yeah, the doctor said I should get a lot of sleep the first week to help with healing."

"You look great, you know. Much better than I thought you'd look less than a week after surgery."

"Thanks. I've come to accept that my face won't be perfect, but then again, it never was in the first place."

"Nobody's perfect, Murphy. And I'll bet in a few months, no one will be able to see any of your scars. And if they do, they're not looking hard enough."

I absorb his meaningful words and smile.

On our way out, Caden gives me a quick tour of the clubhouse, which is just a fancy term for locker room, a place that is normally off-limits to anyone who isn't with the organization. Then we track down Harold and thank him profusely.

We walk to the nearest intersection and I look around as Caden hails a cab. I adore New York at night. The lights, the activity, the endless stream of pedestrians. I close my eyes and inhale. I'm not sure why I do it. I think the city just has a certain smell. If busy were a scent, this would be it. And I love it.

When I open my eyes, Caden is studying me. He holds the door of the cab open for me and we scoot in. "What made you finally do it?" he asks. "Move to the city."

I fumble with the ring on my thumb. Kelly's ring. The only one I never take off. "One of my friends from high school was always encouraging me to do it."

"Sounds like a good friend," he says. "Do you still keep in touch?"

I shake my head sadly. "She was my *best* friend. She died in late February," I tell him. "We were in the middle of an Indian summer. Kelly and I were out jogging when she complained about a sharp pain in the back of her neck. Turns out she got stung by a bee. She didn't even know she was allergic. I tried to get her back, to keep her breathing, but the doctor said there was nothing I could have done."

"Jesus, Murph. That's horrible. I'm sorry to hear that. You've experienced a lot of loss in your life. But that explains why you had the guts to follow your dream. Life's too short not to."

I nod. "Yeah, that's what Kelly always said. My other friends, Tami, Megan and Hannah, they had all taken jobs in other cities or got married and moved away. Kelly and I were the only two left, and when she died, there was nothing more to keep me there."

"No boyfriend?" he asks.

"No. I had a few on and off. Nobody I cared enough about to bring home to my mother."

"How did your mom take your leaving?"

"She didn't want me to go. She thought I was making a rash decision too soon after Kelly died. But she's gone a lot. She's a travel agent and she's always taking trips here or there, either to scope out places or because she won them from her company because she's so good at what she does."

He stares me down. "You still haven't told her what happened, have you?"

"No. She'd only worry about me more than she already does. But I'll have to face the music soon enough, there will be no more hiding it when she starts to get insurance statements after my medical bills begin rolling in."

"About those, I'd like to take care of them," he says, looking guilty.

"What? No. Besides, my mom has really good insurance."

"We'll see," he says, refusing to look directly at me.

"We will not *see*, Caden. Thanks to the job you got me, I can pay my own way. You've done enough. You've done more than enough."

He narrows his eyes at me. "You sure do have a stubborn streak, don't you, Danny-girl?"

"Danny-girl? What is it with you and all your nicknames?"

"You know, Daniel Murphy."

I look at him with a blank stare.

He laughs. "Oh, I have so much to teach you. Daniel Murphy plays second base for Washington. Great player. Good guy."

"Maybe I need to come up with a nickname for *you*," I say, as the cab pulls up to my building.

A smile grows up his face. "I think I might like that," he says. "But my name's pretty boring."

"Your name is anything but boring," I say. "It's quite original. What do your friends call you?"

"Nothing really. The guys on my team call me *Kessler*, or just *Kess*."

"Maybe I'll try it out sometime. Or maybe I'll come up with another one."

"Give it your best shot, Murphy Brown."

I swat him as I exit the cab.

"Thank you, Caden. I had a really good time tonight."

"Mission accomplished then," he says, getting out behind me.

I shove Caden back into the cab, remembering how he almost got mobbed by girls when someone recognized him earlier. I was genuinely fearing for his safety. "Don't get out. I don't want people to swarm you."

He sits back down but instructs the cabbie to stay put until I'm inside the building. Then he turns back to me. "I'll see you Saturday. I gave Lexi your number and she's going to call you this week to set things up."

"I'm looking forward to it, now that I know what … wait, what is that stick you hit the ball with called again?"

His laughter trails after me as I walk away.

When I walk into my apartment, three heads turn my way. I find it hard not to roll my eyes when I see Tony sitting on the couch with Kirsten and Tori. They were probably having some kind of threesome.

I walk past them into the kitchen without saying a word. I grab a bottle of water and head to my bedroom when Tony stands up, blocking my path. "What's with the Hawks hat?" he asks.

I reach up and take the hat off my head. I study it for a second. "Oh, I forgot I was wearing it."

"You don't wear ball caps," he says. "And you don't like baseball."

I crinkle my nose at him in disdain. "And yet you took me to a game," I say dryly.

"Can I have it?" he asks.

"Do I look like I was born yesterday?" I say, pushing my way past him.

I shut my door and lean against it proudly, thinking of how that was the first conversation I'd had with him since he became my ex. I can almost hear Caden's voice in my head. *Good girl.*

Chapter Thirteen

Caden

As a favor to Sawyer's cousin, Rob, Sawyer and I are on a triple date with Rob, his girlfriend, and a few of her visiting friends. As luck would have it, *bad* luck, the friend I got paired with is a huge baseball fan. I give Sawyer the evil eye for the second time tonight when the girl takes yet another selfie of us at the dinner table.

It's not that I don't like baseball fans. I do. If it weren't for them, we wouldn't be able to do what we do. But I like them more from a distance, not when they are draping themselves all over me.

Like the older gentleman at the bar. He's been staring at us all night. He obviously recognizes us, but he's nice enough not to interrupt our dinner. He's the kind of fan I'd gladly sign an autograph for if he asked us on our way out.

"Want to head back to my place?" Rob asks the group. "My roommate is out of town. We can have a few drinks or something."

When Sawyer looks over at me, I give him a punishing stare, making my answer crystal clear.

Sawyer is a nice guy. Like me, I think he's wary of women and their intentions. But he takes it to the extreme. Instead of a three-strikes rule – his dates never get past *one.*

"Come on, man. One drink," he pleads.

It's not that I think he necessarily cares about hooking up with the girl he's with, I just think he's trying to appease his cousin. Rob is in the construction business and he renovated Sawyer's townhouse for barely more than cost when Sawyer moved here two years ago.

"Fine. One."

Brandy, my … uh, *date*, claps her hands and squirms in her chair, apparently excited that the night isn't going to end after dinner. "Maybe we should go back to *your* place, Caden. Rob's is hardly big enough to hold all of us."

I refrain from looking at Sawyer, because I know we'll start laughing if I do. I don't take girls to my place. Lexi and a few of her good friends, they are the only females who have ever been there. I'm very protective of my privacy. "It's not clean. Better not."

Brandy brushes off my comments. "Who cares about that? It's not like we're going to see your bedroom with your skivvies all over the floor." She leans over to me and whispers, "Not unless you want me to."

I look at Rob, who thankfully reads my expression and saves me from Brandy. "My place is just around the corner. We'll go there. And it's clean," he says, shrugging an apology at me.

I take my ball cap out of my back pocket and put it on my head when we leave the restaurant. Sawyer does the same. Even though it's clearly a Hawks hat—I mean what else would we wear—it does provide some camouflage if we pull it down low enough over our foreheads.

Brandy plucks the hat from my head and puts it on her own. "Can I have it?"

I study her for a second, thinking how it doesn't look that good on her with her poufy hair. I carefully remove it from her head and return it to mine, pulling it down low. "I'd really like to wear it myself if you don't mind."

I think about last Saturday night and how I gave Murphy my hat. I'm not sure I've ever seen a girl look so natural, and … so fucking amazing wearing one. There's nothing natural about Brandy. Not her lips, not her voice, not her tits that are practically falling out of her dress. And there is definitely nothing amazing about her.

I need to text Murphy. Find out how her first day at the gym went. I hope she likes it there. Mason did me a real solid hiring her. They were in a bind and needed someone immediately. I talked him into getting someone from a temp agency until Murphy could start. For all I know, she might hate it. It's far from a modeling gig. But the people there are great. It's where I work out in the off-season.

"Oh, my God, Caden Kessler!" a woman squeals as she passes us in the other direction. "And, holy shit, Sawyer Mills!" The girl backtracks and runs to stand in front of us. "Can I please get a picture with you? My brother would freak out. He's a huge fan. I mean, I'm a huge fan, too. But he's like your *biggest* fan."

I look at Sawyer and he nods. Both of us are pretty good at fan interaction. I don't mind signing autographs and taking pictures as long as everyone remains calm. Sometimes, though, it can get out of hand, like now, on a crowded Friday night. I glance around and hope nobody heard her yell our names. I see a few onlookers, but nobody else is approaching us.

"Sure, we can do a quick picture," I say.

The girl moves to stand between Sawyer and me, giddy with excitement.

"Uh." The friend who is aiming her phone at us looks to my right. "Would you mind stepping out of the picture please?"

I look to see that Brandy is still standing next to me—hovering. She pouts before moving out of the way. But as soon as the girl thanks us, Brandy comes right back over and threads her arm around my elbow, as if claiming me.

"Are you Caden's girlfriend?" the fan asks nicely.

"I am tonight," Brandy says proudly.

I have to keep my jaw from dropping at her temerity. "I don't have a girlfriend," I announce. "Brandy is my date."

"Well, thank you," the girl says, before walking away and giggling with her friends.

I start walking. "Come on, let's go before a crowd gathers."

When we get to Rob's place, Brandy raids the kitchen, coming out with all the alcohol she can carry. "You guys up for a game?" she asks.

Sawyer looks at me skeptically. "What did you have in mind?" he asks her.

She shrugs. "Whatever you want. Truth or Dare, Quarters, Strip Poker."

What are we—sixteen?

Rob gives his girlfriend, Kayla, a scolding look. She finally speaks up. "Brandy, would you quit it. They are not playing Strip Poker with you. *I'm* not playing Strip Poker with you. What's *with* you tonight, anyway?"

"She's drunk," Kayla's other friend says. "And she stupidly took a Xanax earlier to chill out because she was nervous about meeting Caden and Sawyer."

"Was not," Brandy whines.

I pick up a deck of cards from Rob's coffee table. "How about just plain old Poker?" I ask.

One drink and an hour later, Sawyer and I get up to leave. Tomorrow we have a double header.

I smile thinking that Murphy and my sister will come watch the second game. Lexi tries to make as many games as she can, but with her job as an assistant to a well-known author, and her two little girls, it seems like her appearances at Hawks Stadium are few and far between.

I told Melanie that the person I hit with my home run ball was coming to another game. I asked her to give Murphy the royal treatment. I know Murphy doesn't want anything from me, but I figure this being her first Hawks Stadium suite experience, she won't know the difference.

Brandy walks me to the door and pulls me aside before I can make my escape. "Don't you want a kiss?" she asks, looking up at me through her eyelashes.

I shake my head. "I don't kiss on the first date."

Her eyes light up. "Oh, so you want a *second* date?"

"Don't you live in Oregon or something?"

"No. I'm from Seattle," she says. "But you never know. If I find a job here, maybe I'll move to New York."

"Oh. Well, good luck with your job search, Brandy," I say, turning to walk through the door.

"You'll look me up when you're in Seattle, right?" She pulls out her phone. "What's your phone number? I'll text you and then you'll have mine."

Not a fuckin' chance.

"I'm sure Rob or Kayla will be nice enough to provide me with your number if I need it," I tell her.

Looking dejected, she puts her phone away. Then she leans close and whispers in my ear. "You don't know what you're missing, Caden Kessler. Everybody says I'm the best fuck they've ever had."

I pull back, put a hand on her shoulder and look at her with serious eyes. "Wow, Brandy. That's impressive. I'll bet if you put that on your resumé, you'll find a job in no time."

On the way downstairs, I get out my phone, hoping to see a text from Murphy about her day.

"Do you have a wife in labor that I don't know about?" Sawyer asks me, motioning to my phone.

"What the hell does that mean?"

"You've been looking at your phone every five minutes all night long, like you're waiting for someone to call you. Or like maybe you want to call someone."

I look at him like he's crazy. "I have not," I say.

He silently laughs as we hail a cab.

Well, I haven't.

Have I?

Chapter Fourteen

Murphy

"Thanks again for coming with me," I tell Lexi as we make our way to the suite in Hawks Stadium. "I don't have many friends here yet."

"I'm happy to do it," she says. "It's been almost a month since I've been to one of Caden's games, so I was due. Plus, I know what it's like to be new to the city and not know anyone."

I laugh. "Oh, I know people. Just not anyone I'd consider a friend."

"What about Caden? From the way he talks about you, I'd say *he's* your friend."

"Yeah, well, he may just be the only one."

"Not true," Lexi says, hooking her arm around my elbow. "Now you have *two*."

Lexi Kessler Stone is someone I knew I would like from the moment I saw her. She greeted me with a hug and proceeded to immerse me in conversation as if we'd been long-lost BFFs. Her smile is infectious and welcoming, and although she's supermodel gorgeous, the way she carries herself is not intimidating in the least.

"Thanks. That means a lot to me," I say.

"Here it is," she says, pointing to a sign labeled 'Suite 19.' "This is going to be fun."

I show our tickets to the attendant at the door and we are ushered through into what looks like a swanky cocktail party, only instead of cocktail dresses and suits, the party-goers are all wearing Nighthawks shirts.

I look down at my plain white t-shirt. I thought about wearing the jersey Caden brought me in the hospital, but it was a men's large and it looked ridiculous on me. And since I haven't gotten paid yet, I couldn't afford to get a Nighthawks shirt in my size.

Lexi looks around at the other people in the suite and then at me, laughter dancing in her eyes. "You don't stand out at all," she says, sarcastically.

"I know, I'm sorry," I say guiltily, thinking the least I could have done was wear one of the hats Caden has given me.

"Drinks?" A waitress asks, circulating through the suite.

Lexi leans over and whispers in my ear. "In case Caden didn't mention it, drinks and food are included in this suite, so don't be shy."

"Why else do you think I'm here?" I say, jokingly. Then I realize how bad that must have sounded. "I mean, I came for the game, obviously. It's just that I lost my job and I recently started a new one and I won't get paid for a week, so I was really looking forward to having some real food."

Lexi gives me a sympathetic look. "You don't have to worry," she says. "I won't tell Caden you just came for the food. I know good and well what it's like to live from paycheck to paycheck. I know how it feels to be without a job."

"You do?"

She nods. Then she calls over the waitress. "So, what will it be, Murphy? Coke, tea, champagne?"

"Are you kidding?" I ask. "Champagne, of course."

Lexi laughs as the waitress hands us some pre-poured glasses from her tray. "I knew I was going to like you," she says.

"Old Man Murphy?" a woman coming through the door shouts over the noise in the room.

I cover my mouth to avoid spitting out a mouthful of champagne. I look around at the now-silent room, embarrassed, but making every effort not to fall down laughing. I walk over to her. "I'm Old Man Murphy."

The lady looks down at the box and then up at me in total confusion.

"I mean, I'm Murphy. Murphy Cavenaugh." The woman continues to stare at me. "It's a long story … er, an inside joke." I feel heat creep up my face as I scramble for an explanation.

She laughs and hands me the box. "Lucky for you," she says. "Murphy Cavenaugh suits you so much better, dear. This is for you. It's from Mr. Kessler."

"Oh, thank you," I say, accepting the package.

She hands me a business card. "I'm Melanie. If there is anything you need, anything at all, don't hesitate to text me during the game."

I look back at Lexi to see her watching our exchange. "Okay, I appreciate that."

"Enjoy the game," she says before walking out of the suite.

I take the box over to a table and open it to see what's inside. Then I look around at the ceiling of the suite. "Are there cameras in here?"

"Cameras? Why?" Lexi asks.

I pull out the Nighthawks shirt and show it to her. "Do you think Caden could see that I wasn't wearing a Hawks shirt?"

Lexi laughs. "You don't know my brother well enough to know this yet, Murphy, but when he plays baseball, he doesn't think about anything else. Even before games, he has a ritual that he does to get ready. To get him in the right frame of mind. So there is no way he would have seen you even if there *were* cameras in here."

"Oh." I look down at the shirt in my hands. "I wonder how he knew then."

"Knew that you wouldn't have any Nighthawks stuff?" she asks. "*You*, the girl who hates baseball? Yeah, I wonder."

"Okay, fine," I pout, conceding her point. "I guess I'd better go put it on."

By the time I come out of the bathroom, the game has started. Some people take seats right in front of the glass, but I hang back, picking at the hors d'oeuvres and sipping champagne. I realize there is quite possibly one inch of solid glass separating me from any potential fly balls, but it still makes me uneasy.

Lexi stands next to me, watching the game from the back of the suite. "Caden's probably batting fifth," she says. "You know, in case you were wondering."

"Does that mean he will get to bat this time, before his team is in the field?"

"Hopefully, unless the guys before him all strike out."

I nod. "He's trying to teach me about baseball," I tell her.

"I know. He told me. I think he's quite enamored with you, Murphy."

"Enamored?" I shoot her my crazy eyes. "No. I'm just his charity case, Lexi. That's all."

She smiles, shaking her head as if she has some kind of private joke.

"What?" I ask.

"Caden hasn't told you how I met my husband, has he?"

"Your husband, the doctor?"

"That's right."

I shake my head. "No, he hasn't."

"I was once a charity case, too, you know. It's not necessarily a bad thing, Murphy. Plus, my brother feels genuinely guilty for putting you in the hospital. And let's be honest, it's not like he can't afford whatever he's done for you."

"I don't care how much money he has," I tell her. "I don't want to be beholden to anyone."

"Beholden?" She turns to face me, head on, ignoring the game. Then she laughs once again. "Murphy, you and I are more alike than you know. I think we're going to be great friends."

There is cheering from the crowd as one of the players runs around to second base.

Lexi pulls on my elbow, dragging me to the front by the window. "Come on, Caden is up."

I find myself getting nervous when we reach the front of the suite. Strangely enough though, I'm not nervous about getting hit, I'm nervous about Caden being up at bat. I look down at the tens of thousands of fans in the stadium and I wonder how anyone could stand up at the plate and hit a ball with all those people screaming and cheering.

He whacks the ball and I find myself yelling and clapping. Then I realize I'm the only one in the suite doing it. I turn to Lexi, embarrassed. "He hit the ball, didn't he?"

"It was a foul ball," she says, pointing over to left field. "That counts as a strike."

I shrug. "Sorry," I say to the people sitting next to me. They chuckle as if they know it's my first time watching a game.

Caden swings and misses, giving him a second strike. Then he swings and hits the ball again. Before I embarrass myself by cheering a second time, I look around. Again, nobody is cheering. "Another foul? Does that mean he's out? Third strike?"

She shakes her head. "Nope. You can't get out on a foul ball. You can hit them all day long and not get out. Well, unless somebody on the other team catches one of them."

He fouls off another and I find myself tensing up as I watch the guy in left field dash over to try and catch it. Caden does it again, hitting the ball straight up in the air, and I grab Lexi's arm waiting to see if the catcher will get a hold of it.

Lexi laughs. "Pretty intense, huh?"

Then he swings and misses and gets called out. "Oh, no," I say, feeling bad about his strike out.

"It's okay," Lexi says. "They get out more than they get a hit."

"They do?"

"Yup. If they only get a hit a third of the time, they are doing well."

"I have a lot to learn," I say.

Someone taps my shoulder. I turn around to see Melanie. She hands me another box. "Mr. Kessler has invited you and Mrs. Stone to wait for him outside the clubhouse after the game."

"Oh, okay, thank you." I turn to Lexi. "That's the locker room," I say, proudly. "Bet you didn't think I knew that."

She laughs and points to the box. "What's in this one?"

I open it and pull out a giant foam finger with the Nighthawks logo and a large #8. I put the box aside and roll my eyes. "A little over the top, isn't he?"

"I think he just wants everyone to love baseball as much as he does," Lexi says.

I can't help myself as I watch intensely every time Caden is behind the plate as catcher. I worry he will get hit with the ball and get hurt like I did. I know he wears that pad thing and a face mask, but I heard some guys in the suite discussing how the pitcher throws close to one hundred miles per hour. That is crazy. I wonder if Caden has ever gotten hurt. He seems to expertly know where the pitcher will throw the ball.

By the time Caden gets up to bat again, I'm really getting into the game. I don't know if it's Lexi and her encouragement, or the fans that surround me, but my heart pumps wildly when he steps up to the plate.

He swings twice and misses twice. I find myself getting bummed out. Then, on the third swing, I hear a *crack* and everyone in the stadium stands up and yells.

Lexi grabs me and hugs me in a tight embrace while jumping up and down. Everyone in the room is high-fiving everyone else. I'm caught up in the excitement as I cheer and even wave my foam finger around in the air. Then I walk up to the glass and watch Caden as he runs around third base. We're pretty far away up here, but I think I can see a smile on his face. Then, right before he touches home plate, I could swear he glances up at the suite.

Lexi comes and stands next to me. When I look over at her, she's studying me.

"What?" I ask.

She looks back down at the field where her brother is joining his team in the dugout. "Oh, nothing," she says, a huge smile overtaking her face.

Chapter Fifteen

Caden

As usual, when we emerge from the clubhouse, there is a large crowd of friends, family and fans who have waited around to see the players. Security does their best to keep any overeager fans from getting to us, but it seems there are always one or two of them, mostly women, who end up breaking through the crowd to get to the target of their obsession.

I used to think it was funny and flattering. But I've since found out some of those women are downright scary. How could someone I don't even know possibly think I'd just drop everything and go out with them? Sleep with them? *Marry* them? They can be delusional. So I've learned to be approachable without being too nice. Because *too nice* can get you into trouble. *Too nice* can be misconstrued by irrational fans.

Sawyer, Brady and I all walk out together. As we always do, we stop to sign autographs, pose for pictures, and shake hands.

"I love you, Caden!" a woman screams from behind the crowd.

I point in the direction the voice came from. "Back at ya!" I shout, making the ASL sign for *'I love you'* with my right hand.

As more and more players come out of the clubhouse and leave, the crowd thins. I say goodbye to Sawyer and Brady knowing I'll see them on the plane tomorrow when we head down south to Tampa.

Suddenly, I find myself being thrown back into the wall as a woman hurls herself at me. I have no choice but to catch her so she doesn't hurt me, or herself.

"Sorry," Drew says as he runs over and peels the fan off me. "I didn't mean to let her get past, Mr. Kessler."

"But he loves me!" the woman screams as Drew pulls her away. "You saw it. Everyone saw it. He said he loves me."

Shit. Really?

I hang my head, realizing once again how literally these deranged fans take things. I intentionally never say *'I love you'* back, because I refuse to minimize the meaning of those three words the way some fans do. I will only say those words to one person—if at all.

I scan the crowd until I find familiar faces. Safe faces. And I smile when I find them.

Lexi and Murphy are leaning up against the far wall, waiting patiently for me to finish up. I walk away from the crowd earlier than I usually do, still stunned by the overzealous fan. When I make my way to the girls, I feel my smile grow larger when I see Murphy wearing the shirt I had sent to her. Not only that, she's still carrying the large foam finger.

I give my sister a kiss on the cheek and then I do the same to Murphy. Then I hear a few screams behind me, from women asking me to kiss them, too.

"Are you okay?" Murphy asks.

I look back to where Drew was dragging that woman away. "I'm fine."

"She *jumped* on you, Caden," she says, concern etched into her face.

Lexi laughs. "Good thing my little brother is a top-notch catcher."

Murphy doesn't find her joke funny. "Does that happen a lot?"

I shrug.

"Oh, my gosh, really? You should have a bodyguard or something."

"It's fine. I'm fine."

When I'm looking at Murphy, it dawns on me that she's had her hairline stitches removed and that she looks great. But then I realize her cheeks are pink. Pink from the sun. I narrow my eyes at her. "Murph, you look sunburned. How in the hell did that happen? Weren't you in the suite?"

"It's a nice day," she says. "Lexi and I walked here."

I take the hat off my head and fit it onto hers. "You have to protect your face from the sun. It'll help reduce the scarring."

"Who's the lucky girl?" someone behind me shouts.

"Are you his girlfriend?" shouts another.

"Caden, can I have a hat?" yet another asks.

Girls are freaking out over me giving Murphy my hat. What the hell is the big deal? It's a *hat*, not an engagement ring.

I ignore the comments, but I can tell Murphy is bothered by them. However, she doesn't acknowledge any of the incessant questions. "It's going to be dark soon," she says, going to remove the hat. "I don't think I'll need it."

I stop the movement of her hand. "Keep it. Wear it. Doctor's orders."

"I wouldn't argue with my brother if I were you," Lexi says. "Believe me, it won't end well. He's as stubborn as a mule. Plus, I'm pretty sure Kyle would tell you the same thing. You need to protect your face from the sun while it heals."

I laugh when Murphy rolls her eyes and fake pouts.

"Whatever, *Doc*," she says.

"Doc?" I ask.

She shrugs. "Just trying out nicknames."

"Keep trying, Old Man Murphy."

Lexi laughs at our exchange. "Oh my gosh! I get it now. The box. *Old Man Murphy.*" She smacks me playfully on the arm. "You are terrible. I thought maybe Melanie had been hitting the booze." She gestures to Murphy. "And I've never seen so many shades of red on a face before."

She asks Murphy, "You need a nickname for him? I have a few from our childhood. *Rat, Bug, Tool, Squirt*, *Homer*, take your pick."

I roll my eyes at my big sister as the girls share a giggle.

"Oh, how could I have forgotten?" Murphy says. "Congratulations on your home run."

"Thanks. I'm just glad it didn't hit anyone this time."

"Me, too. And the guy who caught it gave it to a kid," she says, smiling.

"I know. Sawyer told me."

"Did you sign it for him?" Lexi asks.

"Yeah. Hey, speaking of my home run," I say to Murphy. "I think you need to come to all my games. You seem to be a good luck charm. And you have to wear *that* shirt and the finger."

She looks down at her shirt and then at the finger she must have forgotten she was 'wearing.'

Lexi leans over to her and explains, "Baseball is a superstitious sport. When something goes well, you have to do the same thing in hopes that it will be repeated. That was number twenty-seven, right, Caden?"

"Lucky twenty-seven," I say, sharing a nostalgic smile with Lexi. "Come on, let's get out of here. I'll buy you girls a drink and then I'll get you home."

As we make our way out of the stadium, I notice a guy lurking at the entrance. He looks familiar. He's staring right at me. At us.

Although I know he's probably just a fan wanting an autograph, I go into protective mode since I'm with Lex and Murphy. I keep looking over at him to see if he's going to follow us. I even pull out my phone, ready to summon Drew or his security team in case we need assistance.

I can't shake the feeling that I know him from somewhere.

"How about Klingmans?" Lexi asks. "They make good margaritas there."

Oh, shit. I know why he looks familiar. Klingmans was the restaurant Sawyer, Rob and I went to on our triple date. And the guy standing over by the entrance, staring at me, is the same guy who was sitting at the bar there last night—staring at me.

Great. Looks like I have another goddamn stalker. I send a quick text to Drew, hoping he can scare the guy into backing off. But when I look up from my phone, he's gone.

So much for unwinding after the double-header. I ruin my time with the girls because I spend the next few hours looking over my shoulder.

Chapter Sixteen

Murphy

"You seem to be getting the hang of things around here," Trick says, giving me her schedule for next week.

Trick is one of the full-time personal trainers at the gym. She's funny, smart, and super strong. And I'm not exactly sure if she's a *she*. But I don't know her well enough to ask.

The past few weeks working at the gym have been a lot of fun. Much more fun than modeling. Okay, so the pay is considerably lower, but if I'm being honest, having a steady paycheck is more exciting to me than living off ramen noodles ninety percent of the time and living like a queen the other ten percent.

I mean, who knows what would have happened if I'd been able to take the job with that high-end clothing line. I keep thinking back to what Caden said about living on borrowed time. In model years, twenty-three is over-the-hill. I might've gotten in a few good years, but at the end of it all, what would I really have had?

It's only taken me two weeks to realize I want more out of life than getting on the cover of a magazine and then being remembered as a has-been. And it's only taken that same two weeks for the owners of the gym to take notice of me.

The other day, Jayden, the manager, asked me to help with some paperwork since the membership coordinator is on maternity leave. I think she was impressed with how organized and detail-oriented I was. I told her I had taken some business courses at the community college back in Iowa, and then the next day, I was informed the owners wanted me trained as an assistant to the coordinator. It doesn't mean any more money. Not yet anyway. But who knows what could happen. This is the biggest gym in the city. The staff is huge and business is booming.

"I've been trying hard to keep up with all your schedules. With fourteen trainers, that's practically a full-time job in itself," I tell her.

"Well, you're doing a great job," she says. "You are so organized. I'll bet your apartment is always neat and clean, isn't it?"

"Ha! Hardly. I live in a two-bedroom apartment with four other girls, all of them models. That equals a lot of clothes and makeup lying around. Not to mention the fact that getting any quality bathroom time is just unheard of."

Her jaw drops. "You live with four models? You must be one tough chick."

"You don't know the half of it. My cheating ex is always hanging around because he's now dating the girl I share a room with."

"No fucking way."

"Way." I nod.

"I have a cheating ex, too. In fact, she just moved her lying cheating ass out of my apartment last week." She studies me for a second, drawing her brows together. "You know, I have a spare room. It may not be much, but it beats sharing a bedroom with a model." She sticks her finger down her throat to let me know just how highly she regards those in my former profession. "And it takes me all of five minutes to get ready in the morning. No makeup and other crap you'd have to weed through to use the bathroom."

"I don't know," I say, hesitant about moving right in with another person I barely know, considering how well it went the last time.

She sees her next client walk through the door. "Just think about it. Joan paid me rent through October, so I have more than a month before I'm in dire straits on my mortgage, and I won't even make you pay rent until November, you know, in case you have to give some kind of notice to your other roommates."

"Okay. I'll think about it," I say as she walks away with someone who I now know is an Olympic skater.

There are a lot of sports stars who come here. Probably because one of the owners is the starting quarterback for the Giants.

My phone vibrates in my pocket so I pull it out to check the text.

#8: Ready for your next lesson? I want to take you to a game.

Me: Isn't your season over?

#8: Thanks for reminding me that we didn't make the playoffs.

Me: Sorry.

#8: I'm joking, Old Man Murphy. You aren't working Saturday afternoon, are you?

Me: What did you have in mind?

#8: I'm taking you to a Yankees game.

Before I can answer him, an attractive woman who has blonde hair with inky-black tips approaches the counter. "I'm looking for Murphy Brown," she says.

I roll my eyes, but I'm also grateful she didn't ask for *Old Man Murphy*. "Let me guess. Caden sent you?"

"Kind of, I mean he told me about you, but I didn't think he knew I'd come in," she says. "I'm Piper Lawrence. Did he tell you to expect me?"

"He didn't tell me anything, but he's the only one who calls me Murphy Brown. I think he has some obsession with an old TV show or something."

"Your name isn't Murphy Brown?" she asks.

I hold my hand out to her. "Murphy Cavenaugh. Are you by chance related to one of my bosses?"

She leans in close and whispers, "I'm married to the *best* boss. But don't let my sisters hear you repeat that since they are married to the other two."

Just like when I met Lexi, I feel an instant connection with Piper.

As if reading my mind, Piper says, "You know, I'm friends with Lexi Stone. Between her and her sisters-in-law, and me and *my* sisters, we can throw some pretty fun girls' nights. You should definitely join us."

I smile thinking of how completely different that would be from when I was hanging out with my pretentious roommates. "I'd really like that. Thank you."

"I have to run and get my daughter from school," she says, pulling a piece of paper from the printer and writing on it. "But here is my number. Text me so I can have yours. We'll set something up."

Before she turns to leave, she stares at my face and I think maybe she's looking at my scars. They're starting to fade, but I'm still self-conscious about them.

"Caden's right," she says. "You *are* gorgeous."

She spins around and walks out the front door, leaving my jaw slightly agape.

Chapter Seventeen

Caden

We play one hundred and sixty-two games in one hundred and eighty days—and that's if you don't make the playoffs. It's grueling. We rarely get a full day off during the season. Then, the day after the season ends … nothing. We go from Mach Two to zero overnight.

It's hard on some of the guys, especially the ones who are married with kids. They go home to wives who are used to taking care of everything. For eight months, their wives paid the bills, took the kids to school, and managed the household. Then baseball season ends and their husbands come back, and for lack of anything better to do, they jump right into being the head of the family.

A lot of people think athletes mainly get divorced because of infidelity. While it's true to some extent, it's more likely they just can't adjust to the twice-a-year rapid changes in lifestyle.

Me, on the other hand, I love the change. In the spring, I can't wait to immerse myself back into baseball. In the fall, I can't wait to slow down and enjoy the things I didn't get to all summer long. Things like going to the beach, hanging out with friends, and lazy Sundays.

Some players can't stand to go to games if they aren't the ones down on the field. Me—I welcome the chance to be a fan instead of a player. I get caught up in the excitement just like everyone else does. Sitting in the stands makes me feel like a kid again. I only hope some of my enthusiasm will rub off on Murphy.

When she emerges from her building wearing the Hawks shirt I gave her a few weeks ago, I smile. We're going to watch the Yankees play the Nationals and she's wearing *my* team. Not that I'm any better. I'm wearing a Nighthawks ball cap.

As we make our way to the subway to go to Yankee Stadium, I notice how well her scars are healing. Then I look up at the bright afternoon sun and frown. "Please tell me you put on sunscreen."

Her hand reaches up to touch the scar beneath her eye. "Yes. I did."

I take my hat off. "That's not good enough." I put it on her head. "You need this, too."

"Caden, no. You need to wear it. You might get recognized. Do you really want to be swarmed at the game?"

We pass by a street vendor and I see something. I smile at Murphy before I pull her to the side and get out my wallet. I pay the proprietor and then tear the tag off the hat before putting in on my head.

Murphy laughs at me. Or, rather, she laughs at my hat. The one that's embroidered *'I heart New York'* with a picture of the Statue of Liberty on the back.

"That hat is hideous," she says. "You need to trade me. I'll wear the stupid New York hat."

"Not a chance," I say, batting her hand away.

"Won't you be embarrassed if you get recognized?"

"I don't give a shit what people think about me, Murph. Well, unless they think I'm a bad ball player."

She shakes her head. "No way would anyone think that, Caden. You are really good."

I raise my eyebrows at her. "Based on your extensive knowledge of the sport?"

"No." She swats my arm. "Based on the fans who swarm you wherever you go. Based on the face time you get on ESPN. Based on your Wikipedia page."

I stop walking and look at her with a smug smile. "You Googled me, Murphy Brown?"

"I was doing research," she says. "Don't flatter yourself."

We arrive at the stadium and are herded in among tens of thousands of other fans. Murphy gets a few stares because of her Hawks attire, other than that, we seem to get lost in the crowd. And that's just fine by me. We stop at the concession stand and buy a couple of beers and a big salty pretzel. Then I lead her through a tunnel to find our seats.

When we emerge from the tunnel into the open stadium and Murphy sees where we're going, she stops walking and the person behind her collides into her back.

"Sorry," she tells him, before leaning against the wall to let people pass.

I see the concern on her face before she sighs, looking at the ground. She's scared to go back out in the stands. I wonder if she thought we'd be in a suite. Maybe I should have prepared her. Maybe I should have asked her. Maybe I should have gotten a damn suite.

Shit. I screwed up.

I lift her chin so she has to look at me. "Murph, it's going to be okay. The odds of you getting hit by another ball have to be one in a million."

She looks out at the stadium and then back to me, fear in her eyes.

"I've got your back, Murphy. I promise I'll never let anything happen to you."

She nods unconvincingly, so I grab her hand and turn back in the other direction. "Come on. I'm sure we can find a suite to watch the game in."

She doesn't let me pull her. "No. Suites are expensive."

I raise my brows at her.

She rolls her eyes. "I know you probably have more money than God, but that doesn't mean you should spend it frivolously." She looks back out into the stadium. "It's fine. I'll be fine." She looks up at me. "Just promise you'll try to catch a ball if it comes our way."

I laugh. "*Try* to catch it? Have you read my Wikipedia page? Because if you have, you'd know that I'm ranked in the top five catchers in the league. I think you're safe with me."

"You're right. I'm being silly," she says. "Okay, let's go."

I lead the way to our seats behind the dugout on the third base line.

Halfway through the game, it dawns on me that the only time Murphy will look at me, or at the scoreboard, or at other fans, is when the ball is not in play. She doesn't take her eyes off the ball until it's safely back in the pitcher's glove. And she flinches every time a foul ball gets within fifty yards of where we are sitting. I guess I can't blame her.

I take every opportunity to educate her on the game. And she seems genuinely interested in learning about it.

During a change of innings, she takes a long look around the stadium and then turns to me. "I can see why you wanted to sit here instead of in a suite."

I nod, knowing exactly what she means. Suites are nice, especially in the dead of summer when it can be a hundred degrees outside, but there is nothing like sitting in the stands, being part of the crowd, experiencing the game.

"It's pretty great, isn't it?" I ask, hopeful she'll agree.

"It is now that I know what's going on," she says. "But I must admit, it's not nearly as exciting without you on the field."

"Yeah, having a personal interest makes it even better."

"You have no idea," she says. "I was so nervous every time you came up to bat."

I study her. "You were?"

She nods, looking out at the sea of people surrounding us. "I don't know how you do it," she says. "How do you get up there in front of all these people and not freeze?"

"Says the girl who is a fashion model."

"Was," she says, touching the side of her face. "*Was* a fashion model. And just so you know, I would throw up before every interview or photo shoot."

Guilt grips my heart. "You will be again, Murphy. If you really want it, it'll happen."

"We'll see," she says with a casual shrug, not looking as upset as I thought she would. "I'm not even sure that's what I want anymore."

"I used to throw up before every game, you know."

"Really?"

"Yup. I still get nervous. Most players do. I think being nervous makes me a better player. Being nervous means you have something to lose. But I've found ways to relax before I take the field."

"Oh, right. Lexi mentioned something about you having pre-game rituals. What is it that you do? Do you always eat the same meal? Meditate? Watch yourself hit home runs on video?"

I laugh. "No. But you just described some of my teammates."

Before I get into boring her with my pre-game habit, a foul ball pops up and I know it's headed our way. I can tell from the spin it had coming off the bat that it won't hit us, but when I glance at Murphy, she looks terrified. I put my arms around her and cover her with my body as a guy three rows down catches the ball.

"It's okay," I tell her. "Someone caught it."

She has a death grip on me as she looks up into my eyes and thanks me for protecting her. Of course I did. I always will.

"I'm never sitting in the stands without you," she says.

"Are you telling me I have to buy you suite tickets to every game next season?"

"You are not paying for me to sit in a suite, Caden. And I can't go to every game. That's ridiculous."

"The hell it is. I hit a home run in both the games you came to. You're my good luck charm."

"Haven't you hit like twenty-something others this year?"

"Doesn't matter." I shake my head. "It's a superstitious game. If I think you being there is good luck, you will be."

I hear people cheering around us when two things happen. One: I realize Murphy is still in my arms, and two: Murphy and I are being displayed on the JumboTron for all to see.

"Damn it," I say, pulling away from her. I grab her hand. "Let's go."

I try to protect her from the fans mauling us on our way out. I politely refuse any requests for pictures or autographs as we hurry through the tunnel and make our way outside the stadium. We run down the street and around the corner before we stop and lean against the wall.

Murphy looks at her phone. "Wow," she says, smiling. "Three whole hours it took them to recognize you. I guess the hat worked."

I take the touristy hat off my head and throw it into the nearest trashcan before we head out to catch a train back to Murphy's.

"I had fun today," she says. "I might even do it again sometime."

"Absolutely." I look at my watch. "I'd ask you to join me for dinner, but I kind of made plans."

She raises an inquisitive brow. "A date?"

"Her name is Laney. She's a flight attendant. I've been out with her twice before. I'm doubling with Sawyer." I get a bright idea. "Hey, maybe you could come. Triple date."

She looks at me like I'd asked her to go to the moon with me. "And just who shall I bring?" she asks, laughing. "Oh, how about Tony? Or maybe Corey, the guy who keeps hitting on me at the gym."

"A guy keeps hitting on you at the gym?"

She shrugs. "A lot of guys do, but he's the most persistent."

I feel a twinge deep inside, but ignore it. "What if I set you up with one of the guys from the team?"

"I'm not going out with a baseball player," she says.

"What's wrong with baseball players?" I ask defensively.

"Nothing, I guess. But I'm not going out with *anyone* right now, Caden."

"What if it would just be platonic? I hate going on dates. The more the merrier if you ask me. I never know what to talk about. And all they ever want to talk about is me."

She laughs. "You are being ridiculous. You never run out of things to talk about when we're together."

"That's different. Friends are different. Come on, will you at least think about it? It might be fun."

"Fine. I'll think about it. But only if they understand it's platonic. And not tonight. Tonight, I have plans with your sister."

"Lexi? That's great. What are you two doing?"

"She's hosting a girls' night for me and some of her friends. To tell you the truth, I'm pretty excited about it."

I open the door for her. "Have fun tonight. And keep next Saturday night free."

"I said I'd *think* about it, Caden."

"Saturday," I say again, allowing the door to shut between us before I head home.

Then, when I turn around to hail a cab, I run smack into someone. When I see who it is, alarms go off in my head.

It's the same guy from the restaurant. The one from outside the stadium that day. I sidestep around him, keeping a close eye on his hands as I don't know what to expect from this stalker.

"Caden," the man says.

I hold my hand up to keep him back. "Sorry, I'm in a hurry," I say, quickening my steps to the curb.

A cab pulls up and I get in before the man can follow me.

"Caden, wait!" the man shouts. "Don't you recognize me?"

I study him as the cab slowly pulls out into traffic. He walks on the sidewalk next to the cab, giving me a better chance to look at him. He gives me a sad smile. And that's when it hits me.

It hits me and my whole world changes. As the cab drives away, I realize the man left in its wake is none other than my father.

Chapter Eighteen

Murphy

When I enter my apartment, I'm more than a little disappointed to see Tony in the living room. *Again.* I swear he's over here more now than when we were dating. He's lying on the couch tossing a baseball to the ceiling and then catching it. I flinch as he does it over and over.

As I walk behind the couch to my room, I reach out and grab the baseball out of the air so he'll stop throwing it.

"Careful," he bites at me. "That's a home run ball."

I study the ball as it dawns on me what he said. My jaw falls open in disgust. "Are you kidding me?" I yell. "I was lying there bleeding and you took time to pick up the damn ball?"

He tries to grab it from me, but I hide it behind my back.

"Do you know how rare it is to get a home run ball?" he asks.

"Ugh!" I pout petulantly.

"Give it back, babe," he says.

"Do *not* call me babe, you two-timing bastard."

"Me? Two-timing? What about *you?*" He points to the television which is tuned to ESPN. "How long have you been fucking Caden Kessler?" he asks.

I'm rendered speechless. I can only stare at him in surprise and confusion.

"I saw you, Murphy. He had his arms around you. It's all over ESPN and social media."

"Not that it's any of your business, but I'm not sleeping with him. Unless you've forgotten, it was his ball that hit me. And unlike some people, *he* came to see me every day in the hospital."

"But you're not fucking him. Right."

"I don't care what you think, Tony."

Kirsten walks into the room with two glasses of wine. "Oh, hi, Murphy. Nice hat. Boyfriend give it to you? Does he have any single friends?" She giggles on her way over to Tony.

I roll my eyes and refuse to acknowledge her questions. If they want to think I'm with Caden, who am I to tell them otherwise?

After Kirsten puts the wine on the table, Tony pulls her on top of him and she straddles him while he kisses her senseless. Neither of them is bothered by the fact that I'm standing right here. When Tony opens his eyes and stares at me while he's still kissing her, I realize this display of affection is all for me.

I shake my head and turn around to walk away. I couldn't care less whose throat he sticks his tongue down anymore.

"Murphy!" he shouts out after me. "Ball."

I look down at the ball still in my hand. Then before giving it too much thought, I cock my arm back and launch the ball across the room, right through a plate glass window. I can hear it bounce off fire escapes before landing in the alley six floors below.

I don't stick around to hear their shrieks of displeasure. Instead, I pull my suitcase out of the closet and throw all my stuff into it.

When I go into the bathroom to get the rest of my things, Kirsten is yelling at me about the broken glass and Tony is pissed at me over the baseball.

Dragging my heavy suitcase behind me, I stop at the door, throw Kirsten my key and say, "I hope you two will be very happy together. If ever two people deserved each other, it's you."

"What about the window?" Kirsten calls out after me.

"Send me a bill," I say, right before the door slams shut behind me.

Walking down the hall, two things occur to me. One: it will probably cost me a week's salary to fix the window; and two: I'm homeless.

~ ~ ~

Lexi looks down at my over-sized suitcase and laughs. "Well, that's a unique hostess gift."

My face blanches. With all the worrying I did on the way over, I plain forgot to pick up a bottle of wine for her. I close my eyes in shame. "Oh, gosh, Lexi. I'm so sorry. I'm a terrible person. I was going to pick something up and then there was Tony and Kirsten and the ball and the window." I notice she's still staring at my suitcase. "It's not what you think. I'm not crashing here or anything. But I left. I threw my key at her so I can't go back. I'm going to a hotel later tonight. I promise. I just didn't have anywhere to leave my suitcase."

She smiles at me before reaching down to pull up the handle of my suitcase. "You are not getting a hotel room," she says, dragging my heavy bag behind her.

"Of course I am."

I follow her down the hallway where she turns into a beautifully-appointed bedroom. "You'll stay here, Murphy. For as long as you need to."

I look around her guest room that looks like it's been decorated by one of those shows on HGTV.

"Wow. This is nice," I tell her. "But I can't—"

"It's already been settled," she says, cutting me off. She puts her hand on my shoulder. "I know what it's like to not know where you are going to stay. I know what it's like to be scared and alone in a big city. You're staying. Now come on, I need some help with the drinks."

I follow her out into the kitchen and notice how quiet it is. I look around. It shouldn't be that quiet in here. She has two small children. "Where are your kids?" I ask. "I was looking forward to meeting them."

"With Mrs. Mitchell," she says. "Kyle is working tonight and I wanted to be able to let loose and have fun with the girls. I think Piper's daughter is there, too. One big sleepover."

"That's nice of her to watch your kids for you."

"That woman is a saint. Between Baylor, Skylar and Piper, she already has six grandchildren of her own, but I swear she considers my kids and my sisters-in-law's kids as her grandchildren as well. I lost my own mom when I was in college, so she's taken me under her wing."

I gasp. "You lost your mom? Caden told me your dad was out of the picture, but I didn't know you'd lost your mom, too. I'm so sorry."

"Thanks. I know you lost your dad at a young age. Caden told me. Are you and your mom close?"

I nod. "Yes. I miss her sometimes, but not enough to move back to Iowa."

She laughs. "Kind of different from New York City, huh?"

"Like night and day."

"Did you tell your mom about the accident yet?" she asks as she hands me glasses from her cabinet.

I draw my brows at her in confusion.

"Caden and I are very close," she explains. "We talk about anything and everything. I hope that's okay."

I shrug. "It's fine. It's not like I'm telling him military secrets or anything. And, no, I haven't told her. I'm sure she'll be calling me any day now once the insurance statements start to roll in."

She shakes her head at me with a smile. "I'd love to listen in on *that* conversation," she says. "How do you think she'll take it?"

"She'll insist I move back to Iowa. That's why I didn't tell her. But now I'm healed. Well, except for some scars, but I'm good. I have a job. I don't have a place to live, but she doesn't need to know that. Plus, I think one of the trainers at the gym is looking for a roommate and I'm pretty sure I will be able to move right in. I might not need to stay here for more than a night or two."

"I'm not worried about how long you need to stay here, Murphy. It'll be fun."

The doorbell rings and all three Mitchell sisters walk in. Over the past week, Piper, Skylar and Baylor have all come into the gym to make my acquaintance. Their husbands are my bosses so I tried to make a good impression on them, but I got the idea they didn't care about good impressions. They all befriended me immediately and I'm grateful that my circle of friends is expanding considering I just walked out on my previous one.

The doorbell rings again and in walks a statuesque redhead and a beautiful brunette. Lexi grabs my hand and pulls me over to them. “Murphy Cavenaugh, I’d like you to meet my sisters-in-law, Charlie and Mallory Stone.”

“Nice to meet you,” says Charlie, the tall redhead as she pulls me into a hug. “I’ve heard a lot about you.”

I sneak a look at Lexi who shrugs and says, “One big happy family.”

Mallory hugs me next. “Any friend of Lexi’s is a friend of mine.”

“Thank you. It’s so nice to meet both of you.”

“Come on,” Lexi says, leading us all to the kitchen. “Let’s get some drinks. I have a feeling Murphy has a great story to tell us about a ball and a window.”

Chapter Nineteen

Caden

Lexi is still in her robe when she answers the door. "I didn't wake you, did I?" I ask.

I couldn't wait any longer to come over. I have to know if she's seen him. Our dad. Is he stalking her, too? Lexi has a picture of him that she's kept ever since he left. Our mother threw all his photos in the trash, but my not even three-year-old sister fished one of them out and tucked it in the back of her closet where Mom wouldn't see it. That picture is the only reason I knew who the man was last night.

"No," she says, yawning. "I've been up since Kyle brought the kids back from Jan's earlier."

I laugh, eyeing the remnants of *'girls' night'* on her kitchen counter. "Looks like you might need to go back to bed."

She winces. "Do I look that bad?"

I kiss her on the cheek. "Beautiful as always, Lex."

"Now I *know* you're full of it." She walks into the kitchen, clearing a bunch of glasses away before she pulls a bowl out of a cabinet. "I was about to make pancakes. Want some?"

"I could eat. Thanks."

I see tiny eyes peek around the corner and I smile. Two-year-old Ellie darts over to me and I pick her up and swing her around in circles. She squeals. I love to hear her make noises like that. I keep it up until I'm too dizzy to continue.

"If you make my kid puke on the floor, you're cleaning it up," Kyle says, coming from the back hallway with his other daughter in his arms.

"Hey, bro," I greet him, leaning down to plant a kiss on three-month-old Beth.

Lexi stops mixing the batter and looks at someone coming down the hallway. "Sorry," she says. "We didn't mean to wake you. It can get pretty loud in here."

I watch Murphy walk into the kitchen, surprised to see her here. She's wearing yoga pants and a tank top. Her hair is tousled and there is a smudge of black crap down one cheek. She sees me and her eyes bug out. Her hand immediately comes up to cover the scar under her eye, like she's ashamed of anyone seeing her without makeup.

I get up and walk over to her, pulling her hand away from her face before I give her a kiss on the cheek. "Morning, sunshine." I laugh, looking between the two hungover women in the room. "I guess I don't have to ask if you had fun last night. A sleepover?"

"Don't ask," Murphy says. Then she turns to Lexi. "Please tell me you have coffee."

Kyle puts the baby down and fetches her a cup. Then Ellie comes up behind me and clings to my leg. She's curious about Murphy, but still a bit wary of strangers so she's hiding from her.

I get down on my knees as I say and sign to Ellie, "This is our friend, Murphy. She looks good in Uncle Caden's baseball caps, just like you do."

"Hello, Ellie," Murphy says behind me. "What a beautiful name you have." When Ellie doesn't talk back, Murphy looks at me. "Should I go put my hat on so she's not scared to talk to me?"

I realize now that my back was turned to Murphy when I was signing and she must not know Ellie is deaf. So I turn to the side as I say and sign, "Ellie isn't scared to talk, Murphy. She's deaf."

"Oh." Murphy looks between us. Then she sits on the floor in front of Ellie and asks me, "Show me how to say hello. We need a proper introduction."

I see Lexi's face break into a smile before she whispers something to Kyle.

Then I teach Murphy how to say *'hello'* and a few other easy signs. Ellie is delighted that Murphy is trying to communicate with her. There are so many people who only bother to talk to her through the adults in her life.

Beth cries, and since Lexi is cooking and Kyle has left the room, I pick her up. I bring her over to the chair where Murphy is looking at a picture book with Ellie. "This is my other niece, Beth."

"She's adorable," she says, turning to my sister. "You make gorgeous babies, Lexi."

"Thanks. I think so too," Lexi says.

"Want to hold her?" I ask.

Murphy looks like a deer in headlights. "Oh, no. I'd probably drop her. I've never held a baby before."

"They're tougher than you think!" Lexi shouts from the kitchen. "Case in point—my little brother there was dropped on his head as a baby and he didn't turn out half bad."

"I wasn't dropped on my head, Lex. I rolled off the sofa onto the carpet. Big difference. You tend to embellish that story every time you tell it."

"You were six months old, Caden. You can't possibly remember."

"And you were not even three, Lex. You don't remember either. You only know what Mom told us, and that is I *rolled* off the couch."

"Whatever," she says. "The fall obviously affected your memory."

Murphy laughs at our sibling banter. She studies my nieces and says longingly, "They are lucky to have each other. I always wanted a sister."

"Feel free to adopt mine," I tell her. "She can be a pain in the ass."

"I heard that!" Lexi yells. "And don't cuss around Ellie. I swear she's starting to read lips."

"*Ass* is not a curse word, Lex."

"It is too," she asserts.

I roll my eyes.

"Don't roll your eyes at me, little brother. When you have your own kids, you can cuss like a trucker in front of them if you want. But in my house, *ass* is a bad word."

"Caden, get your lazy ass off the floor and help me set the table," Kyle says, winking at Murphy as he walks back in the room.

"See?" I say to Lexi.

She throws a pancake at her snarky husband.

Kyle walks over and plants a kiss on her lips and swats her behind. "Just kidding, sweetheart."

Ellie toddles over to her toys, picks up a Hawks hat, climbs back onto the chair, and places it on Murphy's head.

"How do I say *'thank you'* in sign language?" Murphy asks.

I touch my chin with my hand and move my hand outward, showing her how to do the sign. Murphy turns to Ellie and repeats it, making Ellie smile.

"That reminds me, earlier you said you brought your hat here? To girls' night?" I ask Murphy.

"I brought *everything* here," she says. When I eye her inquisitively, she adds, "Long story. But, hey, how was your date last night? Her name was Laney, wasn't it?"

I shake my head at the thought. My date was a disaster. Pretty much because all I could think about was my dad showing up in New York. Why, after all these years, is he trying to contact me? He's a drug addict. There is only one reason I can think of why he'd show up. Money.

It's why I need to find out if Lexi has seen him. I'm not sure she would come right out and tell me if she had. She doesn't despise him like I do. She has a few memories of him teaching her how to swim and how to pump herself on a swing. I have no memory of him at all. I have no desire to ever see the bastard.

"Uneventful," I tell her.

"Sounds wonderful," she says sarcastically.

"Girls' night probably would have been more fun," I say.

"Girls' night was epic," Lexi adds, putting a plate of pancakes on the table and then rubbing her temples.

"Thank you, Lexi. Leave the dishes for me. I'll clean up," Murphy says.

Lexi turns to me. "See, Caden—*that* is what a considerate houseguest does."

"I'm considerate," I tell her.

"If by considerate, you mean leaving your dirty skivvies on the floor, then yes, you are."

Murphy laughs around her bite of breakfast as I explain to her, "I crash here sometimes when I come for dinner. I love to be here when the kids wake up. It's my favorite time to see them, when they're in their pajamas with messy bed-heads. They aren't yet old enough to have mascara smeared down the sides of their faces, but I'm sure that will come."

Murphy's eyes go wide. "Do I have mascara on my face? Why didn't anyone tell me?" She wipes under and around her eyes to try and clean it up. She misses the smudge completely.

I put my thumb in my mouth and then wipe the smudge away for her.

"Did you just wipe your spit all over my face, Kessler?" she asks abhorrently.

I hold up my hands in surrender. "Just trying to help," I say. "It's gone. Your face is good as new."

She looks down at her plate. "Well, I'm not sure about *that*."

I put my hand on her arm. "Your face is perfect, Murph. Beautiful and with character."

"Thanks," she says, smiling.

I look over to see Lexi staring at us, her eyes darting between Murphy and me. She smiles and then looks over at Kyle who is smiling, too. They share a look. I know what they're thinking.

And they're wrong.

There is entirely too much smiling going on at this table so early in the morning.

Chapter Twenty

Murphy

Today has been the best day. Good things always happen in threes.

First, I was cleared by my doctor this morning to resume any and all physical activity. No more restrictions on leaning over or heavy lifting. I'm looking forward to starting a workout program at the gym that has become my second home.

Second, Jayden informed me that I'm getting a raise. She said she's been impressed by how many of the membership coordinator duties I've taken over while Stephanie is on maternity leave.

And lastly, I'm moving in with Trick after work today.

Trick is great. She's a few years older than me, but looks like a teenager with her petite but muscular frame and her flat chest and boyish figure. She has piercings in both her lip and her eyebrow and she tends to favor neon hair colors. This week's color is green.

I've learned a lot about Trick since agreeing to become her roommate this morning. Mostly, that her real name is Sally. She warned me of that because she hasn't yet changed it legally and all the mail will be addressed to her with that name. I had my suspicions that she was technically a girl, but now I know she prefers to be considered transgender.

"Murphy," a familiar male voice calls out from behind me. I finish putting a load of folded towels on the shelf and turn around to say hello.

"Hi, Corey. How are you today?"

He gives me a crooked smile. Corey is a frequent patron of the gym. He comes in four or five times a week to run and swim. Based on the brief conversations we've had over the past weeks, I've pieced together that he's in his upper-twenties, divorced, and works in security. He's built like a Mack truck and is easy on the eyes.

"Better now that I'm talking to you," he says with a wink.

Corey has been flirting with me since I started working here. I'm nice to him, but I don't flirt back. I don't flirt with anyone these days.

"How's the foot?" I ask, knowing he'd suffered a sprain a while ago and is just recently able to get back into running.

"It's good. My doc cleared me of all restrictions this morning."

"That's good to hear. Same for me," I say.

"You had restrictions?" he asks.

I point to my face. "Yeah, after my face was injured, I couldn't do any heavy lifting and I wasn't supposed to bend over too far."

"Oh, wow. What happened?" he asks.

"Long story."

I don't like to get into it with people I don't know. I tend to keep to myself. I'm not even sure why I mentioned it. I guess because of the comment he made about his doctor. Maybe Corey and I have things in common. Maybe I'm ready to date again. I mean, it *has* been six weeks. I study him. I take in the sharp angles of his face. The thick veins corded around his biceps. Surely his good looks would have me breathing heavily if I were ready.

But, no. I realize being in his presence does nothing to me. I might as well be standing here talking to Trick.

I guess I just need more time.

"Well, maybe you'll tell me your story over dinner sometime," he says, with a raised brow.

I shrug. "I just got out of a bad relationship, Corey," I explain. "I'm not quite ready to jump back into anything yet."

He laughs. "Dinner doesn't have to mean jumping into anything, Murphy. But, I get it. I've been there." He leans around me and grabs one of the towels off the shelf. "The invitation stands. Whenever you're ready."

"Okay. Thanks."

I watch him walk away, trying my best to urge my subconscious to increase my heart rate over his swoon-worthy backside.

Working the front desk allows me to talk to a lot of patrons. I get to observe how they interact with others. I see who the players are and I know who is here to further their social games versus their physical ones.

Corey isn't a player. I don't see him hitting on every girl in the gym like some of the other guys. In fact, I'm not sure I've seen him hit on anyone other than me since I've worked here. He's nice. He's good looking. He's fit. Maybe I should give him a chance.

"Hey, Murph."

My eyes close briefly and my pulse quickens when I hear his voice. See – this is the reaction I want when I talk to Corey.

Oh, God.

"Caden, hi." I turn around and paste on a friendly smile. Because that is what I am to him. His friend. Or his charity case, I'm still not sure which.

I will my autonomic nervous system to get out of overdrive.

Trick comes up behind Caden and wraps him into a hug. "If it isn't my favorite client," she says.

He laughs. "I'll bet you say that to all your clients. That's why you make the big bucks."

She winks at him. "You talking to my roomie?"

Caden looks between Trick and me, furrowing his brow. "Roomie?" he asks me.

"Moving in tonight," I tell him.

"That's great, Murphy. I'm happy for you. What did your old roommates say when you told them?"

I look at Trick and smile. She heard the whole story from me this morning. "It's not so much I told them as I threw the key at Kirsten and stormed out."

"You *what?*" he says, smiling. He's been wanting me to move out of that place since he met me.

Trick starts laughing and then regurgitates the entire story, even winding up and miming throwing a baseball and using shattered-glass noises to give him the best visual experience.

Caden's jaw falls open. Then he doubles over laughing. Then, just like friends do, he puts his fist out for me to bump. "Somehow it's satisfying for me to know that the same ball I hit you with was used to break the window."

"You have no idea just how satisfying," I say. "But it was kind of disturbing to know he saw me on TV with you at the Yankees game."

He shakes his head. "Don't worry about that. I saw it too. With you wearing my hat, only people who know you well would recognize you."

"Good." I breathe a sigh of relief.

He draws his brows at me. "Why does it bother you so much to be seen with me?"

"I don't know," I say with a shrug. "I just don't think whom I choose to hang out with is anyone's business."

He smiles. "Couldn't have said it better myself. Hey, if you need any help moving in, I'm free."

I nod to my large suitcase behind the main counter. "I think I can handle it."

"No furniture? No … stuff?"

"I didn't know how long I'd be able to stay in New York at first. I knew if I didn't find work, I'd have to go back to Iowa. And I didn't want to move twice, so I packed light. My old place was furnished. And Trick owns her apartment and is renting me her second bedroom."

"That's great. But do you know Trick hates to cook?" He turns to her. "I'll bet you only have takeout menus and paper plates in your kitchen."

"And a blender." She laughs. "I love protein smoothies. But Caden's right. I've got two left feet in the kitchen. Wait, do you cook, Murphy?"

"I do," I tell her, impressed that Caden would remember a small detail that we only talked about once.

"Well, I like you even better now," Trick says. "Except that you won't be able to cook squat unless you can do it on the one cookie sheet I have for reheating pizza."

"That's okay. I can hit a flea market this weekend and pick up everything I need." I wrinkle my nose and look between them. "Uh, do they even have those here?"

"Do they have flea markets in the city?" Trick asks, sarcastically. "Wait until you see my eclectic furniture. Then you tell me."

"Oh, good."

"I don't want you going by yourself," Caden says. "Those places can be dangerous. I'll go with you."

I roll my eyes. "Flea markets are not dangerous. Have you ever been to one?"

"No. But they sound shady."

"Well, they're not."

"I still think I should go with you. You never know."

"I can take care of myself, Caden."

He shakes his head and blows out a frustrated breath. I can see he's about to argue with me, but I get saved by a gym patron who has a question.

Good. Because I don't need Caden Kessler wasting any more of his pity on me.

Chapter Twenty-one

Caden

Trick pulls on my arm. "Come on, big guy, let's go do your workout. Can't let you get soft in the off season, now can we?"

"Catch you later, Murph. Enjoy your new place."

"I plan to," she says smiling.

As Trick drags me away, I call out to Murphy, "We're still on for a double date on Saturday, aren't we?"

"Caden—" She blows out a regretful sigh.

"I bet you thought I forgot all about it." I pull away from Trick and jog back over to the front desk. "Come on, Murphy's Law, you said you would."

"I said I'd think about it, Caden."

"Please?"

"Is your date with that Laney again?" she asks.

"What? No. Laney is history." *It was our third date.*

"I thought you said you weren't a player," she says, narrowing her eyes at me.

"I'm *not*. Hell, I didn't even sleep with her if you must know the truth. She just wasn't for me. I'm not sure anyone is, but I can't just not date."

"I'm not dating," she says with a stern look.

"For a whole six weeks, Murphy. That's not *not* dating, it's just taking a break because that bastard broke your heart."

"I wouldn't say *broke* it," she tells me. "He might have chipped it a little maybe, but he definitely didn't break it."

I'm relieved to hear that Tony didn't devastate her. She seems okay on the outside, but I've always wondered about what lies beneath her strong exterior.

"Caden!" Trick calls impatiently.

Without looking away from Murphy, I hold up a finger to my trainer to make her wait. "I date to be social. And I've told you before, I don't date much. Mostly just in the off season. I don't like distractions when I'm playing. Come on, Murph. It would mean a lot to me."

She lets out a long, acquiescing sigh. "Fine. Who's my date?"

"Brady."

"Brady? As in your starting pitcher?"

I might be slightly impressed. "Have you been watching ESPN again?" I joke.

"No. I've heard you talk about him."

"Yes, *that* Brady."

"And he knows it's strictly platonic?"

"Yeah. He's taking a break, too," I say, unconvincingly.

"Really? How long has it been for him?"

I start to walk backwards toward Trick, but then look down at my watch. "Let me see, by the time Saturday rolls around, he'll have been on a break for about twelve hours."

"A player?" she yells. "You set me up with a player?"

"I didn't set you up," I tell her. "Because it's not a date, Murphy Brown. Relax."

She picks up the nearest thing she can find and throws it across the room at me. I catch the rolled-up hand towel and toss it back. "Saturday," I say. "We'll pick you up at your new place at seven."

I turn back to Trick. "Do you really have nothing but paper plates and a blender?" I ask.

She nods before she puts me through a grueling sixty-minute workout with weights. Then she programs a treadmill for me. "After this, I want you doing laps in the pool. Try to do as much backstroke as you can, we need to keep those arms limber."

"Yes, boss," I say with a wink. "Hey, thanks for letting Murphy take your spare room. I'm glad she's getting away from those bitches that were her roommates."

"She's the one who's doing me a favor. You'd think I'd be able to find *one* person in this progressive city who'd want to live with a trans, but no. Joan really screwed me over when she left. I won't fall for that again."

"You and me both," I say. I look over at the front desk. "Best to stick with friendship. It's safe."

Trick follows my gaze. "Just friends, huh?" she asks. "And you're double dating with her this weekend?"

"Yup."

She laughs as she hits the start button on my treadmill, but she walks away before I can invite her along. The more people that go out with me, the better. I was being truthful when I told Murphy that I date to be social. If I only went out with the guys, I wouldn't be going out much at all. Unlike me, most of them love to have a girl on their arm.

Brady and Sawyer are probably my best friends on the team. And while we are alike on the field, we couldn't be farther apart in what we want from women. While Brady has a girl in every city, Sawyer has a girl for every night. A *new* girl. *One and done*—that's Sawyer's motto. While *I'm* afraid women won't like me for who I am, *they* use their celebrity status to bed everyone with a skirt. And mark my words, it will get them into trouble. Eventually.

While I'm running, I think back to my conversation with Lexi yesterday morning. When Murphy went to take a shower, I casually mentioned our father when Lexi gave me a good segue by bringing up Murphy's dad. I asked her what she thinks became of him—the guy who ran out on us before I could even walk.

She told me she Googled him once. I did, too, the night I saw him. But there are just enough Shane Kessler's in the world to leave it a mystery. I've thought about having Ethan Stone, Kyle's brother, dig into what became of our dad as Ethan is a highly respected private investigator.

It was clear to me, however, that she hasn't been contacted by him nor has she seen him lurking like I have. I was relieved. Maybe he doesn't know she's married to a multi-millionaire. Because if he did, I'm sure our deadbeat father would be after *her* money as well.

I vow to reach out to Ethan this week to have him look into it. The last thing I need is for Lexi to be in danger again. Her going through what she did with Grant Lucas several years ago was enough drama for a lifetime. I'll never be able to thank Kyle and his brothers enough for what they did for her. What they did to bring her back to me.

When my thirty minutes are up, I grab my towel and then almost run smack into a guy as I step off the treadmill. But he doesn't even notice me. He's too busy staring at Murphy, who has come over to help someone clear a jam from one of the weight machines.

I watch the guy as he appraises her. He's not looking at her like Brady and Sawyer look at their sexual conquests. He's admiring her. Revering her. And although I want to hate the guy for how he's staring at her, I can't help but respect him just a little for not outright ogling her like most men do.

He finally notices that he's blocking my way. "Sorry," he says. Then he peels his eyes away from Murphy and looks up at me. "Oh, hey, you're Caden Kessler. Sorry I got in your way, man. I can't keep my eyes off her."

I decide to play dumb. "Your girlfriend?" I ask.

He laughs. "I wish. Been trying for weeks to get her to notice me. Even asked her out today."

I stiffen. "How'd that go?"

"She shot me down. Said something about a past relationship. You know her?" He looks at me hopefully. As if I could put in a good word or something.

"Not really," I lie.

"Just as well," he says, shrugging. "If you knew her, there would be no way in hell anyone else would have a chance with her."

"You overestimate my abilities. Not everyone wants to date a professional athlete, you know."

"I guess," he muses.

"Well, good luck, uh …"

"Corey," he says, holding out his hand.

Corey. He's the guy Murphy mentioned last week when I brought up going on a double date. I wonder if she wants to date him. Then again, he said she shot him down.

I shake his hand, sizing him up as I do. I find myself wanting to protect Murphy. He seems to be a nice guy. Nicer than Tony, that's for sure. But then again, serial killers are nice, too. It's how they lure their victims. "Good to meet you, Corey."

"Yeah, you too," he says, stepping on his treadmill. "Good luck next season."

"You a Hawks fan?"

He raises his arm and shows me a Nighthawks tattoo on the side of his ribcage. *Damn.* I can't help but like the guy now. "Nice," I say. "Thanks for showing your support."

"Always," he says, before putting in his earbuds.

The whole time I'm doing laps in the pool, I can't decide if I want to encourage Murphy to date the guy, or warn her away. But I also find myself wondering why I'm even thinking about her at all. And why the hell am I so irritated about Corey expressing an interest in her?

After I shower and leave for home, I all but run into the man who is my father when I round the corner at the end of the block. I throw him against the brick building, holding my hand against his throat. "Why are you stalking me?"

"I'm … I'm not. I just didn't—"

"Leave me alone, you deadbeat scumbag. And don't even think about contacting Alexa. If you try, I'll file a restraining order faster than you can fail a drug test."

"It's not like that, son."

I tighten my grip on him. "Don't call me son. You lost that right twenty-five years ago. You'll get nothing from me. Not one penny. Go back to whatever rock you crawled out from under and stay there."

"Is there a problem here?" a police officer says from his perch on a horse.

I pull away and put my shaking hands down by my side.

"No," my dad says, followed by a long, drawn-out sigh. "No problem. I was just leaving."

He turns to walk away, shoulders slumped as he shuffles down the sidewalk. I finally take a moment to study him. He's wearing khakis and a dress shirt. He's sporting Doc Martens for Christ's sake. *Probably stolen ones.*

Once he turns the corner and I can no longer see him, I breathe.

Then I pull out my phone and call Ethan.

Chapter Twenty-two

Murphy

I'm putting away the last of my clothes when Trick calls out to me from the other room telling me I have a delivery.

"Be right there!" I shout.

I look around the room that is my new home. I smile at the queen-size bed. I can't wait to sleep in it. It's much better than the twin I had at the old place. And this room—it's all mine. No back-stabbing slut to share it with.

I wasn't sure what to expect coming to Trick's place. She said she pretty much furnished it with flea market findings. And seeing how eccentric she is, I guess I thought the apartment would be decorated in neon colors or something. Quite the contrary, she's found some wonderful antique pieces with tons of character. My bed has a wrought-iron headboard with an incredible Greek-mythology-inspired inlay that looks hand-painted. My dresser has been crafted out of distressed wood and each handle has been carved into letters that, together, spell 'H O M E.'

I pull out the last things from my suitcase—the four hats Caden has given me, and the framed picture of Kelly and me taken the day of high school graduation. I put them all on top of my dresser.

I walk out into the living room to see a huge box sitting on the coffee table. I look around to see if there are any other deliveries, because surely this one is not for me.

Trick sees me looking confused and points to the box. "It's for you."

I rip off the envelope taped to the top of the box and pull out the card inside.

Old Man Murphy,

You said you didn't have any 'stuff,' and now that you've decided you are a bona fide city girl, I thought you should have some. Happy housewarming!

Caden

"It's from Caden," I tell Trick. "He got me a housewarming gift."

I look at the box cautiously.

"Well, don't just stand there," she prods. "Open it!"

"He's done so much for me already," I say, sitting down and staring at the large box. "I really don't like him spending money on me."

"It's not like the man can't afford it, Murphy. You know that, don't you?"

I roll my eyes. "I know. But I don't want to feel indebted to anyone."

"Indebted?" she says abhorrently. "Believe me, Caden has no ulterior motives here. He's a nice guy. I've known him for over a year."

"I know he's nice. Maybe too nice. I've been his charity case for almost two months now."

"Charity case?" Trick walks over to her bookshelves and grabs something before coming to sit beside me. She hands me an old book. "It's a first edition by my favorite author. Caden gave it to me last spring because he knows how much I love the writer. Do you have any idea how much that must have cost?"

"No," I say, carefully leafing through the pages of the book that must be decades old.

"Me neither," she says laughing. "But if I had to guess, it's worth a lot more than you or I make in a month. Did he give it to me because I'm a charity case? Because he wanted something from me?"

I shrug. "Maybe he wanted you to take it easy on him at the gym."

She snorts through her nose. "Hell, no. Caden urges me to push him more than any of my clients. Well, except maybe Mason. But he's not really a client. He's my boss." She slaps the side of the box. "He gave this to you because you're his friend. And you read the card, it's a housewarming gift. Accept it gracefully, Murphy."

I nod at her words, running my hand along the side of the sealed box. I stand up so I can reach the top of it and peel the packing tape away. When I open it and see the contents, I smile.

"What is it?" Trick asks.

I pull out item after item, unwrapping them and placing each one on the coffee table. "Pretty much everything I need to cook us a gourmet meal."

My mouth waters thinking about all the food I'll be able to whip up. I've missed cooking. I didn't get to do much of it at my old place. It was too crowded there and the kitchen was tiny. Trick has a great kitchen. I'm already thinking about how I'm going to email my mom and have her send me all my favorite recipes.

When I get to the bottom of the box, I see he's even thought to include eight place settings of dishes and silverware and a few serving pieces.

"Caden should be your first dinner guest," she says.

"*You* should be my first dinner guest, Trick," I tell her, grateful for the opportunity to live in such a nice place with a nice person.

"Okay," she says with a smile. "Caden can be your second."

"You wouldn't mind if I had people over?"

"Not at all. You're not my houseguest, Murphy. You *are* paying me rent, you know. I want you to feel comfortable here. And that includes being able to invite your friends. That goes for boyfriends, too. Or girlfriends," she says playfully and with a wink.

I laugh. "You don't have to worry about any boyfriends. I'm taking a break from that."

"What about Corey?" she asks. "He seems to be finding a lot of excuses to talk to you lately."

I nod. "Yeah. He asked me out today but I turned him down."

"What about the double date you have on Saturday?"

"Purely platonic," I tell her. "I'm just playing wingman, or whatever, for Caden."

"Is that what he calls it?" She laughs, shaking her head. "Hey, why not have them over here?" she asks. "Cook for them. Your first dinner party. I'll be at a concert with some friends. The place will be all yours."

I study her for a beat and then look at the spread of kitchenware on the table. "That's brilliant, Trick. If I'm busy cooking, I won't have to make awkward conversation with the guy he set me up with."

"Awkward conversation with Brady Taylor? That man doesn't have an awkward bone in his body. I mean, if you like bones. Which I don't. But if I did, I'd definitely want *his*."

I laugh, picking up my phone to text Caden.

Me: Thank you so much for the housewares. You didn't have to do that.

#8: You're welcome. I hope you can put them to good use.

Me: About that. What did you have in mind for Saturday night? I'd love to cook dinner here. That is if you didn't have anything planned.

#8: Dinner there would be perfect. I'd love it. Why don't I come by early and we can hit the market together?

I blow out a sigh. He thinks I can't afford dinner for four. And maybe I can't. Maybe he's expecting filet mignon and lobster.

Me: I can get groceries myself, Caden. You are NOT buying those, too.

#8: Dinner for four is expensive, Murph. Do you know how much money we would have spent going out?

I can't argue with that logic. But still. He needs to quit doing stuff like that for me.

Me: The menu will be chicken piccata with risotto and asparagus. If that's not good enough for you, I guess I'll be eating for four.

#8: Chicken piccata sounds great, Murphy Brown. What time should we be there?

After we finish our conversation, I get up to put my new stuff away when I glance at the TV programs that Trick is channel-surfing through. Something flashing across the screen catches my eye. "Wait, can you go back a channel, please?"

She clicks back one. "You like this show?" Then she rolls her eyes at her question. "Of course you do. *Duh.* Were you named after it? Was *Murphy Brown* your mom's favorite show or something?"

I laugh. "No. I never even heard of the show until Caden started calling me by that name. Mind if I watch it for a minute?"

She pats the couch next to her. "Take a load off. I'll watch it with you. I love old sitcoms."

A half hour later, I sit staring at the TV, stunned. Because, as fate would have it—or maybe just coincidence—Murphy Brown was sometimes called *'Slugger.'*

Chapter Twenty-three

Caden

Ethan pushes an envelope across the table. "Here you go," he says. "Start from the top."

I open it, removing the contents. On top of the pile, there are a few pictures of my dad. Recent ones that I assume Ethan had someone on his team take. He looks just like he did last Friday when I ran into him outside Murphy's building.

Next, I see a picture of him in a copy of a newspaper article that looks very old. I check the date. It's almost as old as I am. The article is about him being arrested. He had stolen a car. And according to the article, it wasn't the first time. They got him for multiple counts of grand larceny.

I knew it.

Another old picture is his prison photo. He's wearing an orange jumpsuit and holding a number in front of him.

That's my father. Prisoner #004583757 in the Georgia State Penitentiary. *There's a picture for the family album.*

I shake my head. "Shit, Ethan."

I stare at the picture. *Georgia.* No wonder I didn't find anything on him. All my on-line searches were centered around Baltimore, where Lexi and I grew up.

"Keep looking," he says.

Next, I find a diploma issued from a community college associated with the prison. He earned an associate's degree in social work while he was doing time.

Beneath that is an article from an Atlanta newspaper dated fifteen years ago. It shows a picture of my father surrounded by what looks to be an unruly bunch. When I read the article, it talks about how Shane Kessler, social worker and former inmate, now spends his time helping other recently-released inmates stay off drugs and find meaningful employment.

The next paper I come across is a bachelor's degree he earned from Georgia Southern University and the next, a doctorate in social work from the University of Georgia.

What the hell? I look up at Ethan. "My dad's a fucking doctor?"

"Of social work. Yes," he says with a smile. "I don't think he's after your money, Caden. Not that social workers make a lot of money, but he runs his own outreach program in Atlanta. Gets government funding and everything. Good program. I've donated to similar ones in the past. He spends his days rehabilitating criminals. I'm pretty sure that means he's not trying to scam you."

"Wait," I say, leafing through the papers. "You're telling me my deadbeat dad, the drug-addict scumbag who took off and left Lex and me, *this* guy is now some sort of scholar who runs his own business?"

I must look damn surprised because Ethan laughs at me. "And wins awards for it," he says, pointing to another article showing pictures of my dad accepting accolades from the mayor of Atlanta.

"Why the hell did he wait so long to look for us?"

He shrugs. "Don't know. Maybe he's sick. Maybe he's moving here. Maybe he just wants to know his kids again."

"It's too late. I don't want to know him. Too much water under the bridge."

"Don't say that, Caden. Charlie thought the same thing about her dad when we first got together. Turned out it was a huge misunderstanding. They have a great relationship now."

"You think my dad walking out on his wife and leaving his six-month-old son and three-year-old daughter was a misunderstanding?" I bite at him.

"Everyone has shit in their past. He was clearly an addict. Addiction does terrible things to good people. He's obviously turned his life around. Maybe you should hear him out."

I stuff the contents back into the folder. "Thanks, Ethan. I'll think about it."

"Glad to help." He looks at his watch. "I'm heading out for the day. Want to grab a beer?"

"Can't. I'm heading over to a friend's house for a double date."

"Look me up next week then," he says, walking me out.

"Sure thing."

~ ~ ~

Kate and I arrive at Murphy's place fifteen minutes earlier than I told Brady to show up. I didn't want him getting here before me and hitting on her. Even though I was quite clear about this being strictly platonic, I don't doubt he'd try to see if he could push the boundaries. I mean, it's Murphy. She's gorgeous.

Murphy opens the door and incredible smells assault us from inside. I've never had chicken piccata before, and I wasn't about to tell her I didn't know what the hell it was. But whatever it is, it smells heavenly.

"Kate, this is my friend, Murphy."

Murphy smiles at Kate, offering her hand. "Hi, Kate. Come on in." She looks beyond us into the hallway. "Brady's not with you?"

I'm not sure if she looks disappointed or relieved.

"He'll be here in a few minutes," I tell her. "We came separately."

She shrugs. "Oh, okay."

"Where should I put these?" I show her the two bottles of wine I brought.

She takes one from me, examining the label before she scolds me with her eyes. Yes, I spent a lot on the wine. It was the least I could do.

"Thanks," she says, more for Kate's benefit than mine. "You can put them on the kitchen counter. Go ahead and open one if you want."

"Do we need to pass the bottle, or does Trick own wine glasses?" I ask.

Murphy's laugh is a soft melodic giggle that resonates somewhere deep inside me. She has a great laugh.

"We've got glasses," she says. "They might not all match, but we have plenty of them."

"It smells great in here," Kate says, taking a deep whiff of the aromas. "Can I help you with anything, Murphy?"

"No, but thanks for asking. Dinner is being kept warm in the oven and I've just finished with the canapés."

"Cana-whats?" Kate asks.

"Canapés," Murphy says. "They're appetizers. Finger foods to tide us over until dinner."

"Oh. Sounds great," Kate says.

"Go ahead and have a seat," Murphy tells her. "I'll go get them and Caden can open the wine."

I follow Murphy into the kitchen. "Before I forget, I hope you're free tomorrow, because a bunch of us are going to Mason's game."

"A bunch?"

"Lexi and Kyle, Chad and Mallory, and Piper will be there, obviously."

She thinks about it and nods. "Yeah. Sounds fun." She touches the scar under her eye. "And not as dangerous as baseball."

"Don't think I've forgotten about giving you another lesson," I say. "I'm going to make you a baseball lover yet."

She laughs, stretching her head around the corner to peek at my date in the living room. "Kate seems nice," she whispers to me.

"I guess," I say.

"Where did you meet her?"

"She's my batting coach's niece."

"That's nice. Did he set you two up?"

I shrug. "She's been out with a few of my teammates before."

Murphy pins me to the wall with her stare. "Caden," she says in a stern whisper. "If she's just going through your team trying to get any baseball player, you should run far and fast."

I put a hand on her arm. "It's not like that, Murph. She's not a Tony. In fact, the other guys didn't take her out a second time because she wouldn't sleep with them. I think she's more like the girl next door than the girl who wants to trap a ball player."

She blows out a relieved sigh. "Good. Uh, she didn't go out with Brady, did she? Because that would be more than a little awkward."

"No, she didn't go out with Brady."

There's a knock on the door.

I laugh. "Speak of the devil."

"Can you get it?" she asks, picking up a tray of little bread things. "I'll bring these."

I introduce Kate and Murphy to Brady.

"It's a real pleasure," Brady says, holding Murphy's hand far too long. I don't miss how he appraises her like a piece of meat.

I call him over to help me with the wine glasses. "Dude, I told you, do *not* try and hook up with her. Don't even try to kiss her."

He looks around at nobody and then back at me. "What the hell did I do?"

"Are you kidding?" I ask. "You were eye-fucking her just now."

He laughs. "Kessler, I eye-fuck everyone. Don't you know that by now?"

I stare him down. "Don't do it to *her*."

He backs up and studies me. "Maybe we should swap dates then."

"Don't be stupid, Taylor."

"Just sayin'," he says. "You seem way more into *her* than the one you're with. Mind if I eye-fuck *your* date then? She's hot too. What did you say her name was again? I was too busy picturing Murphy squirming under me."

If I didn't know he was kidding—well, half kidding—I'd run his ass right out of Murphy's apartment. "Just be cool, Brady."

"I'm *always* cool, Kessler."

I shove two glasses of wine into his hands thinking this could be a very long night.

Chapter Twenty-four

Murphy

Sitting in a suite watching the Giants game is a lot like sitting in a suite watching a Nighthawks game. But without the stress of seeing Caden play.

I've never been much into sports. Growing up in Okoboji, Iowa didn't lend itself to it. We had one hundred and fifty students in my entire high school—not much to pick from if you wanted an award-winning football or baseball team.

Still, I find sports are kind of growing on me. Maybe it's from working at the gym and seeing all the sports stars come and go. I glance over at Caden, who's deep in conversation with Kyle and Chad as they discuss Mason's last play.

"Which one are you ogling?" Lexi whispers, coming up beside me to catch me staring.

I snap my eyes to hers. "I wasn't ogling," I pout.

"It's okay to ogle, you know. They're all hot, if I do say so myself."

I glance back at the three men. She's right. The amount of testosterone and unbridled attractiveness there could bring any woman to her knees. Mallory's husband, Chad, laughs loudly and I turn back to Lexi. "You could have warned me that your brother-in-law is a Hollywood A-lister."

"A little star-struck, are we?"

I shrug. "Maybe just a little. I mean, he's been in like ten movies, Lexi. *Good* movies. Movies you stand in line for on opening night. Isn't that unreal? And here he is just laughing and watching football with the rest of us like a regular guy."

She studies me, shaking her head. "Says the BFF of one of the hottest sports stars in New York."

"That's different," I say. "And we're not BFFs."

"That's up for debate," she says. "But either way, do you go around introducing yourself as 'the best friend of Caden Kessler of the Nighthawks'?"

I cringe. "Of course not."

"Then why would I introduce myself as the sister-in-law of the famous Thad Stone?"

I nod. "Touché. But I think it was the name that threw me. I'd heard Mallory talk about her husband, Chad, before. I guess I didn't realize he was the same guy."

"Are you two talking about my husband?" Mallory asks, joining us at the bar.

"I think Murphy was a bit star-struck to find out who Chad is."

"You wouldn't feel that way if you had to use the bathroom after him every morning." She waves a hand under her nose, making us laugh with her.

We're watching the guys interact with each other when a woman comes up to them, asking not Chad, but Caden, for an autograph.

"See?" Mallory says. "I love it when that happens. The girl didn't even notice Chad. Keeps his ego in check."

I can't tear my eyes away from Caden and his fan. Kyle takes a few pictures of them with the woman's phone. Then she hugs Caden and he hugs her back. It reminds me of last night, watching Caden with Kate. They didn't touch much, maybe a hand on an arm or an elbow to the ribs. But the fact that I noticed every little touch was surprising. And the fact that it bothered me was bothersome.

Brady was quite the gentleman for the most part—when he wasn't staring at my chest that is. He earned more than a few kicks under the table from Caden when he was caught doing it. It was almost comical how Caden was trying to protect me from the man-whore of the western world. He must have felt bad knowing he assured me our date was platonic. I guess he thought it was his duty to uphold the 'platonic-ness' of it.

Caden glances over and winks at me. Then something happens. Heat creeps up my face and my heart stops beating for just a fraction of a second. That's all it took really, just a fraction of a second to realize that what I'm feeling for him is not what one friend feels for another.

It was an innocent gesture on his part. I'm sure he winks at everyone. The fan who is now sitting back with her friends on the other side of the suite—did he wink at *her?* I think back to last night and try to remember if he winked at Kate. Surely, he must have.

A glass is shoved into my hands. Lexi laughs and says, "Looks like you need this more than I do."

I take a drink of her beer and then turn around and focus all my energy on the game.

I concentrate on the game so my mind can't fester over the fact that my pulse races every time I'm near him. Or the fact that when he left another hat at my place last night, I secretly wondered if he did it on purpose as I added it to my growing collection. Or the fact that seeing him with another woman last night made me jealous.

Or the fact that I've fallen for my best friend.

No. This can't be happening. I down the rest of Lexi's drink and go to the bar in search of another.

Hands come up and touch my shoulders, causing shivers to travel down my spine. "Having fun?" Caden asks, in a deep masculine voice that twists my insides into knots.

My eyes close and I'm glad my back is turned to him so he can't see the visceral reaction my body is having to his words. His touch.

I stiffen and try to compose myself. "I am," I say. "Thank you for inviting me."

He starts to massage my shoulders. "You're so tense, Murph. Everything okay?"

I take my beer from the bartender and turn around, shrugging his hands off my shoulders in the process. If he only knew what his touch was doing to me, he wouldn't have put his hands on me. "Yeah. Just tired, I guess."

"Tired? We left your place before eleven."

"I stayed up too late watching TV," I confess.

"Me too." He laughs quietly. "They had a late-night *Murphy Brown* marathon."

My face heats up. I'm not sure why knowing he was watching the same show embarrasses me, but it does.

"What?" He sees my reaction. "No way. Really?"

I shrug. "Had to see what all the fuss was about. I mean, it *is* your favorite show and all."

"I haven't watched it in years," he says. "But, yeah, it might just be my favorite show." He winks at me.

"Why were you watching TV?" I ask. "Didn't you and Kate … um, didn't you go out for a drink or … something?"

Oh, God. Could I be any more awkward?

Caden laughs. "No, we didn't go out for a drink or … *something.*"

I try not to smile too broadly at his admission. I try not to think about how I watched TV last night to get my mind off what he and Kate were most likely doing after they left my apartment. And now, knowing he took her straight home—it feels better than the day I got that modeling contract.

We walk over and sit down to watch the second half of the game.

"Speaking of baseball," Caden says.

I look at him and roll my eyes. "We weren't speaking of baseball."

"Yeah, but now we are," he says, elbowing me in the ribs. "When is your next day off?"

"Not until next Sunday," I say. "I picked up some extra hours this week to cover for someone."

Caden looks disappointed. "You work six days in a row?"

"Yes. But they aren't all full days. I only work until noon on Thursday."

"Good. I'll pick you up at the gym at noon on Thursday."

I look at him sideways. "Are you going to tell me why?"

"For your next lesson."

I laugh. "I've seen you play plenty of times, Caden. I believe I've gotten the gist of it by now."

"But you only went to two games. And the first one doesn't count since you didn't even watch it." He cringes and I know he's thinking about his ball hitting me. Then he stares me down, a slow smile dancing up his face. "You watched my games on TV, didn't you, Murphy Brown?"

"I may have caught a few on ESPN," I admit, more heat creeping up my face.

He slaps his knee in excitement. "I knew it! Come on, fess up, it's a great game, isn't it?"

"I'm not sure I'd call it *great*. But it is growing on me."

"What's a walk-off grand slam?" he asks me.

"Um … some sort of home run?"

He laughs. "*Some sort?* Yeah, you need another lesson. Thursday. Twelve o'clock."

"Fine. But you have to feed me first," I say.

"I know just the place."

The suite erupts in cheers and we look down to the field to see that Mason has just thrown a touchdown pass. Caden jumps over the back of his chair to go high-five the other guys.

He leaves me to my thoughts. Thoughts that convince me I'm going on a date on Thursday. A date with my best friend.

Lord help me.

Chapter Twenty-five

Caden

After my workout and shower, I sit in the café in the gym and wait for Murphy to finish up her shift. I can just barely overhear the conversation she's having with her boss, and from what I can make out, it sounds like she's been given a lot more responsibility than a front-desk receptionist would normally have.

I'm glad they've figured out she's much more than a pretty face. She's been working here for over a month now. Sometimes I wonder if she will go back to modeling when her scars fade. She never talks about it anymore. It's almost as if she left that life behind when she moved out of her old apartment.

I see someone familiar come through the front door of the gym and I go on high alert. Tony walks to the front desk with a smirk and throws an envelope down on it. He has a few words with Murphy and I can see she's uncomfortable, so I get up and head over.

"What's up, Murphy?" I ask. Then I look at Tony as if I just noticed him. "Oh, and look, it's the lying, cheating bastard."

Tony looks at me funny. I guess he doesn't know that I know who he is. "You don't know dick about me," he says.

"I don't?" I say, coming around the desk to stand right next to him. "Let's see. I know you were feeling up your girlfriend's roommate while your girlfriend was getting hit by my ball on what was supposed to be a night celebrating *her*. I know you and the aforementioned slut were carrying on behind Murphy's back. I know you kissed her the very day Murphy got injured and was lying in a hospital bed."

"Whatever. Like I said, you don't know shit," he says.

"I saw you in the hospital cafeteria, you asshole. I heard you on the phone saying you were going to dump her because her face got messed up. I saw you stick your tongue down her roommate's throat right there in the food line."

Tony looks surprised, but not the least bit guilty. He nods to the envelope on the counter. "The bill for the window you smashed," he says to Murphy.

I swipe it from her when she picks it up. I open it and then I open my wallet and take out five hundred-dollar bills and slap them on the counter in front of him. "That should cover it."

"You aren't paying for the window I broke," Murphy scolds me, pushing the money back to me.

"It was my ball that broke the window," I say. "I'm paying."

Tony grabs the bills off the counter. "Must be nice to have a sugar-daddy," he says.

I lean towards him, putting my chest inches from his. I look down on his face that only comes up to my neck. "You got what you came for. I suggest you leave. Now."

"Gladly," he says. But before he reaches the door, he turns back to me. "She was a shitty lay anyway. A cold fucking fish. But maybe you already know that."

He walks out the door leaving Murphy horrified. There were at least five people within earshot who are now looking at her in sympathy.

She smiles awkwardly. "Let me go clock out and get my purse," she says, quickly leaving the scene.

I'm on the phone with Sawyer a few minutes later when Murphy comes out from the back. "Gotta go, I'm taking Murphy to lunch."

"Murphy, the girl you hit with your home run ball?" he asks.

"One and the same."

"I'd like to meet her," he says. "You should bring her along this weekend."

I look at Murphy as she tries to ignore my phone conversation. "I'll ask her. But she doesn't date."

Murphy furrows her brow at me. She heard her name and knows we're talking about her.

"She went out with Brady last weekend, didn't she?" Sawyer asks.

"As *friends.*"

"At least that's what she told you," he jokes.

I ignore his misplaced humor. "Goodbye, Mills."

"Later, bro."

"What was that all about?" she asks.

"My friend, Sawyer—you've heard me talk about him before—he wants you to come out with us on Saturday. Make it a triple date."

"Why would you need *me* when you already have a wingman?"

"Wingman, huh?" I laugh. "More like a buffer. Something between me and my dates in case I need an out. Come on. It'll be fun."

"I'm not going out with Brady again. He stares at my boobs."

"Brady stares at everyone's boobs," I say laughing. "I'll find you someone else then."

Murphy looks behind me and smiles. "What are you doing Saturday night?" she asks someone over my shoulder.

I turn around and see Corey walking up to us. And he's got a big damn grin on his face.

"I might be free," he says, looking between us. "Why do you ask?"

"Want to go on a triple date?"

He looks confused. "I thought you two didn't know each other."

"We've recently become friends," I say, before Murphy can respond.

He appraises me like he knows I'm lying. Then he looks back at Murphy. "Sounds good. Just tell me when and where to pick you up."

"She'll meet you there. Just leave your phone number at the front desk and she'll text you the details," I say, swinging my large bag over my shoulder as I pull Murphy towards the door. "We're late for something."

"Has anyone ever told you you're pushy?" Murphy asks as we walk to the subway.

"Just think of me as your overprotective big brother."

I think I see a frown cross her face before she shakes it away and hides it with a laugh. I'm sure she always wanted siblings. I can't imagine having grown up without Lexi.

"Are you going to tell me where we're going?" she asks.

"To Mitchell's."

She smiles. "Oh, great! I've been wanting to eat there but was saving all my money to pay for the window." She puts a hand on my arm and looks me directly in the eyes. "And since I ended up not paying for it, *I'm* buying."

"But—"

"Don't give me your shit, Caden. I don't care that you make a gazillion times what I do. I'm buying or no baseball lesson."

I laugh quietly. She's kind of sexy when she's mad. "Gazillion?" I ask.

She rolls her eyes.

"Fine," I say, pouting. "You can buy lunch. You drive a hard bargain, Murphy's Law."

~ ~ ~

An hour later, with our bellies full, we walk through Central Park on the way to our destination.

"I wanted to ask you about something you said to Tony earlier," she says.

I was wondering if she was going to bring it up. "Okay, shoot."

"You said you saw him kissing Kirsten at the hospital. And you said you overheard him say he was going to break up with me."

I nod my head. "I did."

She lets out a huge, frustrated sigh. "Why didn't you tell me, Caden?"

"I did. Well, I sort of did. I showed you the video of when you got hit, and then you came to the same conclusion."

"You should have told me. I don't like deception." She kicks a mound of dirt on the sidewalk.

"Deception? No, it wasn't like that. I didn't even know you, Murph. I wasn't about to walk in there and tell you your boyfriend was a lying, cheating scumbag. You would have thought I wanted in your pants. It wasn't my place to do it. But I got the job done in a way that didn't make me the prick. People do tend to kill the messenger, you know."

"I guess you're right. But please don't keep anything from me again," she says, looking me straight in the eyes.

I hold my hand out to shake hers. "Deal. And we're here."

I open the gate to one of the many ball fields and wave her through. Murphy narrows her eyes at me. "Aren't we going to get into trouble? I mean, I'm not sure we should be here. Are we trespassing?"

"It's fine. I reserved it."

"You reserved an entire baseball field?"

I put my bag down by the dugout. "I did."

"What, like there is some on-line signup sheet to use the Central Park baseball fields?"

"Kind of. You need to get a permit to use one," I explain.

"A permit?" she asks, surprised. "That sounds like it would take a while, yet you only asked me about coming on Sunday."

I shrug. "I know people, Murph."

"Who are you, John Gotti?" She laughs at her own joke about the infamous mobster.

"Come on," I say, grabbing some gear and pulling her to home plate. "Let's get started."

She looks at the bat in my hand and pales. "I know you don't think you're going to throw a baseball at me."

"Relax." I raise my other hand and show her my catcher's helmet. "You'll be fully protected."

"I'm not wearing that, Caden." She takes it from me. "It's ugly." She examines it closely, turning her nose away. "And it smells."

I laugh. "I'll remember to spray it with my cologne next time." I take my hat off and put it backwards on her head.

She takes it off and turns it around, placing it on her head with the bill facing front. "Why did you put it on the wrong way?"

I remove it once more and place it back the way I had it. "Because this is how you have to wear it under a catcher's helmet."

"Ewww," she says, crinkling her nose at the smell as I carefully put my helmet over her head.

I pat her on the top of the helmet. "Looking good, Slugger."

She laughs. "Did you know that's what Murphy Brown's co-worker called her?"

I smile and wink. "Kind of apropos, don't you think?"

I can't be sure, but I think I see her blush. I stand back and admire her. Then I take out my phone and snap a picture of her before she can protest. Somehow, I know this will be one of my favorites.

"You better not show that to anyone. I mean it, Kessler. I will hang you by your toenails until the life drains out of you."

She stares me down through the facemask of my helmet and I realize how much I like the way she looks wearing my gear. I realize I love the way my last name sounds coming out of her pouty lips. And as wrong as it is, I realize I love the tiny scar under her eye. It's as if she's been branded by me. Something inside me shifts. I feel like I've been punched in the gut. I all but double over when it hits me.

I want her.

I want her like I want baseball.

Chapter Twenty-six

Murphy

Lexi and I stroll down Fifth Avenue, window shopping. I'm pushing Ellie in a stroller and Lexi is wearing Beth in a baby sling.

I love spending time with her kids, especially Ellie. Caden has been teaching me a few signs every time we're together. I know how to tell her she's pretty. I can ask her if she's hungry or sad. And I can understand some of the basic signs she does.

I'm impressed by how proficient Caden is at sign language. He loves his nieces and would go to the ends of the Earth for them.

As if thinking of him has caused some cosmic shift in the universe, I look in a storefront window and see a life-sized cutout of none other than the very man who has been invading my dreams. I don't even realize what I'm doing when I stop and stare.

"What's the story with you and my brother?" Lexi asks, looking between me and the cutout.

I peel my eyes away from the likeness of him. "There is no story," I say. "We're friends, Lexi. Same as you and me."

She giggles. "Yeah, except I'm pretty sure you don't want to get me into bed."

My jaw drops. "Who says I want to get him into bed?"

"The drool on your chin, maybe? Or how about the way you couldn't take your dreamy eyes off him at Mason's game. Or the way your face lights up every time we talk about him."

I turn my back to the window and lean against it, closing my eyes. "God, Lexi. Am I that pathetic?"

"No, Murphy, you aren't pathetic. It's just that my brother is *that* awesome."

I shake my head. "You won't say anything, will you? I don't want him to know. It would ruin things."

"How would it ruin things?" she asks. "I think it's wonderful."

"We're friends, Lexi. Good ones. We have a great time together. If he knew I was having feelings for him, he'd run in the other direction."

She smiles at me. "I think you're wrong. He'd run straight into your arms."

"What? No. He's not looking for a relationship, Lexi. Plus, he's dating other women. Your brother does not like me. Not in that way."

"I think you're both living in denial," she says. "He looks at you the same way you look at him."

"He does not."

She nods emphatically. "He does. And he only dates to be social."

"But Kate, the girl I met last weekend, she seemed so nice. Definitely girlfriend material."

"No way," she says. "You know she won't make it past the third date. No one does."

I cock my head and look at her. "What do you mean no one gets past the third date?"

Beth starts fussing and Lexi fishes a pacifier out of her bag for her. "He hasn't told you?"

"Told me what?"

"About his three-strikes rule?"

I furrow my brows. "What's his three-strikes rule?"

She rolls her eyes. "Caden never takes a girl out more than three times. He claims it's because he doesn't want to get trapped by anyone, so I guess he never keeps a girl around long enough to fall for her. He's afraid people won't like him simply for who he is underneath his celebrity."

I nod remembering how he told me something like that in the hospital. Then I turn around and study the pseudo-Caden in the window. "Still … it's a stupid rule. How will he ever find out if anyone likes what's underneath? You can't possibly get to know someone after only three dates." I look back at Lexi. "Never?"

She shakes her head in affirmation. "Not since he's been with the Nighthawks."

I give her a confused look. "Well then knowing he has this three-strikes deal, why in the world are you encouraging me to tell him I like him?"

"You've already answered your own question. Caden can't possibly get to know someone in three dates. But you he already knows—and very well by the way he talks about you. There would be no reason for the rule when it comes to you, Murphy."

I look up at the fake-Caden. "It would be too big a risk. I could lose him as a friend. I care too much for him to do that. Plus, I think you're wrong about how he feels. In fact, I'm going on a triple date with him and one of his teammates tonight."

I can tell Lexi tries not to laugh. She locks her lips together to form a thin line. Then she asks, "What do I have to do for an invite? I'd pay good money to see that go down."

"I'm sure Caden won't mind if you come. He's always saying he wants more people along when he goes on dates."

"I'm kidding, Murphy. I've got plans with Charlie and Mallory that involve kids, pizza, and a sleepover. We often do it when Chad is out of town and Kyle is working an overnight shift."

"Sounds like more fun than my triple date."

She laughs. "We'll invite you the next time we get together. So, which one of his teammates did he set you up with this time?"

"He didn't have to set me up. There's a guy at the gym who's been asking me out. Corey will be my date."

Her face breaks into a slow, devious smile. "Oh, Murphy, now I really *do* wish I was going. I'll bet there will be so much sexual tension between you two that you could cut it with a knife."

"That's ridiculous," I tell her. I see Ellie getting impatient and asking for a snack, so I get a pouch of goldfish out of the diaper bag and hand it to her. "I'm telling you, Lexi, he doesn't see me that way."

"And I'm telling you I've known my brother a lot longer than you have. Trust me. He wants you." She tugs on my arm to get us walking again. "Now, come on, we have to find you a killer outfit to wear. One that will send him over the edge. There's nothing like a little jealousy to get a guy to admit his feelings."

I roll my eyes, but I let her drag me to five shops anyway. After all, if what she said is true, if there is even a sliver of hope that he wants to be more than friends, I want to look my very best.

~ ~ ~

Lexi was wrong. Caden has spent more time staring at my date than he's spent staring at me. And Caden was right the other day when he said he's like my protective older brother. He keeps asking Corey questions about his job (he works in security), his apartment (third-floor walkup in Midtown), and his family (two sisters and a brother). It sounds like a job interview. He's vetting the guy for me.

I feel kind of sorry for his date, Maggie, as she's getting ignored. I don't miss how Maggie keeps trying to hold hands with Caden, but he brushes her away.

From the little information I've learned about her, I know she works in the fashion industry and is the best friend of Sawyer's date, Angela.

Oh, and I've learned she's a slut. Or at the very least, she's exactly the kind of woman Caden wants to avoid. She keeps dropping names of famous people she's managed to date. I guess she thinks that will impress us. But the only person at the table who seems impressed is Angela. Probably because she's doing the same thing. In fact, they mentioned dating the same guy and I wonder if they had some kind of twisted threesome. The two girls do seem very close.

In the past, had I met someone in the fashion industry, I might mention that I was a model. You never know who might be able to get your foot in the door. Oddly, though, I purposefully keep my lips sealed about my former profession—if you can even call it that. I only had a few modeling jobs for second-rate magazines that barely paid me enough to cover the rent.

I realize I haven't thought about modeling lately. Not since I moved in with Trick. I'm kind of in love with my new job. It's low stress. It more than pays the rent. And I get along well with all my bosses and co-workers. I'm even beginning to think this might lead to an actual career for me. With all the new responsibilities they have entrusted to me, I feel there is plenty of room to grow. After all, I work for one of the biggest, most exclusive gyms in the city. How did I get so lucky?

I reach up and touch my scar and then look over to catch Caden watching me. He winks at me and smiles. Then Corey puts his arm around the back of my chair and rests his hand on my bare shoulder, caressing my flesh with slow circles from his thumb.

Caden's smile disappears as his eyes hone in on the movement of Corey's hand. Then Caden gets up abruptly and excuses himself to the men's room. I can't help but smile. It was the first sign of jealousy I've ever seen from him. Maybe it's the first sign of hope I see for *us*.

Corey mistakes my smile for being happy that he's touching me. I don't shrug his arm away. I don't see any harm in letting him leave it there. But it's not like I'm planning to go home with him. Even if I weren't lusting after Caden, I still wouldn't go home with Corey. And maybe it makes me a bad person to use him as a pawn to try and reveal Caden's true feelings—if there are any. I swear, however, this was not my intention when I invited Corey to be my date. But that was then and this is now.

"Do you think Caden fell in?" Sawyer says, after Caden doesn't come back to the table.

"Maybe he climbed out the window," Angela jokes, nudging her friend.

Maggie laughs. "He'd be missing out if he did," she says. "I have big plans for us later." She makes an obscene gesture with her hands, giggling with her friend. "*Big* plans."

My back stiffens.

"Are you okay?" Corey asks.

You mean other than picturing little Miss Slutty underneath the man I want?

"I'm fine. I just need to hit the ladies' room."

I run into Caden in the back hallway. He's sitting down on a bench outside the bathrooms. He's slumped over looking at the floor, his forearms on his knees. I sit next to him. I think Angela was right. He's hiding from Maggie.

"Maggie's a bit much, huh?" I ask.

"To say the least," he says. "How about Corey? You two seem to be getting along."

I shrug. "He's nice I guess."

He looks up at me, pinning me to the wall with his stare. "You going to see him again?"

"I'm only on a date with him because you asked me to tag along. Remember?"

"So, you aren't going to see him again? Are you going to go home with him?"

My jaw drops. "Of course I'm not going home with him, Caden. You know me better than that."

He lets out a deep, relieved sigh. "Good. He's not right for you anyway."

I bite my lip, trying to keep from smiling. *Maybe Lexi was right.*

"What about you?" I ask. "It sounds like Maggie has big plans for you later." I shake my head, once again, picturing the two of them together. "And in case you're wondering, those were her exact words."

"Jesus, really?" He looks right and left down the hallway. "Can we climb out the window or something?"

I laugh probably more than I should.

"What? I'm serious. Don't think I haven't done it before," he says. "Well, I haven't actually climbed out a window. But I have used a back door. Sawyer will understand. Hell, he will probably thank me for it. Maybe he'll take *both* of them home."

"Oh, my gosh. I was thinking the same thing."

"So, can we bolt?"

I shake my head. "I won't do that to Corey. He really is a nice guy, Caden. He doesn't deserve that. I was the one who invited him."

"You're right. You're a better person than I am, Murphy Brown."

I stand up and hold out my hand. "Come on, let's head back. It's getting late and we only have to stick it out for another hour."

When he grabs my hand, something happens. I'm not sure what, but it might have something to do with music and birds flying and clouds under my feet. The touch we share is electrified. Intense. *Scary.*

He must feel it too, because the way he's looking at me right now, it's the way you get looked at before your first kiss. Before you get picked up and carried over the threshold. Before you lose your heart to someone forever.

Our hands part and the moment dies. But before we rejoin the others, he calls me back. "Murphy, that's one hell of a dress. You look … incredible isn't even a strong enough word."

"Thanks," I say, blushing. "You're not half bad yourself."

He winks at me again and I melt inside.

Please, God, let Lexi be right.

Chapter Twenty-seven

Caden

I'm on my third episode of late-night *Murphy Brown* reruns. I glance at my phone to check the time and wonder if Murphy is also watching them. I hope she is. In fact, I might go so far as to bet on it. Maybe it's become our thing. And anyway, I had to do something to take my mind off tonight.

It was torture watching that guy put his hands all over Murphy earlier. Okay, so maybe his hands weren't *all* over her. But the way he touched her shoulder; the way he put his hand on the small of her back when we entered the restaurant; the way he would lean close every time he talked to her—I've never in my life wanted to be another person so badly.

And I've never been so relieved than when she told me she wasn't going to go home with him. But what happens if he asks her out again? What happens when the *next* guy comes along? There is no way in hell I'll be able to watch her do that again. And I only know one way to keep it from happening.

The problem is—she's my friend, maybe even my *best* friend. I don't want to ruin what we have. I've never had so much fun with a girl who isn't my sister. Hell, I've never had so much fun with *anyone.*

She's all I've thought about since I took her to Central Park on Thursday. If I'm being honest, I thought about her long before then. I guess I've been denying it for a while.

But it goes to reason that she might not even want me. She's given me no indication that she wants a relationship. No indication that she's interested in me beyond the friendship we have. In fact, she's flat-out said she's taking a break from dating.

But that touch we shared tonight. And the way she was looking at me when we shared it. That's not the way you look at your friend. That look got me hard. That look had me thinking about long walks and shared holidays. Christ, that look had me thinking about white dresses and black tuxedos.

What is happening to me?

I pull out my phone and scroll through my pictures. I look at the picture of Murph and me sitting in the stands at the Yankees game. I smile at the picture I took of her last Sunday when she was laughing with Lexi. I stare at the photo I snapped of her wearing my gear.

It's the last one that brings my dick to life for the second time tonight. I don't fight it this time. I reach my hand into my sweat pants, stroking myself as those brilliant blue eyes of hers stare at me from behind my facemask. I watch her and think of the incredible dress she was wearing tonight. I've never seen her look so alluring. Her long, wavy hair was down around her shoulders, covering her bare neck that I longed to grip with my hands so I could pull her to me.

And her breasts. My God, the rounded globes pushed up and showed just enough flesh to be enticing without being slutty.

I stroke myself faster and my breathing becomes heavier. I think about the time when we were lying under the stars at Hawks Stadium. I think even then, I had the urge to touch her. Kiss her. But she was off-limits, raw from a failed relationship. But the way she looked at me tonight when she offered me her hand—it was far from the look of a broken woman. It was intense. And I swear we shared more unspoken words with that one look than the countless conversations we've had.

My balls tighten as I once again think of her breasts and what they might look like if her magnificent dress was in a heap on my floor. As I wonder what her tall and fit body would feel like under mine. I give myself a few last tugs before I stiffen and shout out with my release.

I put my phone down and go in the bathroom to clean up. When I'm done, I brace my arms on the counter and lock eyes with my reflection. "Face it, Kessler, you've got it bad."

I grab a beer and watch the end of an episode. Then I stare at my phone, wanting so badly to pick it up and ask her out. But I can't. I can't take Murphy on a date. For as long as I can remember, I've had the rule. Nobody gets past it. I've broken it for no one.

What if I date her and then get spooked after number three? I've no doubt dated some great girls over the years. Girls who clearly were not after me because of my fame and my bank account. But I ditched them. All of them. What if I do that to Murphy? What if I ruin everything right along with our friendship?

But if I don't try, will Corey or someone else take the opportunity? Hell, for all I know, Corey's at home rubbing one out too.

Shit.

The thought of another guy getting off to a picture of her—to the mere thought of her—makes me something I've never been before … territorial. And I know for sure I don't want anyone else having her. So despite the late hour, or the early one, I pick up my phone.

Me: Text me as soon as you wake up.

Murph: I'm up. Is everything okay?

My heart pounds in my chest. I didn't expect her to respond. I thought I'd have the night to think about how I was going to play this. Damn, I'm nervous as hell. I don't even get this nervous when I'm at bat and forty thousand fans are watching me.

Murph: What's wrong, Caden? You're scaring me.

Me: Nothing. Sorry. Just didn't expect you to be awake at this hour. What are you doing up so late?

Murph: You'd laugh at me if I told you.

I smile because I already know.

Me: You aren't watching channel 144, are you?

Murph: No.

Murph: Okay, yes.

Murph: Wait. How'd you know it was on 144? Unless you're watching too.

Me: I'm watching it too.

Murph: LOL

Murph: Why did you want me to text you tomorrow? Uh, today.

Here it goes. My fingers hesitate before I type out the text. I close my eyes for a second, hoping I'm not about to make this stupid move that will make it monumentally awkward for us if she shoots me down.

Me: I've been thinking.

Murph: Easy, boy. Don't go pulling a muscle or anything.

Me: Can I finish please?

Murph: Sorry.

Me: I've been thinking that maybe you should come over to my place for dinner.

Murph: Another double date?

Me: Not a double date. I don't bring girls here. It would just be you and me.

Murph: In case you haven't noticed yet, Kessler, I'm a girl.

Me: I'm well aware, Murphy Brown. Believe me, I'm well aware.

She doesn't text me right back. Did I scare her off? Is she getting the picture? Is she trying to figure out how to let me down easy?

Murph: You want to cook for me?

Me: Well, I was kind of hoping you would help with the cooking. And maybe we could have a nice bottle of wine. And then we could watch a movie or something.

Murph: Let me get this straight. You want me to come to your place so we can cook dinner together. And drink wine. And watch a movie. Caden, that sounds awfully close to being a date.

Me: Not a date. Just a thing.

Murph: And when will this *thing* be happening?

Me: When is your next day off?

Murph: Wednesday.

Me: I'll pick you up Tuesday at seven.

Murph: Okay, it's a date.

Me: No. It's not.

Murph: LOL. Whatever you say, Kessler.

Chapter Twenty-eight

Murphy

"I think the apartment is clean now," Trick says from her perch on the barstool where she's been watching me. "In fact, it was clean two hours ago. We could eat off the floor. Would you sit down already?"

I put the dust rag away and grab a bottle of water before I plop down on the stool next to her and quench my anxiety-driven bone-dry mouth.

"You look as nervous as a whore in church," she says, laughing.

I put my forehead down against the countertop. "I'm going to screw this up, aren't I?"

She puts a comforting hand on my back. "You aren't going to screw anything up, Murphy. Just be yourself. That's the person he wants to be with. Nothing has changed."

I look at her like she's crazy. "*Everything's* changed, Trick."

"You said yourself you aren't even sure this is a date. Maybe it's not. Maybe this is you guys testing the waters or something, you know, before you decide to dive in."

Maybe she's right. Earlier, I let her read our texts from the other night. The ones where he called it a '*thing*.' What does that even mean? He doesn't want to call it a date. Maybe that's because he's not sure he wants it to be one. *Oh, God.* That's even worse. It's going to be like an audition or something.

"I think I'm going to be sick."

I run into the bathroom and splash some water on my face. I look at the girl in the mirror and shake my head. What happened to the calm, confident woman who could walk a runway? "Get it together, Murph," I say to myself, pulling out my makeup to do one last re-touch. "It's just Caden."

I try to convince myself this is no big deal. That going to the apartment of one of the most recognized professional athletes in New York is just an everyday thing for me.

"Murphy!" Trick calls from the other room. "Caden's here."

I give myself one last look in the mirror. One last mental pep talk before I walk out there and try not to make a fool out of myself.

I blow out a big breath and open the door. Caden smiles when he sees me. I walk over to him, picking up my purse along the way. He takes a few steps forward and kisses me on the cheek. My flesh burns where his lips touch me. He's kissed me like this before. But those were different. Those were friendly kisses, the same as he'd give his sister. Those weren't lingering ones like this one. They weren't followed by him taking a whiff of my hair. They weren't punctuated by the inviting stare he's giving me right now.

He touches my arm. "You ready to go?"

I smile and nod. Like a love-sick schoolgirl, I lost the ability to speak as soon as he put his hand on me.

Caden says goodbye to Trick and escorts me into the hallway. He grabs my hand on the way to the elevator.

Caden Kessler is holding my hand. Oh, my God!

His hand is big and soft, except for the calluses on his palm up by his fingers. He holds my hand confidently in his, like we've done it many times before. Like he hasn't just caused my insides to flip upside down and inside out. Like he hasn't just confirmed my deepest desire and my greatest fear all at once.

We stand silently, waiting for the elevator to arrive. I stare at our entwined hands in the shiny chrome doors. When I look up, he catches my eyes in our reflection. He leans close to me. "This isn't a date, Murphy Brown." Then he squeezes my hand and runs his thumb up and down across mine.

"I know," I tell him, finally finding my words. "It's just a *thing*."

When we arrive at his apartment twenty minutes later, I realize the only time he let go of my hand was when he paid the cabbie. But he finally releases me when we walk through his door. I walk to the center of the room and spin around, taking it all in. I'm not sure what I expected, but it wasn't this.

My eyes take in the view from his living room. It's nice. Much nicer than the view at Trick's place. But it's not at all what I envisioned. It's so … normal. I figured he'd have an unobstructed view of the Freedom Tower, or maybe a prized location overlooking New York Harbor.

I look at his kitchen where I'd expect to find an oversized refrigerator, a wine cooler and top-of-the-line countertops. But it looks just like Trick's, only bigger. His living room is tastefully decorated, with a large L-shaped leather couch overlooking the view and a regular-sized flat-screen TV in the corner.

As someone who plays baseball in televised games, I was sure he'd have a big-screen TV.

"What?" he asks, seeing my reaction.

"For a guy who makes a gazillion dollars, I guess I thought you'd live in the penthouse suite with a maid and a butler."

"I told you before, Murph, I could be living on borrowed time. I'm not about to blow my money on frivolous things and then end up homeless when I can no longer play." Then he chuckles. "And I *do* have a housekeeper. Her name is Maria. She comes every Monday."

"You said you never bring girls here. Why?"

"Same reason I don't give them my phone number. It makes me too easy to find."

"But you gave me your number the day we met. And now here I am, standing in your apartment."

"You're different, Murphy."

"Why am I different, Caden? Why didn't you bring Kate here? Kate was nice. I find it hard to believe you haven't dated other nice girls. Girls who aren't after you for anything but who you are."

He shrugs. "You never can tell. Even with the nice ones. I've seen it happen too many times. Ball players get married and then end up divorced, paying child support for kids they never get to see and alimony to a woman they've come to despise."

"Lots of people get divorced, you know," I say. "Ball players haven't cornered the market."

"I just … it just scares me I guess."

"What scares you?"

He looks at some pictures of his nieces on the bookshelf. "I couldn't imagine having kids and not seeing them."

I can't help shifting my feet nervously. "Are you sure you don't?" I ask.

"Have kids? I'm sure," he says, staring me down with truthful eyes. "Came close once."

"Really?"

He nods. "I'm sure any shrink would tell you that's why I'm like this. About four years ago when I was playing for the Hawks' triple-A team in Vegas, I got a girl pregnant."

"I'm sorry," I say. "What happened?"

He motions for me to follow him into the kitchen where he opens a bottle of wine. "She was a typical groupie. It's amazing how many women hang out around minor league ball fields just waiting to sleep with anyone in a uniform."

I take a glass from him and sip some wine as we each find a barstool. "They're all a bunch of Tonys, just wanting to go along for the ride when someone hits it big."

"Exactly," he says. "See, you understand. It's one of the reasons I've always trusted you. You never wanted anything from me. You've been taken advantage of, too. You know how it feels."

I look around his apartment again. "Is that why I'm here? Because you trust me?"

"Yes. Well, that and I couldn't stop thinking about how you looked in that dress on Saturday night."

I blush. He has no idea how much I was hoping that dress would affect him. "So, the groupie?"

"She turned up pregnant after we'd been together a few times. I was young. Barely twenty-two. I didn't know what I was going to do. She wasn't even my girlfriend. I couldn't imagine marrying her, but I knew I'd have a hard time not seeing any kid I'd brought into the world."

"What happened? She didn't get an abortion, did she? I mean, she wouldn't have if she were trying to trap you."

"She had a miscarriage shortly after she told me. It was a blessing in disguise. And a huge wake-up call for me. I made sure that would never happen again."

I tilt my head to the side, studying him. "You telling me you're celibate, Kessler?"

He laughs at my question. "No, Old Man Murphy, I'm not celibate. But I never trust a woman to take care of birth control. And I always double wrap."

I almost spit out the drink of wine I'm taking. "Double wrap?"

"Yeah, you know—" He mimes putting on a condom and I feel my face turn a deep shade of red.

"I know what you mean, Caden. I don't need a visual."

The last thing I need right now is to picture him naked, rolling on a condom. I'm barely keeping it together as it is. Because whatever this *thing* is, I like it. I like *him*. I like his apartment. I like *my* apartment. I like my job. I like the way he's looking at me right now. I like the way he makes me feel. And I realize for the first time in a long time, I'm truly happy.

He winks at me and stands up, holding out his hand to me. "Come on. Let's make some steaks."

Chapter Twenty-nine

Caden

Watching Murphy eat is making me hard. Every time she cuts a piece of steak, she licks her lips. The lips I want to claim as mine. I've been thinking about kissing her all night. Every time she puts the wine glass to her mouth. Every time she talks. Every time a gorgeous smile cracks her face.

I wonder if she would be okay with me kissing her. Technically, this isn't even a date. Can I kiss her if it's not a date? Would she be mad if I did? Be upset if I didn't?

"I finally told my mom," she says. "I told her everything. About the accident, my roommates, my new job."

"What did she say?"

"She's coming out here in a few weeks. Says she wants to spend Thanksgiving with me, but I know she's going to try and get me to move back to Iowa. She was pretty freaked out."

I tense up. "But you don't want to go, do you?"

I find myself holding in a breath until she answers.

She shakes her head. "No. I love my job." She puts down her fork and looks me in the eyes. "I'm not sure I ever thanked you, Caden. When you first got me the job, I knew it was out of pity and I had no choice but to take it. I never expected it to turn into anything. But now, Jayden keeps telling me I have a head for business and I think I might be offered a promotion soon."

"That's great, Murph. And just so you know, nothing I've done for you was out of pity. Kindness maybe, but not pity." I push my food around on my plate. "So, you love your job. Is that the only thing keeping you here?"

"No way. I *love* New York. I loved it even before I moved here. It's where I belong. And now I have Trick and Lexi and—"

"Me," I interrupt. I put my hand on top of hers and look her dead in the eyes so she understands my meaning. "You have me, Murphy. That is, if you want me."

Her hand trembles underneath mine and I think I hear her breath hitch.

The kitchen timer goes off, alerting us that dessert is done.

I laugh as I get up from the table. "Saved by the bell, Murphy Brown. Stay here, I'll get dessert."

I clear our plates and bring them to the kitchen, looking back to see her taking some very large swallows of her wine.

I put the hot peach cobbler in front of her and take my seat. "Speaking of parents, my dad is in New York," I say. "At least he was a few weeks ago."

Her surprised eyes snap to mine. "What? I thought you didn't have any contact with him."

"I don't. But he approached me on the street near your old place and then we had a confrontation outside the gym. I had Ethan do some digging and it turns out he's not a drug addict anymore. He did some time in prison and I guess now he helps people get rehabilitated when they get out of jail. Owns a business and everything."

"That's great, Caden. What's he like?"

I shrug. "Don't know. I haven't contacted him."

"You think he wants your money or something?" she asks.

"At first I did. But now …" I look out the window and onto the city.

"Now you're scared of what could happen if you take that step," she says. "Everything is good in your life right now. You don't want to rock the boat."

I stare at her introspectively, wondering if she's talking about me and my dad or me and *her*.

"Maybe," I say.

"Do it, Caden. I would give anything to have my dad back, and now you have this opportunity to have yours. What if it turns out to be the best thing that ever happened to you? But you'll never know unless you take the chance."

I want to take her words and throw them right back at her—tell her that's exactly why we should try this thing.

She pushes her plate away. "I'm stuffed," she says, finishing off her wine. When I put down my fork, too, she grabs our plates and walks them over to the sink to wash them.

"Leave them," I say, coming up behind her.

My body is almost touching hers. My breath flows over her neck. I can see the fine hairs on her arm stand at attention. But she keeps washing. And I keep standing where I am—close enough to feel the heat between us, but far enough so she doesn't feel my own growing reaction.

She finishes and turns around. I brace my arms on the counter on either side of her, caging her in. "I have a very important question to ask you, Murph."

Her eyes close briefly and she takes in a shaky breath as she looks up at me. I pull a hand away from the counter and brush my thumb across the scar on her cheekbone. We lock eyes and I try to convey everything I want to say, but am afraid to.

I drop my hand and smile. "Comedy or sci-fi?"

"What?" she asks, looking confused. And maybe a bit flustered.

"Movies," I say. "Do you prefer comedy or sci-fi?"

She blows out a relieved breath and then she giggles. "What if I say romance?"

Damn I love that sound. I find myself searching for something funny to say so she'll make it again.

"I'd say you're out of luck. Because the last time I checked, I'm a guy."

And there it is.

"I'm kidding," she says. "I wouldn't make you watch a romance."

"Come on." I grab her hand and pull her towards the hallway.

"Uh, Caden?" she says, hesitating. "Where exactly are you planning on watching this movie?"

"My theater room."

"You have a theater room?" Her eyes go wide before she rolls them. "Of course you do."

I escort her down the hall and into the first door on the left. I flip on the lights and let her look around. The walls aren't lined with movie posters, they are lined with old jerseys of mine. I kept one from every team I'd ever played on, all the way back to T-Ball.

"Oh my gosh," she says, walking from jersey to jersey, touching some of them. Then she turns around, biting her lip in thought. "Did the Nighthawks make you change your number?"

Every jersey hanging in this room has #27 on the back. It's been my number since I was a kid. Right up until my sister went missing a few years ago. "Eight was Lexi's favorite number," I tell her. "She grew up bugging me to change it, but I never did. Not until she was gone."

"So, you changed to number eight for her. What an incredible gesture. And it worked. She came back." She smiles and looks at my jerseys again. "Lexi and I have become close and I know a little of what happened to her, but I didn't know that."

"Not many people know why I changed my number," I admit.

"Thank you for telling me."

I lead her over to my collection of DVDs. "Now, what are we going to watch? You pick."

She peruses the titles and settles on a comedy. Then she looks at the screen that takes up an entire wall. "I knew you had a massive TV somewhere," she says, laughing.

"A guy's got to have priorities," I say, walking her over to the first row of seats.

I look down at my theater-style seating and curse myself for not putting a couch in here, or at the very least, seats with retractable armrests. How in the hell am I supposed to put my arm around her? I didn't think this through very well.

Maybe she doesn't *want* me to put my arm around her.

But when I look at her, she's eyeing the seats the same way I am. We share a smile, both aware of what the other is thinking.

I put in the movie and dim the lights. Then I grab a few bottles of water from the mini-fridge and take the seat next to her. I hand her a bottle. "I can make popcorn if you like."

"I'm full, but thanks. Water is all I need."

The movie starts and I immediately grab her hand and hold it the entire two hours. Neither of us moves. My arm almost goes numb from leaving it in the same position for so long. And when the movie ends, I can't even say I watched it. I was too busy looking at our hands. Watching the way we would take turns rubbing our thumbs across the other's knuckle. I was too busy thinking of how or when or where I was going to kiss her tonight.

Because I *am* going to kiss her tonight. There is no doubt in my mind. I *have* to kiss her. I have to kiss her as surely as I have to breathe.

I stand up and pull her along with me.

"That was good … I think," she says, looking embarrassed at the admission.

I laugh. "I didn't watch much of it either."

The room is still dim, but not dim enough that I can't see the way she's looking up at me. She wants this. She wants it, too. But, like me, she's plagued by hesitation and uncertainty. My heart races as I pull her close and put my hands on either side of her face as I lean down toward her.

"Caden …"

"Don't think about it, Murph."

"That's the problem," she says with a sigh. "It's *all* I think about."

Those are the last words she utters before my lips crash down on hers.

Holy God. Kissing Murphy is unlike anything I've ever experienced. Her soft lips immediately part for mine, allowing our tongues to mingle, tasting each other until we are left gasping for air. My hands leave her face and find her shoulders, her arms, her back—all the places I've longed to caress but couldn't until now.

She puts a hand on my chest in the tight space between us. Her other hand makes its way to the back of my neck as she winds her fingers through my hair. Seductive throaty noises come from her when I break the kiss for air and let my lips explore her neck.

My hands trace every soft curve of her sides, longing to feel what's underneath, but needing to take it slow. When my lips find hers again, we mold together, feasting on each other like there's no tomorrow.

My hard dick is straining against the fly of my jeans and I pull her even more tightly against me. I don't care if she can feel it. I want her to know what she does to me. I need her to know I think of her as so much more than a friend.

Before crossing a line I don't want to cross tonight, I break our seal and put my forehead down on hers as we breathe heavily into each other.

"That was …" I can't find the words.

"Yeah," she says, catching her breath.

I give her a squeeze. "Don't get any ideas, Murphy Brown, this isn't a date, you know."

She laughs, putting her hands on my chest. I wonder if she can feel my heart thundering underneath them. Because I'm not sure it's ever beaten this fast.

I lean back so I can look at her. "But if I asked, would you be open to having another … *thing* with me?"

She shrugs. "I don't know. It might take some convincing," she says, moving a hand to the back of my head and tugging on the ends of my hair.

"Gladly," I say, leaning down for a replay of what I'm sure was the best damn kiss of my life.

Chapter Thirty

Murphy

A hand waves in front of my face. "Earth to Murphy," someone says.

I look up, embarrassed that my boss has caught me daydreaming as I watch Caden run on a treadmill on the other side of the room. "Sorry, Jayden. Did you need something?"

"Did you get a chance to work on that spreadsheet?"

"Yup. I finished it this morning. Check the printer."

"You finished it?" she asks, her mouth agape.

"Uh, yeah," I say nervously. "Isn't that what you wanted?"

"Yes. But I didn't expect you to finish it *today*. Next week maybe."

"Oh. Well it was easy enough once I broke Stephanie's code about the different membership types."

She laughs. "I was going to put in a call to her to ask about it, but I'm always afraid I'll wake the baby."

"When is she coming back from maternity leave?" I ask. "I'm eager to meet her."

"Two weeks. I can't tell you what a godsend you've been in her absence. I'm not sure what we would have done without you." She nods to Caden on the treadmill as she walks back to the office. "You can go back to your drooling now, Supergirl. You've earned a few extra minutes of mindless gawking."

I shamelessly look back at Caden, happy he can't see me staring at him. Was it only a few days ago that he kissed me? I think I've replayed that night a million times in my head. It was perfect. The best first date I've ever had.

My eyes fall to the counter and I sigh. '*This isn't a date.*' His words echo through my head. I wonder, not for the first time since that night, if he only wants a friends-with-benefits thing. I mean, he did call it a *thing*.

Then again, I remember what he said that night about me having him if I want him. Did he mean have him as my boyfriend?

And then there is the whole three-strikes rule Lexi told me about. What if we go out three times and he tosses me aside? What if we have three incredible, perfect dates like on Tuesday and then he freaks out and falls behind his tried-and-trusted albeit stupid rule?

I really need to talk to someone about this. I would normally go to Lexi, but she's his sister and as such, will be far too biased to look at things rationally. Maybe I can talk to Piper. Then again, her husband is good friends with Caden. And Trick is Caden's trainer. I look around realizing there isn't anyone I can talk to about Caden because all my friends are his friends. Because everything I have in my life right now is because of him.

Oh, God. A sick feeling washes over me. What if we don't work out? I could lose all my friends. Maybe even my job.

Before I melt down into a full-on freak-out, someone walks up to the desk, pulling me from the rabbit hole. “Hi, Murphy,” Corey says, smiling.

I’ve been avoiding him this week. I’m not sure how to act around him after having asked him out last Saturday night.

“Hi, Corey. What can I do for you?”

“I haven’t seen you around much lately,” he says. “I thought maybe you were avoiding me.”

I pick up a pile of papers on the counter in front of me. “I’ve been busy. They have been giving me more responsibilities around here.”

“That’s nice. So, uh, would you like to go to dinner tomorrow night?”

“I’m sorry, I’ll be working.”

“How about Saturday?”

I look over at Caden. He’s just finished his run and is wiping his face with a towel. He looks over to see me talking with Corey and he leans against the wall, arms crossed in front of him. He doesn’t look pleased. In fact, he looks … jealous.

I’m not sure why that makes me so happy, but it does.

“I’m sorry, Corey. I appreciate the invitation, but I can’t.”

He looks briefly at the ground and kicks an invisible spot. “Are you dating someone?”

I glance over at Caden again to see him watching me intently. “Not dating, but, well I have this … thing.”

“Thing?” he says, following my eyes over to Caden. “I knew it. You’re sleeping with him, aren’t you?”

“I’m not sleeping with *anyone*, Corey.”

“Whatever. It’ll never last. He’s a baseball player, Murphy. He’s got women throwing themselves at him. Not to mention he’ll be gone half the year. You’ll never see him during baseball season.

That is, if he keeps you around that long. Relationships between famous athletes and people like us never work out, don't you know that? You're the receptionist at his gym for Christ's sake."

I reach up and touch my scar, not wanting to let his words get to me. In one short conversation, he's brought up every fear I have about whatever this is Caden and I are doing.

I see Caden making his way towards us. "I'm not in a relationship with him," I say. "We're friends."

"Don't let him use you, Murphy," he says.

"Excuse me," Caden says, pushing his way past Corey even though there is plenty of space to walk around him. Caden comes behind the desk and drapes his arm around me. "Everything okay here?"

Corey eyes the hand touching my shoulder. "I was just talking to your *friend* here," he says. "Or should I say *girlfriend?*"

I stiffen at his words. Oddly, Caden does not.

"And now *I'm* talking to her. Nice to see you again, Corey. Enjoy your workout." Caden's passive-aggressive words dismiss him.

"I guess I'll see you around," Corey says to me before walking away.

"Yeah, we'll see you around," Caden says, squeezing my shoulder and molding himself to my side.

I watch Caden as he watches Corey walk across the weight room. "You didn't have to do that, you know," I say, peeling myself away from him.

"Do what?" he asks innocently.

"Rescue me, or whatever that was. I can handle Corey and every other guy who asks me out."

"Just how many guys are asking you out, Murph?"

I shrug.

He gives me a look of concern. "Seriously, how many?"

"He's the third one this week," I say.

"Three? In one week?" His hand comes up to run through his hair. "What did you tell them?"

"That I wasn't interested."

"Good. Keep telling them that," he says with a possessive stare. He checks the clock on the wall. "I have to go. I have a thing."

I stiffen. He has a *thing?* My heart lodges in my throat.

He sees my reaction and his hand comes up to scrub across the stubble on his jaw. "Shit, Murph. That's not what I meant. I'm meeting someone. My father actually."

My deep sigh is audible and I detect the hint of a smile on his face when he sees how relieved I am.

He leans close. "Believe me, you are the only one I want to have a *thing* with."

While I'm inhaling his musky scent, it dawns on me what he said. "I'm so glad you decided to meet with your dad. I hope it goes well."

"Do you have any words of advice for a guy who's about to meet the father he never knew?"

I stare at his gorgeous face, wondering if he got his looks from his father. "We don't get to choose our family, Caden. And we will only ever have one mother and one father. If this guy can't be your dad, nobody else can. I think you should be open-minded. Give him a chance. We've all made mistakes in our lives. We shouldn't be defined by them."

He nods. "Thanks, Slugger."

I laugh at the *Murphy Brown* reference.

He leans in and gives me a kiss on the cheek. A sexy, lingering cheek-kiss that warns all the other guys to stay away.

And then, just like how Caden watched Corey walk away, I follow Caden's every step to the locker room, appreciating how his prominent calf muscles flex with each long stride. How the strong lines of his back ripple under his tight shirt when he tosses his towel into the bin. How he looks over his shoulder at me to catch me staring.

When he rounds the corner, I slump over and knock my forehead on the counter a few times, berating myself for becoming a love-sick puppy.

"Oh, my God, are you Caden Kessler's girlfriend?"

I look up to see two patrons standing near the counter. The women are wearing workout clothes that look like they were purchased from a children's clothing store. Their breasts almost spill over the too-tight sports bras, and the boy shorts they're wearing barely cover their entire pubic region. These girls are obviously not here to work out.

"Uh, no," I say.

"But you *want* to be," the taller one declares.

"Is there anything I can help you ladies with?"

"Besides getting us his phone number?" the short one says, giggling.

I don't bother to answer.

"No, really," she says. "Like, can you get it for us? I'm sure you have it on your computer somewhere. Oh, do you have his address, too?"

"Member records are private," I tell them.

"Maybe we could come to an agreement," she says. "I'll pay you. How much is it worth?"

My jaw drops. "I don't care how much you offer me, I'm not giving you his number."

"Everyone has a price," the tall one says, eyeing me up and down. "Surely a lowly desk clerk such as yourself could use an extra few hundred bucks."

"You would pay a few hundred dollars for his phone number?" I ask, both surprised and appalled.

The shorter one looks excited. "Sure. How about we make it three?"

"Oh, my God. No!" I grab some papers off the counter and turn around.

"Bitch," one of them says. "Like *she* has a chance with him."

They walk away laughing.

Chapter Thirty-one

Caden

I finish the rest of my drink and order another. Every time the damn bells jingle when someone comes into the bar, I crane my neck and look to see if it's him. I had Ethan track down my dad's phone number and set up this meeting.

I'm not even sure what I'm going to say to him. Part of me wants to just meet him and then tell him to get lost. Tell him he has no right to be in Lexi's or my life. But the other part of me, the part that Murphy appealed to—that part wants something I've never had. A father.

The waitress puts another Jack and Coke in front of me. I thought I might need something a little stronger than my regular beer for this monumental meeting. Plus, liquor mellows me out. I don't want to get riled up and end up causing a scene. When she steps away, I see him. He's looking around the bar at every patron until his eyes meet mine.

He freezes. I freeze. We stare.

He walks over with a cautious smile on his face, nodding his head along the way. He stops and stands at the end of the booth. "Caden, thank you for meeting me."

He holds out his hand but I can't shake it. He *left* us. He just up and left the three of us and my mom had to work two jobs to feed and clothe us. That is not the kind of man whose hand I want to shake.

His smile falls. "Maybe we can work up to that," he says.

I nod to the other side of the booth. "Have a seat, Shane."

His surprised eyes snap to mine. He sits and says, "Maybe we can work up to that, too."

"To what?"

"You calling me Dad."

I snort an incredulous breath out my nose. "Don't count on it."

"Listen, Caden. I know I was a terrible father. I know I have a lot to make up for. You asking for this meeting is one of the best things that's happened to me. I've wanted to reach out to you for years. Especially when your mom died. But a few weeks ago, when you pushed me against that wall, I thought that was it. I thought there wasn't a chance in hell you'd ever give me another look. And then your friend called me. And now here we are."

"Wait. You know my mom died?"

He nods. "I've been keeping tabs on you for years."

"Alexa?" I ask, having to keep my voice low because what I really want to do is crawl over the table and strangle him for stalking my sister.

"It about killed me when she went missing a few years back."

"Then why now?" I ask. "Why did you come to New York and follow me around?"

He pulls out his wallet and removes a picture, sliding it across the table. It's a picture of me when I was younger. I don't remember it and I have no idea how in the hell he got it.

"What can I get you?" the waitress asks him.

"Club soda with lime, please."

The waitress walks away and he looks around the bar and laughs. "Been a while since I've been in a bar. Good to see they haven't changed much."

I ignore his statement and pick up the picture. "Where did you get this? Did my mother send it to you?"

"Shannon? No, she never sent me anything. It's not a picture of—"

"Well why the hell would she send you anything?" I cut him off. "You left her. You left us."

"No, son. I didn't."

I grit my teeth. "Do not call me *son.*" I take a drink and slam my glass back down on the table. "And what the hell do you mean you didn't?"

"Caden, your mother threw me out. With good reason, I might add. I was a drug addict. Cocaine. And my addiction drove us right to the poor house. Came home one night and she had thrown all my belongings on the front porch. Said never to contact her again. I thought about fighting her, because damn, I loved you kids, but I knew no judge would give custody to an addict. It killed me, Caden—the thought of not seeing you and your sister. So, I did everything I could to make some money so I could be a good dad to you and come back and fight for you one day." He shakes his head, clearly disgusted with himself. "But I did a lot of stupid things back then. Cocaine had a tight grip on me and I messed up. I couldn't even steal cars without letting the drugs get the best of me. I ended up doing a few years in prison."

"Yeah, I saw your mug shot. How proud you must be."

"I'm not proud of anything, son—uh, Caden. The only damn thing I've done right in my life is have three great kids. Not that I have anything to do with it, I credit their mothers for everything."

Now he has my attention. "Three? You have *three* kids?"

He puts a finger on the picture and pushes it back to me. "This is your half-brother, Scott."

I pick up the picture and stare. He's a goddamn carbon copy of me. "How old is he?"

"Twelve. And he's the reason I'm here. He's had a big growth spurt this past year. He's grown up fast. Grown up to look just like his older brother. And don't think it's gone unnoticed. People are starting to tell him how much he looks like the New York Nighthawks' star catcher. The person he shares a last name with. We never told him the truth about him being your brother. But when you became famous—well it's been harder and harder to convince people you aren't related. And then when my wife got sick …"

"You re-married?"

A sad smile crosses his face. "Dawn is the best thing that ever happened to me. She helped me get right after my release from prison." He looks down at the picture of Scott and frowns. "She died two years ago. Cancer. Scott took it hard, as you can imagine a ten-year-old would. He fell into depression. Doctors couldn't help him. Medication didn't work either. So six months ago, I took a chance. I took a chance and told him about you and Alexa."

I scrub my hand across my jaw. "I have a brother?" I'm still trying to absorb the words. I look Shane in the eyes. "I want to meet him. Is he in town?"

He shakes his head. "No. He's in Atlanta. I've been coming here on business. I'm scouting locations for somewhere to start up a new program. And anyway, I was hoping you and I could repair our relationship before introducing you. Get things off on the right foot."

"Repair our relationship?" I look at him through damaged eyes. "I don't care if my mother threw you out or not, you are the one who cut off all contact. I'm twenty-five fucking years old, Shane, and I've never received so much as a phone call or a goddamn birthday card. What you broke is beyond repair."

"What are you talking about?" he asks, cocking his head to the side. "I sent you cards every birthday, Christmas and Easter. I sent gifts, too. Even from prison. I sent them for years, Caden. Despite the fact your mother told me to stop. She said it hurt you and your sister to get gifts from the man they despised. But I kept sending them anyway, until the one Christmas when the presents I sent you were returned along with a note from you and Alexa asking me not to contact either of you again."

"That's crazy," I tell him. "We never wrote any such letter. And we never got any cards. We never got *anything* from you."

He looks about as broken as a man can look when he hears my words.

"Caden, no. I did. I sent them. I promise you I did." He closes his eyes and sighs in frustration. "She must have hidden them from you. Or thrown them away. I can't believe she would do such a thing. I tried so hard to get you what I thought would make you happy. One year I stood in line for hours so I could get a pink scooter for Alexa—one with those tassels hanging off the handlebars. She loved pink. From the time she could dress herself, she would only wear pink. I think she must have been six or seven that year."

"She was eight," I say, shaking my head in disbelief. "I remember because it was the best present she ever got. She flipped out when she opened it. She never let the thing out of her sight. It—it was from *you?*"

He nods, his eyes becoming glassy with tears. "Did you get any of the others? The pogo stick? The collection of Superman DVDs? The Game Boy?" He runs a hand through his hair. "The … the baseball glove?"

My heart lodges somewhere in my throat. So many things are going through my head right now. Not the least of which is that my mother might have lied to us. She may have passed all those gifts off as being from her. She withheld the fact that my father was trying to contact us all those years. That *she* was the one who kept him from us.

"When?" I ask, needing more concrete information. "How old was I when you sent the glove?"

He thinks on it a beat. "You would have been five. Same age as I was when my father gave me one."

Oh, my God. He is the one who got me the glove? The glove that had me begging my mom to let me play T-Ball? The glove that still sits on my dresser as a reminder of where I came from and what I had to go through to get here.

The glove that made me who I am today.

"I became a baseball player because of that glove," I say through the lump in my throat.

Tears spill over his lashes as he can no longer control his emotions. He reaches over and puts his hand on mine. I don't pull away. I don't pull away because I hear Murphy's words echoing through my head. *What if it turns out to be the best thing that ever happened to you?*

"So," I say, choking back my own tears. "Tell me about my little brother. Does he like baseball?"

My dad laughs. Then we spend the next two hours getting to know each other; making up for twenty-five years of lost time. He tells me about the program he runs. I tell him about my job. He shows me pictures of the step-mother I never knew. I let him scroll through pictures of my nieces—his grandkids—on my phone.

"What do you need from me, Caden?" he asks, when our conversation winds down. "I'll do anything you ask."

I look at the picture of Scott, once again. "I need you to go with me to see Lexi," I say. "And then the three of us are taking the first flight we can get to Atlanta."

Chapter Thirty-two

Murphy

I stare at the picture of Caden and his brother, amazed at how Scott is just a smaller version of Caden. Who could have imagined that his dad reaching out to him could have led to this? Their relationship is far from ideal, however, as Caden has a lot to overcome in his mind before he can fully accept his dad. But he's trying. He's talked about him a lot tonight. And the way he looks when he speaks of Scott—I can tell he's already become the proud older brother.

"Thank you," he says, putting his fork down, full of the dinner we've once again cooked together at his place.

"You cooked half of it," I say, getting up to clear the dishes.

He grabs my arm, pulling me back. "Not for dinner." He nods to the picture of him and Scott. "For that. I wasn't ready to face my father, Murphy. You are the one who encouraged me to do it. And now my whole world has changed. I can't thank you enough."

I smile down at him. "You would have gotten there eventually. All I did was give you a little nudge."

He pulls me onto his lap and I deposit the plates back on the table. My heart beats wildly in my chest. I'm sitting on him in a way girlfriends might sit on their boyfriends. He's staring into my eyes the way one lover would stare into another's.

We haven't talked about it. About *us*. Not since our last date—or whatever. We've texted. We've had conversations at the gym. But, other than the one time he said that the only person he wanted a *thing* with was me, he hasn't mentioned it.

He runs a finger lightly across my scar. "Let's go out for a drink," he says, eyeing my neck like he wants to devour it with his lips.

My mind barely comprehends his words because all it's focused on is his growing erection beneath me. I don't want to go to a bar with him. I don't want to go anywhere but back to his bedroom where I can fulfill the fantasies that have been consuming my every waking hour.

But when my head clears and comes down from the clouds, I realize how monumentally bad that decision would be. I mean, this isn't even a date if you ask Caden.

"A drink sounds great," I tell him, extracting myself from his lap.

We clean up the kitchen before heading out. On the way to the front door, he reaches into a bin, pulling out a couple of Hawks hats. He puts one on his head and then puts the other one on me. He takes care to fit it perfectly to my head and then he tucks my hair behind my ears.

"Have I ever told you how good you look in my hats?"

I laugh. "*Your* hats?"

He shrugs confidently.

"It's not even daylight, Caden," I say, going to remove mine. "Why—"

"Camouflage," he says, putting a hand on the top of my hat to keep me from taking it off.

I frown, wondering if he's afraid to be seen out with me.

He puts a finger under my chin and raises my head up until our eyes meet. "Don't read too much into it, Slugger. What we do together is nobody else's business, that's all."

I nod, willing myself to believe his words. "But where will we go without you being recognized?"

"Someplace dark. We'll sit in the back."

"Are you sure that's a good idea?" I ask, not wanting him to get mobbed by fans.

He eyes me up and down, perusing every inch of me like he's appraising a prized possession. He grabs my hands, pulling me so close that my chest touches his. When he leans down, the bills of our hats collide. "You look amazing. You *smell* amazing. And all I've been able to think about tonight is dragging you back to my bedroom. So, yes, I'm sure we need to get the hell out of my apartment and go somewhere safe."

Heat courses through my veins and I smile thinking that he's been fantasizing about me as well. "I'm not safe with you?" I tease.

A hand comes up to caress my scar and his breath warms my face. "You'll never be safer with anyone else, Murph. I swear it."

He pulls away before his lips have a chance to touch mine, leaving me wanting more. Needing more.

"Come on, let's go," he says, opening the door and pulling me through.

~ ~ ~

I still can't believe Caden has gone unnoticed. Yes, it's dark. And yes, we're sitting off in a corner. But even the whole way here, when we walked along the crowded streets, nobody singled him out.

I've often thought New York City is a good place to get lost. To blend into the crowd. Mallory told me not so long ago that it's why her uber-famous husband, Chad, likes it here so much. The city is busy. People rarely take the time to pay attention to each other. It's especially true on a Saturday night when everyone seems to have a place to go and is in a hurry to get there.

The waitress places our second round of drinks on the table and Caden carefully sips his while I all but guzzle mine. Anything to distract me from the soft under-the-table touches. The strong leg he has pressed against mine. The seductive glances. They all have my body humming.

Caden, on the other hand, is calm and calculated. I've noticed he doesn't drink much. My guess is that he likes to be in control and if he drinks too much, he may give that up.

Suddenly, I have thoughts about getting him drunk and watching him lose control.

"I'd love to be in your head right now," he says, studying me intently.

I look away, embarrassed that I was staring at him, having lewd thoughts about what I want to do to him. What I want him to do to me.

He laughs at my reaction. Then his face breaks into a smile and he stands up, pulling me off my chair and over to the dance floor. "I love this song," he says, twirling me around and into his arms as '*Sweet Caroline*' blasts through the speakers.

I love it, too. In fact, I was in part named after it as it was my grandmother's favorite song. During parts of the song, everyone in the room shouts out "*Ba, Ba, Baaaa*" and then "*So good, so good, so good.*"

I look at Caden and then around the bar, seeing everyone sing along. "Why does everyone here like Neil Diamond?" I ask, confused. "I thought that was a Red Sox thing."

"This is a sports bar. It's a *baseball* thing!" he shouts over the music, laughing. "Just go with it, Murphy Brown. Come on, let loose."

I know the song has been associated with baseball. My friends were always tagging me in YouTube videos when we were younger. But I thought it was only popular in Boston. I mean, I don't remember them playing it in Hawks Stadium the times I was there.

By the time the second verse rolls around, I get into it along with every other person in the bar. Caden pulls me close as we dance to a song I wouldn't think was danceable. But we aren't the only ones on the crowded dance floor so I guess it doesn't matter how stupid we look.

Every time the verse rolls around, Caden and I put our faces close and yell "*Ba, Ba, Baaaa*" into each other, and when he loudly chants "*So good, so good, so good,*" I could swear he's talking about me. About us. And not the illustrious song.

When the song changes to a new one, he tells me, "The next time we play the Red Sox in Boston, you are definitely coming. You have to hear this in person with forty thousand screaming fans."

I can't help but smile, because I know the soonest that could happen is next spring, many months from now. That means he still plans on us having a, um … *thing* by then.

"It sounds like fun. I'll have to check my calendar though," I say, smiling up at him.

"Oh, you're going," he says. "In fact, I'm getting you season tickets. You are my good luck charm."

I look at him like he's crazy. "Season tickets? Don't you play like a hundred games?"

"A hundred and sixty-two," he says. "But only half of them are played in New York."

I stop dancing and look at him nervously. "I know you don't expect me to go to eighty-one games."

He laughs. "Hell no. I expect you to go to *more*. Maybe you can tag along on some road trips." He sees my face pale. "I'm kidding, Murphy Brown. Well, not about getting you season tickets, but about you having to go to all the games."

I swat him in the chest, and he grabs onto my arm, reaching his other around my back and pulling me tightly against him. "But I would have you at every single one if I could. Having you around makes everything better."

"Do you want to hear something crazy?" I ask.

"Okay."

"I was named after that song," I tell him. "My middle name is Caroline. That song was my grandmother's favorite."

He stares at me in disbelief. Then he shakes his head laughing. Maybe he thinks it's a bit too coincidental as well.

"What?" I ask. "I told you it was crazy."

"Want to hear something even crazier?"

"Okay," I say.

"*My* middle name is Neil."

Now it's *my* turn to be speechless.

Our dancing turns into swaying. Our bodies are as locked together as our eyes. I lose all track of space and time as his eyes burn into mine, telling me everything I want to hear. I watch his lips as they come towards me in what seems like slow motion. They can't get to me fast enough. I know what he tastes like. I'm already addicted to him. All I want is more.

But before his lips find mine, I'm blinded by a bright flash.

Caden pulls me protectively behind him, telling whoever took the picture to back off. Then hordes of other cameras come out and countless flashes light up the dark room. Caden pulls my hat down as far as it will go while he quickly escorts me out into the night and into the nearest cab.

I smile when he gives the cabbie his address instead of mine. He doesn't want this night to end any more than I do. And even though his place is only two blocks away, he tells the guy to turn the opposite way and drive around for a minute before heading there.

Caden looks behind us the whole way to make sure no one is following.

"I'm sorry about that," he says, once we're safely in his apartment. "One of the many hazards of my job."

"I'm the one who's sorry, Caden. Those pictures might show up on the news. They will for sure be all over social media. Probably with *me* in all of them." I put my purse on the bar and slump onto a bar stool.

"Do you think that causes me concern?" he asks, wide-eyed.

"Well, doesn't it?"

"Not for the reasons you might think, Murphy." He comes up behind me and wraps me into his arms. He leans down and rests his chin on my shoulder. "In case you haven't figured it out by now, I want this. But I also know what could happen if and when people connect you with me. I told you earlier that I'd always keep you safe, but the truth is, I would fear for your safety if it got out that you have what others want."

I wriggle out of his grip and turn around to face him. Because I need clarification of what I think it is that he's telling me. I look up into his alluring green eyes. "What do I have that others want?"

"Me," he says.

The way he said it wasn't cocky or conceited. It was simply a truth. A fact. Because undeniably, others would kill to be in my position. Maybe that's what he's afraid of.

He brings his hands up to cradle the sides of my face. Then he traces my scar with his thumb—something that's become a habit for him. "That is if you want to have me," he says.

"Caden …"

Before I can answer, his lips claim mine. They claim me even more completely than the other kisses we've shared. His kisses destroy me with each soft touch, nip and lick of his mouth. They destroy me, because now I know for sure that I'm ruined. I'm ruined for any man that would follow him.

He asked if I want him. But it's no longer a question of want. I *need* him. I need him to the very core of my being. This man is my best friend. My other half. My soul mate.

His hands explore my arms and my back as mine weave through the locks of his hair. My legs part for him and he stands between my thighs, pressing himself against me in all the right places. The pleasurable friction causes me to moan into his mouth as he grips me tightly.

He finally breaks our kiss, pressing his forehead against mine. "I want you, Murphy Cavenaugh. I want you more than you could possibly know."

Two things simultaneously go through my mind. One: that is the first time he's ever called me by my given name; and two: this is only our second date. Or maybe it *isn't* our second date. Because for some reason, Caden refuses to classify it as such.

I pull back and sit up straight.

He backs away, looking disheartened. "What is it?"

"What's going to happen after our third date, Caden?"

He narrows his brow at me in question.

I blow out a sigh. "Lexi told me about your three-strikes rule. Technically, we haven't even been on a date yet. According to you, this is just a *thing*. What happens after our third date? I want you too, Caden. But I want you for more than three dates. And I'm not about to go to bed with another guy who's going to dump me in two seconds flat."

He paces around the counter, running a hand through his hair. "It's not like that with you, Murph. You're different and you know it. And I'm not Tony."

"Am I different? How do you know your old habits won't come back to haunt you? What if you get scared and can't help yourself. What if you decide *I'm* a Tony and am only here to trap you?"

"Jesus, Murphy, I would never think that. I know you aren't trying to trap me. Hell, you didn't even want my help when I offered it to you in the hospital. You didn't use my phone number. You didn't get all starry-eyed like most girls. To this day, you won't even text me unless I text you first."

"None of that matters if it's being in a relationship that scares you," I say. "What if your three-strikes rule is to keep *you* from falling for someone, not to keep others at bay?"

"That's ridiculous," he says.

"Is it? Why, Caden? Why is it ridiculous?"

He walks back around the counter and stands in front of me again. "Because it is. And besides, even if that's why I had the rule, it obviously didn't work."

"What do you mean?"

He cages me in with his arms and leans down close. "It didn't work because it didn't keep me from falling for someone."

My heart flips over in my chest. My pulse shoots through the roof. My hands shake.

"So now you know the score of the game, Murphy Brown. I guess the ball's in your court."

I can't speak. I can barely breathe. Could he possibly feel the same way about me as I feel about him? Two weeks ago, we were friends. And now we're talking about wanting … needing … falling.

He leans over me and grabs my purse off the counter before putting it on my shoulder. Then he stands me up and leads me towards the door. "Thanks for a great time, Sweet Caroline. I'm taking you home now. But I hope you aren't working next Friday night, because we're going on a date." He stops walking and looks directly into my eyes. "Our third date."

Chapter Thirty-three

Caden

Murphy leans in close and whispers in my ear. "I guess Brady doesn't think *he's* living on borrowed time."

Her eyes go wide as she takes in Brady's penthouse. It's true. It's impressive. He spared no expense. What I don't tell her is that while I'm focused on making sure I have a future, Brady could care less if he has one. He's impractical. Arrogant. Reckless.

And despite his cocky and roguish exterior, he thinks he's broken beyond repair—his words, not mine.

My dime-store psychoanalysis, based on the eighteen hours of psych I took in college, is that the reason he has a different girl in each city is because he refuses to let anybody in. Because if he doesn't let anybody in, he can't let anyone down.

He hasn't told me much, because he's the most tight-lipped son-of-a-bitch I've ever met, but what I do know is that he was married once and she was the love of his life. And the only reason I know that is because we got drunk together one time and he passed out, mumbling her name, saying how he was sorry and that everything was his fault. Sometimes I wonder if he couldn't keep it in his pants. If he screwed up the best thing he ever had by cheating on her.

Brady is a good guy. A loyal friend who would lay his life down for his buddies. When it comes to women and relationships, however, he's a complete jackass. Every woman he dates knows the score. They know they are one of many. And he never fails to remind them not to expect anything from him.

I'm not sure the other guys on the team even know what little I do about him. He's a closed book. Except for when it comes to his wallet and his dick—both of those are usually up for grabs. It's why he never lacks female companionship.

"Is that … Oh, my gosh, is that an original Monet?" Murphy asks, gaping at the masterpiece hanging over his fireplace.

I shrug. "I wouldn't doubt it." I pull her behind me into his massive kitchen where all the action seems to be. "But, you know, if you really want to see something impressive, well …" I look down at my pants.

She swats me on the back of the head. "Don't push your luck, Kessler."

A smile splits my face. I love it when she calls me that.

"What can I get you?" a waitress asks, carrying a tray of drinks. "If I don't have what you like, Jerry will make you anything you want."

I look around the room and then over at Jerry the bartender and shake my head, laughing. Only Brady Taylor would hire a waitress and a bartender for a party with only a few dozen people.

"I'll have a beer," I say. "Murph?"

"Me, too. A light one if you have it."

"Sure. I'll be right back," the waitress says.

"What's so funny?" Brady asks, walking over to us.

"Nothing. Thanks for having us."

"You have a beautiful place, Brady," Murphy adds.

"You have a beautiful face, Murphy," he says, eyeing her seductively.

I grab her hand. "Back off, Taylor."

"Damn," he says, looking at our entwined hands. "You two together now?"

I feel Murphy stiffen so I give her hand a squeeze. "We are," I say. "So keep your eyeballs in their sockets, my friend."

He laughs and pats me on the back. "I called that one, didn't I? And believe me, there are plenty other things for my eyeballs to focus on."

He's right. There seems to be a disproportionate number of women to men in attendance. There are only a handful of our teammates here, but the harem of beautiful ladies outnumbers them by two to one.

One of the ladies walks up, draping herself around Brady. "Can I have the tour now?" she asks.

His arm snakes around her and he pulls her tight. "Sure thing. It's Lindsey, right?"

She nods.

"You guys want to join us?" he asks, earning a disapproving look from his … *date?*

I take our beers from the waitress and hand one to Murphy. "No, you go ahead. I wanted to show Murphy your amazing view."

"Catch you later, bro," Brady says, pulling Lindsey and her huge smile behind him.

I introduce Murphy to a few of the guys and then on our way to the balcony, we get stopped by a couple girls.

"Caden Kessler, oh, my God, I love you, you are the best catcher."

"Thanks," I say. "I do what I can."

The girl's friend asks, "Can we get a picture with you?"

I look at Murphy, who doesn't seem to be bothered by the intrusion. She holds her hand out for the girl's phone. "I'll be happy to take one."

I smile and wink at her, happy that she's okay with this. I know she'll have to deal with this a lot. She'll have to deal with this and a whole lot more. I'm glad to see it doesn't upset her.

I pose with the girls standing on either side of me. They both stand on their toes and give me a kiss on the cheek when Murphy snaps the picture.

Murphy's mouth puckers ever so slightly. It was so subtle, I almost missed it. But it was definitely there. And I find myself happy that she doesn't want any other woman kissing me. I wiggle out from between the two girls and step back over to Murphy as she hands the phone back to them.

As we walk away, I feel one of them stuff something into my back pocket. I turn around and look at them. "That's not cool," I say.

"I was just giving you my phone number," the brunette says. "I'm Bridgette."

I hand it back to her. "Thanks, Bridgette, but you should probably give it to one of my teammates instead."

I open the door and a rush of cold air engulfs us as I escort Murphy onto the massive wrap-around balcony that boasts one of the best views money can buy.

Murphy goes to the very edge, taking in the lit-up buildings of the skyline. "Wow," she says, looking at the scenic view in complete reverence.

The way she's looking at it makes me want to upgrade my own place so I can see her look like this every time she comes over.

I put my drink down and position myself behind her, wrapping my arms around her to keep her warm. "I'm sorry about what happened inside."

"It's okay. I know stuff like that happens all the time."

"It bothered you when they kissed me."

She shrugs. "It's something I'll have to deal with if we …"

I turn her around so we're face to face. "If?" I say. "There is no *if*, Murph. We're doing this."

She looks up at me, smiling. I'm about to lean down and kiss her when the door opens and someone shouts, "Kessler, get in here!"

I turn around to see Sawyer beckoning us inside. I give Murphy a squeeze and then run a finger across her lower lip. "Come on, let's go say hello to Sawyer. We'll continue this later."

I grab her hand as we gather our drinks and head inside. "Sawyer, you remember Murphy."

Sawyer's eyebrows shoot up when he sees our entwined hands. A huge smile breaks across his face as he kisses her cheek. "How could I forget the home run girl."

Murphy laughs. "Is that what you guys call me?"

"That's what *he* calls you," I say. "I already have enough nicknames for you, Murphy's Law."

"It's nice to see you again, Sawyer," she says. "You're the short stop, aren't you? And you lead the team in stolen bases?"

Sawyer smiles. "Beautiful *and* smart. Looks like you got yourself a winner, Kess. Come on, I need you to settle a debate Spencer and I are having in the kitchen."

"Go ahead, I'll be there in a sec." I turn to Murphy. "Leads the team in stolen bases? I never told you that."

"I may have done a little internet research on the Nighthawks."

I can't help my massive smile. "Admit it, Murphy Brown, you like baseball."

She rolls her eyes at me. "Maybe. Or maybe I just like *you*."

I pull her into my arms. "Good. Because I kind of like you, too." I look down into her eyes, the eyes that are now looking at me the same way she was looking at the skyline. "Actually, I'm not sure like is a strong enough word."

"Kessler!" Sawyer yells from the kitchen.

Murphy can't peel herself out of my arms fast enough. "I have to use the bathroom," she says. "I'll find you in a minute."

I watch her walk away, kicking myself for saying something so stupid.

Chapter Thirty-four

Murphy

I lean against the wall next to the bathroom, waiting my turn. I close my eyes and let my head fall back as my mind replays what he said. *Like isn't a strong enough word.*

He more than likes me? Is that what he meant last week when he said he was falling for me?

But this is our third date. Maybe he *more than likes* everyone on third dates. Maybe that's why he has the rule to begin with.

No, that's not him. That's not us. We're different. I know we are.

But I have to be sure.

I'm wondering what's taking so long in the bathroom when I hear several voices. One girl slips out the bathroom door, but there must be three others still in there, and she left the door cracked. I turn away as one sits down to pee. They are probably too drunk to care that someone walking by could see them. I suppose I could shut the door, but I don't. If they don't care—why should I?

"He is beyond gorgeous," one of them says. "I'd give anything to snag him. Hell, even if I could just have him one time. It would make my entire year."

"So, go for it, Cindy. I mean, it is your birthday and all."

"You're right. God, he would be the best present, wouldn't he? But did you see that tramp he walked in with? I'd have to get past her."

"You are so much prettier than she is, Cin."

"Still, he might not go for it."

I turn and peek through the door to see if they are making any progress. I really do have to pee. I see one girl rustling through her purse. She pulls out a pill bottle, opens it and hands a pill to one of the other girls.

"Here, this will mellow him out. Crush it up and slip it in his drink. Then give him a half hour for it to kick in and we'll distract the tramp so you can get him into a bedroom. It'll be our present to you, right Kylie?"

My mouth hangs open. They want to *drug* someone? Oh, my God. I'm about to go tell Caden what I heard so he can warn all the men who are here. But before I turn away, the girl who is Kylie nods her head then looks speculatively at the others. "I don't know, Caden is a big guy, you might need to give him two."

My heart almost stops when they say his name. Without even thinking, I burst through the door, loudly crashing it into the wall behind it and then I slap the pills and the pill bottle out of their hands, sending them flying across the floor.

"You bitch!" one yells at me.

"Me?" I point to myself. "*I'm* the bitch? You are planning on drugging Caden so he will sleep with you. I'd say *you're* the bitches. Not to mention criminals. You know that's a felony, don't you?"

"What's going on here?" Caden asks, standing in the doorway behind me with Brady and Sawyer behind him.

I motion to the pills scattered across the floor that one of them is on her knees cleaning up. "Caden, they were in here conspiring to drug you."

"What?" I can see fury in his eyes.

Brady and Sawyer look pissed, too.

"That one" —I point to Cindy— "said she wants you for her birthday present and the others were going to help her spike your drink with two pills and then distract me so she could take you to a bedroom."

"You've got to be fucking kidding me?" Sawyer says, eyeing the three guilty-looking girls.

"Oh, relax," says the girl whose name I don't know yet. "We just wanted to liven up the party." She holds her hand out with some pills. "Anyone want one?"

I grab the pills from her and throw them into the toilet.

"What the hell?" she says, leaning down to pick up some others at her feet.

"You were seriously going to give that shit to me without me knowing it?" Caden asks the girls. "Do you think that's funny? I know a girl who had it happen to her. It's anything but funny. What the fuck were you thinking?"

"You're a guy," Kylie says. "It's different."

"How is it different?" Caden asks. "You think because I'm a guy it's okay to fuck me without my consent?"

My skin starts to crawl. "It's called sexual assault in case you were wondering." My angry eyes bounce between Cindy and her friends. "You know … *rape.*"

"*Rape?*" Cindy says, rolling her eyes. "Right. Like little old me could possibly do that."

"Well then," I take a step forward and say to her face, "what do *you* call it when someone is forced to have sex against their will?"

"Whatever," the girl with no name says, then she turns to her friends. "Let's go get a drink."

They scoot their way past Caden and me when Brady takes Cindy's arm. "How about I show you the door instead? You and whoever you came with."

Sawyer escorts the other girls behind them and then Caden puts his hands on my arms. "Are you okay?"

I shake my head because I'm not. "What if I wasn't standing out here? What if I never heard them and they drugged you? Oh my God, Caden."

He pulls me into his arms. "It's okay," he says into my hair as he caresses my back. "I'm fine."

"This time," I say. "But what about next time? What if next time nobody is around to hear?"

He pulls back and looks down at me. "I could say the same thing about you, Murph. You're a beautiful woman. Women get drugged all the time. I personally know one who did. Hell, I know a guy who did, too, although that one didn't turn out so tragically."

"You know two people who've been drugged?" I ask in abhorrence.

He nods. "Sadly, I do. It happens a lot. But they aren't my stories to tell."

"Of course they aren't."

"Are you okay, Murphy?" Brady asks, walking back down the hallway.

"I'm fine. I'm just glad I was standing here when I was."

"We all are," Brady says, crouching down to pick up a stray pill and toss it in the toilet. "Come on. Those bitches are gone and the party is better for it. Let's go grab you guys a drug-free drink."

We both laugh at his joke, but then Caden and I look at each other, knowing what just happened is far from being funny.

We sit around Brady's living room, playing a silly word game where someone holds their phone up to their forehead and the others try to get them to say the word displayed on it.

When it's Brady's turn, he puts the phone to his head and Sawyer says, "Talking about a no-hitter."

Brady shouts out his guesses. "Jinx! Superstition! Not fucking allowed!"

He guessed right—the word was 'jinx.' He finishes his turn and we take a break to replenish our drinks.

"Why can't you talk about a no-hitter?" I ask.

The eyes of every baseball player in the room snap to mine. They all look at me as if I told them the moon is green.

Sawyer throws a bottle cap at Caden. "Kessler … dude, educate your girlfriend."

Caden laughs.

I'm glad he laughed instead of stiffening uncomfortably when Sawyer called me his girlfriend.

"You can't talk about a no-hitter when there is a possibility of having a no-hitter," he explains. "Not even the announcers will say the words. In fact, the players won't even talk to the pitcher between innings once he's getting close to one. A no-hitter is one of the rarest things in baseball and we don't do anything that could jinx it."

"And don't even get me started talking about a perfect game," Brady adds. "That's like the holy-fucking-grail of baseball."

"So you think talking about it will make it not happen?" I ask.

"Yes!" all the players in the room say collectively.

I can't help my giggle.

Caden nuzzles his face close to my ear. "Have I ever told you what that sound does to me?"

Instantly, my body is at complete attention. I'm aware of his hot breath flowing over my shoulder. His firm grip on my waist. His possessive stance at my side.

And I want nothing more than for him to show me.

Chapter Thirty-five

Caden

I can't wait to get her home. My home, her home—I don't care where. I just want to get her alone. I want to kiss her. Put my hands on her. Do whatever she'll let me do for as long as she'll let me do it.

She's gorgeous. And she has an uncanny ability to look elegant even when she's wearing something as casual as jeans and a blouse. Her heels make her even taller than she normally is, and through her fitted jeans, I can see every curve of her butt and thighs. The blue blouse that matches the color of her eyes has the two top buttons undone, exposing just enough cleavage to entice me without insisting she button up and not expose herself.

And her lips. God, those lips. I stare at them whenever she talks. Because I know what they feel like. What they taste like. I know exactly what to do to make them open for my tongue. I know exactly how to kiss her so she'll make those sultry throaty noises.

Shit. I realize I have a rising problem. I look at my phone and see it's almost eleven. Hoping it's not too lame to leave this early, but thinking Brady will understand that I want to be with my girl, I ask Murphy, "Can we get out of here?"

She looks into my eyes, knowing exactly what I'm asking. "My place?" she asks, without any hint of hesitation.

My dick strains against my fly at her words as I grab her hand and shout out thanks to Brady and the quickest of goodbyes to everyone else. Laughter follows us out the door. Murphy covers her face in embarrassment. "You know why they think we're leaving, don't you?"

I put my arm around her and lead her to the elevator. "I don't care what they think, Murph. I only care what *you* think."

"I think I want to take it slow. Until …" She looks up at me with a sad smile.

I nod, knowing precisely what she's thinking. "Until you know you can trust me."

"I'm sorry," she says, looking down at the floor. "I know I should trust you. You've been nothing but a loyal friend and a courteous gentleman, but, well … this is—"

"Our third date. I know." I put a finger under her chin and lift her head until our eyes meet. "I don't want you to worry about what happens after this. You are the exception to the rule, Murphy. I promise you. And I'm not saying that to get in your pants. If you wanted me to wait until our *twenty-third* date, I'd do it. I'd wait that long for you."

She stares at me as if she's trying to figure out how much truth is in my words. Then she does something unexpected. Something incredible. Something she's never done before.

She kisses *me.*

And I let her. I let her take control of the kiss. Of me. Right up until the elevator dings, when I push her in and cage her against the wall. "What are you doing to me, Murphy Brown?"

"Same thing you're doing to me, Kessler."

The twenty-minute cab ride to her apartment seems like an eternity.

She opens the door to a dark apartment and I smile. Good. No roommate. I love Trick and all, but I've shared Murphy enough tonight.

"Do you want a drink?" she asks, putting her purse on the entry table. "I think I have a few beers. Or maybe you'd like a bottle of water?"

"Water is good. I've had enough to drink tonight."

We walk into the kitchen and she grabs two bottles from the fridge. "You don't get drunk much, do you?"

"Habit, I guess," I say, taking a bottle from her and unscrewing the top. "People make poor decisions when they're drunk."

"That's smart," she says, leading us back into the living room. "Someone in your position needs to be careful. Enough bad things can happen even when you're sober."

She looks at me and I know she's still upset about earlier.

"Please don't worry about that."

"I can't help it, Caden. I worry about a lot of things."

"Such as?"

She shrugs. "You getting hit by a ball. You getting mauled by a fan. You getting, um … traded."

"Traded?" I say, incredulously. "Not going to happen, Murphy Brown. Not unless I royally screw up. Which I won't."

I have a hard time not smiling at the fact that she's thinking so far into the future. If I could only convince her I do the same.

"Still. I worry about you getting injured." Her finger comes up to run along her scar.

I lean against the back of her couch and pull her into my arms. "Ball players don't usually get stalked by fans like movie stars do, so go ahead and put that out of your head. And you've seen what I wear behind the plate—my catcher's gear is top of the line. It's going to protect me, Murph. And when I'm at bat, my eyes are laser focused on the ball. I hardly ever take a hit to my body. Catchers rarely do because we're trained to watch the ball all the way across the plate. Taking our eyes off the ball, even for a second, could mean a stolen base, or a run. That helps us when we're at bat."

She leans into me, putting her head on my chest. "I'll always worry."

I chuckle. "Well, I'll always worry, too. About you, Murph. It goes both ways."

A loud noise comes from the other room. I step around her to investigate. I open the door to one of the bedrooms and look around. It happens again and I realize it came from the window. I step up to it and look outside to see some teenagers playing on the fire escape. I check to make sure the lock on the window is secure.

I realize I don't even know whose room I'm in. I never got past the main living area the other times I've been here. I turn around and smile when I see what's on the dresser. I walk over and appraise the six Nighthawks hats sitting in a row. I pick one up and turn it over to see writing on the inside. It's a date.

I look up to see Murphy watching me from her doorway. And she's blushing. "You weren't supposed to see that." She walks over and takes the hat from me, putting it back down where it was.

I pick up another and she tries to take it from me. I hold it above her head where she has no chance to get it. I look inside this one. Another date. She tries to keep me from looking inside all the others. We both laugh when she chases me around the room.

She finally gives up and falls onto her bed, with her arms covering her face. "I'm a silly sentimental girl, Caden. What can I say?"

"Where's the sharpie?" I ask, looking around her room.

"Why?" She eyes me skeptically.

"Just give me the sharpie, Murph."

She rolls her eyes and opens the drawer of her nightstand. Then she tosses me the black marker. I take my hat off and remove the cap of the sharpie with my mouth before I write today's date inside my hat. Then I put all the hats back on her dresser, in chronological order with the new one at the end.

She still looks embarrassed which I find incredibly sexy. "I get it," I tell her. "Some chicks save receipts and movie tickets. You save hats." I crawl on top of her on the bed. "But you'd better get a bigger apartment. Because you're going to have a shitload of hats."

Her face lights up with a smile right before I lean down to kiss her.

This kiss is better than any of the others. It's better because I can feel her entire body underneath me. I can feel her chest rise and fall with each heavy breath she takes. I can feel her writhe and squirm under my weight. I can feel her arch her back and press herself to me in all the right places.

We make out like teenagers in a basement. We kiss until our lips become raw. And when I'm about to die if I don't touch her, I ask if I can.

"Murphy … God, I want you so much. I know we're waiting. And that's okay. I'll wait as long as you want. But, sweetheart, can I see you? Can I touch you?"

She stares up at me, her hair tousled and sexy. She nods. "Only if I can do the same to you."

Holy shit. If my dick weren't already standing at full mast, that would have done it. I get off her and sit up, grabbing my shirt and pulling it over my head. I'm turned away slightly, so she is getting her first view of my back.

She reaches up to touch my #27 tattoo on my right shoulder blade. "This is why you reach around and grab your shoulder before you go to bat, isn't it?"

I crane my neck around and study her. "You noticed that?" It's the one thing I've always done when I go up to bat. But no other woman has ever caught on. Maybe they weren't paying enough attention.

"At first, I thought you had a sore shoulder or something. But then the more I saw you do it, the more I knew it had to be some kind of ritual."

"I got it when I was eighteen."

She traces the number with her fingertip, sending shivers down my spine. "And you'll never change it, not even though you are number eight now. Because being number twenty-seven got you where you are today."

Jesus. This woman.

I turn around and pin her to the bed. "Do you have any tattoos I should know about?"

"I guess you'll have to look to find out."

I eye her top and then her jeans. Then I look into her eyes again. She nods. "It's okay. Go ahead."

I straddle her as I unbutton her blouse, being careful to keep my weight on the bed. The opening of each button reveals more flesh I can't wait to explore. When I'm finished with the last one, I move the blouse aside and admire her beautiful chest.

Her black lacy bra is almost transparent and I can see her stiff nipples and the outline of her areola. My hands come up her body, brushing against the sides of her ribs before I cup her breasts. She arches her back, pushing her chest further into my hands as she moans under my touch.

I run my hand lower across her stomach and play with the button on her jeans. "I won't …" I say, my eyes pleading with her. "I just want to see you."

"It's fine," she says, with a shaky breath. She nods to my pants. "Yours too."

I release her button and move my hands to mine, figuring I should go first. But she brushes my hand away, undoing my pants herself. She looks up at me as she lowers them as far as they will go without me getting up.

I shift off her and remove them the rest of the way. My erection is straining against my boxer briefs and Murphy's eyes widen as she takes me in. Her jaw goes slack and she stares unabashedly. It's fucking erotic. It makes me want to stand here all day just so she can look at me.

But I want to see her more than I want her to stare at me, so I kneel next to her and remove her shoes before I peel the jeans off her body to reveal her matching lace panties.

I want so badly to know if this is what she normally wears or if she wore them in anticipation of me seeing them. And in this moment, I'm not sure which would please me more.

"My God, Murphy. You're beautiful. I'm never calling you *'old man'* again."

I can't stop looking at each soft curve, each tantalizing inch of her creamy skin. She's pure perfection.

"You're beautiful, too," she says.

I chuckle. "Nobody has ever called me that."

"Then they weren't looking hard enough," she says, smiling.

I climb over her and lean down to capture her smile with my mouth. Our bodies mash together, flesh on flesh, separated only by thin scraps of fabric. She moans again when I press my erection into her. I know she can feel how much I want her. Her rising hips reveal how much she wants me.

My lips blaze a trail down her neck, and I lick and suck and kiss my way to her breasts. I pull one of the cups of her bra down and my breath catches at the beauty of her. I taste her creamy white skin and then take her stiff peak into my mouth, sucking on it while she undulates and moans beneath me.

The friction between our lower halves is almost unbearable. I grind into her and she meets me with every thrust. We mimic the act that we've only consummated in my dreams.

I return my lips to hers and kiss her with such fierceness, such emotion, that I almost have to stop. Because this is more intense than anything I've ever felt. I want to make love to her. Of course I do. But if this right here is all she ever gave me, in some strange way, it feels like it would be enough.

"Caden …"

Her head whips around on the bed beneath her. I realize what this friction is doing to her and I reach out and grab one of her breasts, pinching and tugging on a nipple to help push her over the edge.

"Oh, God!" she shouts as I make sure to keep rubbing myself on the exact same spot over and over while I watch her face in complete awe as she experiences wave after wave of pleasure.

Her head falls back against the bed, her body languid and sated as she catches her breath. Me—I'm still reeling over witnessing one of the world's greatest wonders.

She finally looks up at me in surprise. In embarrassment. “Sorry,” she says.

“Sorry?” I say. “That was one of the best moments of my life, Murphy Brown. I might just take back my hat, because this sure as hell is a day I never want to forget.”

She laughs. “Not a chance, Kessler. The hat is mine.”

I laugh with her. But what I really want to do is tell her how I feel. Because the woman lying under me owns more than just my hat. She owns every goddamn piece of me.

But I don’t tell her. Because this is our third date. And I have to be sure.

I have to be sure that when I wake up tomorrow, she’s still the owner of my heart, not just a short-term renter.

Chapter Thirty-six

Murphy

I finish giving Mom the tour of the gym and we head back to the office to get her suitcase. She flew in this afternoon and is staying for Thanksgiving. I tried my best to ignore Corey on the treadmill, but my mom saw him staring and mentioned what a nice young man he looked like and asked if I was dating anyone.

I froze. I didn't know what to say. I'm not sure if I have a boyfriend or not. It's been two days since I've seen Caden, not that it's unusual for us to go that long, but other than a few casual texts he's sent me, it's been radio silence.

Is he pulling away? Letting me down easy?

It's taken every ounce of my willpower not to text him and ask him about it. It's not like I expected a proposal or anything the morning after our third date, but I expected … *something.* A text maybe about how much fun he had. An invitation to go on a fourth date perhaps.

I guess I'm just confused. And too stubborn to call him.

When we reach the office, Jayden hands my mother a drink voucher. "Mrs. Cavenaugh, would you mind terribly if I stole your daughter for fifteen minutes? You are free to wait in the gym's café and have a drink on me."

"Take as much time as you need," my mom says, grabbing her small suitcase and leaving the office.

Jayden closes the door behind her and motions for me to take a seat.

"What's up?" I ask her.

"Murphy, you have really done well for yourself here in such a short time. You fit in with everyone. You are great with the members. I've talked with the owners and we all agree you should get a promotion."

I want to jump out of the chair and hug her. But that wouldn't be very professional of me. I knew this might be coming. A few weeks ago, the front desk supervisor left for another job. When they didn't fill the position right away, I was hopeful that maybe they would offer it to me. They have, after all, been giving me more responsibilities.

Instead of hugging her, I simply smile and keep my cool. "Jayden, thank you so much. I promise I won't let you down. I'll be the best front desk supervisor you've ever had."

"Front desk supervisor? No. We're giving that job to Gregory. We want you to be our new membership coordinator."

"What?" I look at her sideways. "What about Stephanie?"

"Stephanie told us a few days ago that she wasn't returning from maternity leave. At the time, we were about to offer you the supervisor position. But you've done so well learning all the membership duties it made our decision easy."

"But I don't even have a bachelor's degree," I say.

"Sometimes on-the-job training is even better than formal education. Plus, you took some business courses at that community college you went to." She laughs. "Are you trying to talk me out of this?"

"No. Oh, my gosh, Jayden, I absolutely want the job. Thank you for having confidence in me."

"Don't you want to know what it pays before you accept?"

I shake my head. "I don't care what it pays."

She chuckles, pushing a folder across the desk at me. I open it to see the compensation package. My chin all but falls into my lap. The salary for the position comes out to almost double what I make per hour now. And it includes benefits such as medical, dental, and life insurance. All of that and I get three weeks paid vacation.

"You must be kidding." I look back at the salary, barely able to contain my excitement.

She hands me a pen. "Sign it and you'll get your first paid holiday on Thursday."

My hand shakes as I sign the employment contract. "Thank you."

"You earned it, Murphy. Now don't keep your mom waiting. Go. Celebrate."

I leave the office, ecstatic about this amazing opportunity. I leave knowing that even if Caden and I don't work out, I have this. Because I won't be defined by any man. And I refuse to be wrecked if he never calls. If I never get to kiss him or touch him. If I never get to be loved by him.

I turn the corner and run smack into Caden. I look up at him and eat my own words. Because I know I would be wrecked. This man—he wormed his way into my life, into my dreams, into my very soul. He has changed me in the short time I've known him.

He has given me the opportunity for a new career. And I know with one-hundred-percent certainty I will never find another man like him.

He cages me against the wall in the hallway. He leans down, smells my hair and then whispers in my ear, "Do you have any idea how much I've missed you?"

My heart skips a thousand beats at his declaration. He still wants this. Still wants me. And I wonder how this day could get any better.

"No," I say. "I don't. Because I haven't heard from you much. So I wasn't sure until just now."

He pulls away, looking guilty. "God, Murph. I'm sorry. I should have called you. Of course I've missed you. But my dad and Scott showed up yesterday morning and we've been doing all kinds of things. I love showing Scott around the city. I spent the whole day with him today while my dad was meeting with someone from the city planning department. Did you know they might move here? Could you imagine if my brother lived here in the city? Anyway, I just dropped Scott off at Lexi's and I'm meeting my dad here to show him the gym."

I hear him ramble on and realize just how excited he is about spending time with his brother. His dad even. There is no way I can be mad at him for not contacting me when something so monumental is happening for him. He had the best reason for not calling me. His family. I can't be anything but happy for him.

He leans in to kiss me. "And now I get to introduce him to my girlfriend."

My eyes snap to his. "Are you sure you're ready for that?" I ask, cautiously.

"I don't know. Do you trust me?"

"Absolutely," I say without a hint of doubt in my answer. I think I've trusted him since that very first day in the hospital. My heart knew it all along. I guess my head just needed more reassurance.

"Then I'm sure," he says, taking my hand in his and bringing it up to his lips to kiss it.

I smile at him. He smiles at me. Then he reaches up and touches his head. "Shit, I wish I were wearing a hat. This moment definitely deserves a hat."

"What does, your being off the market? Maybe they'll make today a national holiday."

He laughs with me and then leans close. "November 19th," he says. "It will always be the day you officially became my girlfriend. I'm bringing you a hat later, Sweet Caroline. No arguing."

"Okay, but just so you know, my mother came to town this afternoon and she'll be staying with me for a few days."

"Damn it, I forgot about that," he says. Then he looks guilty. "I mean, I'm glad your mom is here, and I'd love to meet her, but now it looks like several more days of cold showers for me."

I giggle. "It's only been two days, Caden. I think you'll survive."

He shakes his head. "I've been taking cold showers longer than two days, Murph." He eyes me seductively. "A hell of a lot longer."

I want nothing more than to crawl into his arms and lose myself in him. But my mom is waiting. I haven't seen her for almost eight months and we have a lot of catching up to do.

I grab his hand. Because I can. Because I'm his girlfriend now and that is what girlfriends do. "Come on, my mom has been waiting for me forever in the café. Now I can tell you both my good news."

"She's here? And what news could possibly be better than you and I becoming an official couple?" he jokes.

We walk to the entrance of the café. I point to the corner booth. "There she is. And she's talking to some strange man. I'll bet she's trying to sell him a river cruise in Paris or something. I swear that woman never stops working."

Caden turns to look at me. "That's not some strange man, Murph. That's my father."

"Seriously?" I cover my laughter so they don't hear us.

I watch them interacting for a beat and then I pull Caden backwards around the other side of the wall. "Oh, my God, Caden. My mom is flirting with your dad."

He cranes his neck around the wall and stares. "How can you tell?"

"Didn't you see the way she touched his arm when she laughed? She's definitely flirting. I've never seen her flirt with a man, Caden. Not since my dad died."

He looks at them again. "He's smiling, Murph. I know I've only just begun to know him, but I haven't seen him smile like that. He's smiling at her the same way I smile at you."

I look at my watch. "I was only gone for twenty minutes."

He shrugs a provocative shoulder. "I guess when you know, you know." His eyes burn into mine.

How can I argue with that?

"So, do we go over there or what?" I ask.

He sighs and rubs a hand down my arm. "Murphy, what would happen if someone wanted to date your mother? I know how close you were with your dad."

I study him as his words sink in. I'd never even considered it because she's never shown any interest in dating after my dad died. "Well, I don't know. I guess it would be okay. I mean it has been eleven years. I can't expect her to never be with another man." I peek around the corner. "But what do we know about him? Is he a good man, Caden? You *hated* him."

He laughs. "Wasn't it you who told me that everyone deserves a second chance? From what Ethan was able to dig up, he's been nothing but a perfect citizen since his release from prison twenty years ago. And we've been talking a lot. I think he's … I think he's a nice guy, Murph."

"Okay. So introduce me."

"I'm glad to hear you say that." He grabs my hand and pulls me along. "Because Lexi told me earlier that you and your mom are invited for Thanksgiving dinner, so things are about to become very interesting."

Chapter Thirty-seven

Caden

Watching my dad interact with Murphy's mom is surreal. They are both in their fifties but they're acting like a couple of love-sick teenagers. Nobody seems to care, however, and I think Lexi is encouraging it, because every time Irene asks to help with the cooking, Lexi claims she's got it all under control.

Murphy takes a break from helping Lexi and sits on the armrest of my chair. She leans over and whispers in my ear. "Do you know that yesterday, she asked me to ask you if your dad said anything about her?"

I laugh and smile, looking over at them. "It makes sense, you know? They both lost someone."

"Yeah, but why now?" Murphy asks. "My dad has been gone for eleven years, Caden."

"I don't know, babe. God works in mysterious ways."

Her face breaks into a slow grin at my use of the endearment. I pull her down onto my lap and kiss her forehead.

"You two are adorable, you know that, don't you?" Mallory says.

"We all knew you'd end up together," Charlie adds.

"I called it first!" Lexi shouts from the kitchen.

I look around at all of them, shaking my head. I turn to Sawyer. "See what happens when you hang out with a bunch of chicks?"

Lexi told me to invite anyone on the team who didn't have a place to go. Most of the guys got invites of their own. All but Brady and Sawyer. And Brady doesn't do 'family shit.'

"Yeah, well, I hope it's not contagious," Sawyer says. "I'm perfectly fine the way I am."

Murphy studies him for a minute. "Doesn't it get old, Sawyer, having a new girl on your arm every night? And I mean that in the nicest possible way."

He laughs. "Sure you do. But, that's the point. It never gets old. No one gets bored. Nobody ever has expectations." He looks out the window. "Nobody ever gets hurt."

Damn. That is the most introspective thing I've ever heard come out of his mouth. I've had my suspicions over the years. The man's been hurt. It makes perfect sense now, why he won't ever take a girl out more than once. I knew his reasons weren't the same as mine. Unlike me, he never gives a rat's ass if girls are using him for what he is. Maybe he likes it that way. It protects him.

Man, if I ever can't play ball. I should be a fucking psychiatrist. I'm good at this. I look at Murphy. Maybe *she's* the reason I'm so good at reading people. Ever since I met her, I've felt more in tune with my emotions.

I practically dump her off my lap in search of my balls. "Who wants to do a shot of Wild Turkey?"

"I'm down," Sawyer says.

"Pour me one!" Kyle calls from down the hallway where he's changing Beth.

My dad takes a break from courting Irene and comes over to join us.

"Want one?" I ask, holding a shot out to him.

He holds up his hand, refusing it. "Never touch the stuff. Not for more than twenty years."

I cock my head and stare, remembering something he told me the day we met in the bar. "You mean to tell me you hadn't been in a bar in that long?"

He nods. "That's what I'm saying. I'm a recovering addict, son. I'm not about to take any chances."

I down the shot myself, realizing he called me son and I didn't tell him not to. I look at him and see that he noticed the same.

He pats me on the back and I think we share a moment.

Scott comes up beside me. "I'll try it," he jokes.

We all laugh. "Come back in about nine years, kid," I say, ruffling his hair.

"If we move here, are we going to live with you, Caden?" Scott asks.

"Well … uh …"

"No, son, we aren't going to live with your brother. He's a grown man with his own apartment. We'll find a nice place of our own, one with good schools around."

"Mallory can help you with that," I say, loudly enough for her to hear. "She used to be a teacher here in the city. Now she travels a lot with Chad when he films on location, tutoring kids of the cast and crew."

"I'll get you a list of the best schools," she says.

"I'd appreciate that," my dad tells her. "Nothing's set in stone yet, but I'm optimistic."

Scott turns to Murphy. "Are you going to travel with Caden like Mallory travels with Chad?"

My little brother is not exactly indirect. If I've learned anything about him in the last few weeks it's that he speaks his mind. And he's a very curious twelve-year-old.

"Um, no, Scott. I have a job." She looks over at me with sad eyes. I'm wondering if this is the first time she's thought about it. We haven't talked about what happens next. About what happens when I leave for spring training in February. About what happens when my life isn't my own for well over half of every year.

"A darn good one, too," her mom says. "Must pay well, because even before she got her promotion, she was able to pay off every single one of her medical bills." She turns to Murphy with prideful eyes. "I'm proud of you."

"What?" Murphy questions her mom with raised brows. "But I never even got a bill."

"They came to me," her mom says. "But they were marked as paid."

Murphy's unamused eyes snap to mine.

Shit. This is not exactly the right time to get into this.

She walks up to me and puts an angry finger on my chest. "You paid them, didn't you?" When I don't say anything, she shakes her head in irritation. "Caden, I told you not to do that. You did enough."

"It was *my* fault, Murphy. It's only right that I should pay for it."

"It doesn't matter. I asked you not to."

I put my hands on her shoulders in an attempt to calm her down. "By the time you told me that, I had already paid. I guess I didn't know what to say or how to tell you."

She shrugs my hands off. "And you thought, what, that I'd be okay with it once you were sleeping with me?"

I glance over at Scott, who is trying not to laugh. "No. Of course not. I wasn't even thinking about you that way back then."

"Great. That makes things so much better," she says, turning to walk away.

I follow her.

"Please don't," she begs. "I just need a minute."

She walks into the kitchen, leaving me a confused, guilty, stupid son-of-a-bitch.

Chapter Thirty-eight

Murphy

"Ugh! Can you believe that?" I say, fuming my way over to the far end of the kitchen.

"Believe what?" Lexi asks, pushing the turkey back into the oven after basting it.

"I know he's your brother and all, but he can be infuriating. He paid all my medical bills, Lexi. After I told him not to."

Lexi laughs. "The way I heard it, he paid them *before* you told him not to."

"You *were* listening," I say.

She rinses off her hands and walks over to the kitchen table, taking a seat and patting the one next to her. "Yes, my brother can be infuriating. Most men can be from time to time. And yes, he paid your medical bills. But, Murphy, he was the cause of your injury and paying those bills was much less of a burden for him than it would have been for you."

I plop down in the chair beside hers. "I can't stand rich people who throw around their money."

She eyes me as if I'm being a petulant child. "He throws around his money, huh? How has he ever done that? Tell me how my rich brother flaunts his money, Murphy."

I shrug thinking about how the man lives modestly even though he's making millions. I finally think of something. "The park. He rented a ball field in the park."

She smiles. "Yeah, he told me about that. But try again, because he said he only had to pay a few bucks for a permit."

"What about the VIP tickets. And the phone—he bought me a new phone."

"He's a ball player. You don't think he has to pay for those tickets, do you? And a phone. Really? You're going to have to do better than that."

"So, you think he's right and I'm wrong?"

Lexi puts her hand on mine. "It's not about being right or wrong, Murphy. It's about finding a balance. It's about not letting the little things turn into big things. Because big things can ruin you."

"You say that as if you have experience with it."

She nods. "You've no idea just how alike we are, do you?"

"What do you mean?"

Kyle comes into the kitchen to check on us. He leans down and gives his wife a kiss, looking at me with empathetic eyes. "Everything okay in here?"

"Everything is fine. Just give us another minute," Lexi says.

When he leaves, her eyes follow him. I can tell how much she loves him just by the way she looks at him.

"He did the same thing, you know," she says, looking back at me. "Kyle paid my hospital bills when I had Ellie."

I look at her, confused. "That's different. He's Ellie's dad."

"Not biologically," she says. "Kyle didn't even know me when I showed up pregnant at his hospital."

"Really?"

Lexi and I have gotten close and we know a lot of things about each other, but this comes as a huge surprise.

"Really," she says. "And when I found out he paid my bills, I freaked. It almost ruined us. It *did* ruin us for a while."

"I'm so sorry," I say.

"It's fine. *We're* fine. I just don't want the same thing to happen to you and Caden. Your relationship is fragile and new. He told me yesterday that you're officially a couple. I think that's wonderful, Murphy. You're the one for him. I know it."

"How do you know it, Lexi?"

She smiles. "Are you kidding? You should see the way my brother looks at you. It's as if you are the Mona Lisa. The game-winning home run ball. The pot of gold at the end of the rainbow."

I roll my eyes. "Caden does not need any more pots of gold."

"Give me a break," she says jokingly. "I was on a roll."

Sawyer comes into the kitchen, looking around. His eyes dart awkwardly over to me. "Uh, can I grab a beer?"

I know full well there is a beer fridge under the bar in the living room. I snort petulantly. "Did Caden send you in here to check on me?"

"No." He looks guilty as sin. "Okay, yes. Hell, I don't know how to do this shit. Your boyfriend is on the edge out there, Murphy. Throw the guy a bone."

My mother walks in and I shake my head. "More reinforcements?" I ask.

"We're all worried about you, honey."

"And we're hungry," Sawyer adds, making us all laugh.

"Fine," I say, getting up from the table. "Let's get things moving then."

My mother puts a hand on my arm, stopping me from helping. "I think Lexi and I can handle this. You have something more important to do."

I look at Sawyer. "Is he still in the living room?"

"He's on the balcony."

I nod, leaving the kitchen and grabbing a throw blanket off the couch on my way to find him.

I wrap myself up and open the sliding door, frozen air assaulting me as I walk through to the outside.

Caden turns around and sees me, worry etching lines across his forehead. "Murphy, I'm sor—"

I hold up my hand to stop him. "There can't be any more secrets," I say. "I know you had good intentions, Caden, but we have to be able to talk about everything or this isn't going to work. First you withheld the fact that Tony was going to break up with me, and now this."

"I didn't know how to tell you," he says guiltily. "It won't happen again."

I pin him with my stare. "Are you sure, Caden? Because you said that once before. I need to be able to trust you."

"You can," he says, his eyes imploring me to believe him. "I screwed up, Murph. And believe me, I won't do it again. More than anyone, I know about three strikes and you're out. I'm not about to strike out with you. I promise."

"Okay." I walk over to him. "You will always have more money than me. That is something I'll have to deal with. I know you can pay for things that I can't. But in the future, we need to agree on what those things are."

He sighs in relief at my mention of the future. "What if I want to get you a birthday present?" he asks with a smirk.

"That's different. Presents are fine. Well, unless you buy me a car or something." I look at his face that is breaking into a smile. "Do *not* get me a car, Caden."

"But anything up to a car is fine?"

"You can be infuriating, you know that?" I swat his chest, causing the blanket to fall off my shoulders.

He picks up the blanket and walks around behind me, pulling my back to his chest as he wraps us both up. "No more secrets," he whispers in my ear.

We stand like this, pressed together and keeping each other warm. And as I look over the city, I realize this is our first holiday together. I turn around and thread my arms around his waist. "When I was little, every Thanksgiving my dad would make us go around the table and say what we were thankful for. I would always say something stupid like how I was thankful for my bike or my new dress. It wasn't until after he died and we stopped doing it that I realized the only thing he ever said he was thankful for was me."

Caden leans down and kisses the top of my head. "It appears your father and I have a lot in common."

"I wish you could have met him," I say, looking up into his eyes.

"Me too. You know that nobody can ever replace him, don't you?"

I follow his eyes as they look into the living room where his father is helping my mother bring a platter of food out to the dining room table. "It's crazy, don't you think? Your dad and my mom?"

"If by crazy you mean perfect, then yes, Murphy Brown, it's crazy."

I have a horrible thought and pull back from Caden. “Oh, my gosh. What if they get married? You’ll be my step-brother. We can’t let that happen. It’s gross.”

Caden laughs, winking at me as he pulls me back to his chest. “We’ll just have to beat them to it, then.”

Chapter Thirty-nine

Caden

After my workout, on my way back to the locker room, I see a familiar face walking towards the front desk of the gym.

I hurry my steps and head him off before he gets there. "Anything I can help you with, Fields?"

Tony steps back and looks around me to the desk. "I was looking for Murphy. She not working here anymore?"

"What's it to you?"

He laughs, handing me a tabloid. "Of course she doesn't. Why work at all if she has you to take care of her?"

I look at the magazine. Plastered on the front cover is a photo of Murphy and me at the club last week. I was afraid this would happen. But since she's wearing a baseball cap, you'd have to know Murphy to know it's her in the picture. You'd have to know her like Tony knows her.

My blood starts to boil. This asshole has been with her. He's had more of her than *I've* had. And it more than pisses me off.

I throw the article back at him. "Not that it's any of your business, but she got another job." I lean close to him so I tower over his smaller stature. "But make no mistake, that doesn't mean I'm not taking care of her."

"What's going on here?" Murphy says, coming from the back office.

Shit. I was hoping that wouldn't happen.

"No longer works here, huh?" Tony gives me a death stare.

"I didn't say she no longer works here. I said she got another job." I put my arm around Murphy and pull her close. "She's the membership coordinator now."

He laughs snidely. "Bet it doesn't pay as much as modeling."

"It pays more than enough," Murphy says. "Now what do you want, Tony?"

"Good, I'm glad you're rolling in money, because Kirsten needs you to cover rent until they can find another roommate."

"What? That's ridiculous. I saw her post a picture on Facebook about her new roomie."

"You saw wrong," he says. "They haven't found anyone yet."

Murphy studies Tony. "He's lying," she says to me.

"Am not."

"Tony, we were together for four months. You don't think I learned a thing or two about you? Like how you chew on the inside of your cheek when you lie?"

"Whatever," Tony says. "I'm not lying, Murphy. Call Kirsten. Find out for yourself."

I laugh. "Oh, like she would tell me the truth—the girl who was screwing my boyfriend behind my back."

"It's not like you and Richie Rich here can't afford it," he says.

I turn to Murphy. "What kind of agreement did you have? Was it in writing?"

"There wasn't a formal agreement. I think the rental is in Kirsten's name. She let the rest of us pay on a month-to-month basis. She was always telling us, or me anyway, how replaceable I was."

"Well, there you go," I tell him. "She paid through the end of last month. She isn't obligated beyond that."

"Really, Murphy? You going to hang her out to dry? Make it so she can't pay rent? She'll be evicted and then all four of them will be out on their asses. I thought you were better than that."

"How much is rent?" I ask him.

Murphy puts a hand on my arm. "Don't, Caden."

"It's not that big a deal," I tell her.

"But he's playing you."

"I'm not playing anyone," Tony says. "At least not any more than the wanna-be model is playing *you*."

I look at Murphy to see if his words hurt her. They didn't. I'm glad to know he doesn't have that power over her anymore.

"I tell you what," I say to him. "You get Kirsten and her other three roommates to come in here and tell Murphy they haven't found someone to fill her bed and that they can't afford to pay the rent. If they do that, I'll cover one month myself."

"Caden," Murphy scolds me.

"It's okay, Murph. It won't happen. You said yourself Jamie was nice enough. I highly doubt this scam-artist can get four women to come beg for money."

Tony shakes his head. "There's no way they can all come in together, they have different schedules."

"I didn't say they had to come together, Fields. They can come in anytime, each one by themselves. If they all verify what you claim to be true, I'll pay Murphy's portion of the rent." I hold up a finger. "For one month. Got it?"

His jaw twitches as he eyes Murphy with disdain. Then he throws the magazine at her feet and turns to walk out of the gym.

"That's what I thought," I say to his back before the door closes. I turn to Murphy. "I want you to watch out for that guy. Tell me if he starts bothering you. He's out for an easy buck and right now, you seem to be his target. If he tries to hurt you …"

"He's harmless," she tells me. "Once, we almost got mugged on the subway and he hid behind me. Some other guy stepped up and ran the attacker off."

"What?" I shake my head in disbelief.

She rolls her eyes. "Yeah, in hindsight I should have dumped him on the spot."

I look at the door the asshole just walked through, wondering how he can even call himself a man.

Murphy picks up the tabloid and studies the photo. She hands it to me. "Why did they have to take one of me laughing? I look like I have a double chin. Now everyone will think you have a fat girlfriend."

I expected her to freak out. Or at least react like she did when she found out our picture was on ESPN. But she doesn't. In fact, she's smiling. "You're *joking* about it?" I ask.

"It's a tabloid, Caden. Nobody takes those seriously."

"So, you're not upset?"

"No. I'm not. I'm going to have to get used to people taking my picture when we're together. No point in fighting it. It is what it is. If we can't laugh about it, it will eat away at us."

"Okay then. If it's going to happen, why not make it happen on *our* terms?"

"What do you mean?" she asks.

"Tomorrow night. Let's put on something fancy and go out to a nice place. Announce our relationship to the world when we're dressed to the nines."

She starts to smile before catching herself. "Are you sure you want to do that, Caden?"

"Sweetheart, I'm about to take you on our fourth date. You might as well tag me and brand your name on my ass." I pull her close to my side. "I'm sure."

She giggles and my dick twitches.

"Then it looks like I have some shopping to do," she says, laughing. "But first, I need to get back to work. And you need a shower."

"I'll pick you up at seven," I tell her. "And in case you were wondering, my favorite color is blue. Keep that in mind when you're trying on dresses."

"Are we talking light blue? Dark blue? Carolina blue?" she asks. "The possibilities are endless. You need to be more specific."

"Just look in the mirror, Murphy Brown, and you'll have your answer."

Her face pinks up before I smile and walk away.

Damn. I can't wait for it to be tomorrow at seven.

Chapter Forty

Murphy

I look out at the view again. I can't keep my eyes off it. I've never been in a restaurant at the top of a tall building before. It's incredible looking down on the city I love. It's like I stepped right into an episode of *Sex and the City*.

"I'm glad you're enjoying the view," Caden says, looking all handsome in his suit. I don't miss the fact that he wore a tie that's the exact shade of my eyes—and the dress I'm wearing. We haven't failed to garner looks from everyone here. Even if he wasn't recognized for who he is, he'd be noticed for how he looks.

I feel guilty for staring at the view and not him. "I'm sorry. I should be looking at my hot date, not out the window."

He smiles. "Look all you want. That way you won't notice the fact that I'm staring at *my* hot date and all her amazing curves."

I look down at my cleavage, once again questioning my decision to go more low-cut than I normally would. But Lexi insisted. She helped me pick out the dress. I've been nothing but self-conscious tonight with all the photos that have been taken of us. I would venture a guess, however, that that's precisely why she wanted me to wear this exact one.

"Have I told you how stunning you look, Sweet Caroline?"

"Only about ten times."

"I just want to make sure you know it," he says.

"Thank you. You clean up pretty well yourself."

"We look good together," he says. "In fact …" He pulls out his phone and leans over as he takes a selfie. "Why should everyone else get all the good pictures?"

He shows me the picture on his phone.

"Will you send it to me?" I ask.

He taps around on his phone for a second. "Done," he says, putting his phone away and wrapping his arm around the back of my chair. He rubs his thumb on my shoulder. "Things may change tomorrow, Murph. As soon as it gets out who you are, your life will change. Are you ready for that?"

"I spent the better part of this year trying to get my face on the cover of magazines," I say, jokingly. "This may not be how I planned it, but then again, life doesn't always go as planned." I twist Kelly's ring around my thumb.

Caden watches the rhythmic motion. "Did your dad give you that ring?"

I shake my head. "No. It was Kelly's. And she didn't so much give it to me as I stole it."

He furrows his brow. "You stole a ring from your best friend?"

"I did. Kelly knew I loved the ring. She got it when she went on a mission trip to India several years ago. She always teased me that she would leave me the ring in her will. And then, well … after we got to the hospital and they brought me in to say goodbye …"

He takes my hand in his. "She wanted you to have it, Murphy. It was the right thing to do."

I nod. "It makes me feel close to her."

"Excuse me," a woman says, looking embarrassed to be bothering us. "I don't want to intrude, but my grandson is a big fan. He's not here because he's in the hospital, but I was wondering, when you are done with your dinner, if I could take a picture of you with his grandfather."

The woman motions across the restaurant to an older gentleman who looks like he wants the floor to swallow him up. He waves awkwardly when we all look over.

"Can I ask why your grandson is in the hospital, ma'am?" Caden asks.

"He's got cancer. Neuroblastoma." She shows us a picture of a bald little boy who can't be more than ten years old.

"Oh, Caden," I whisper, studying the picture.

"What's the boy's name?" he asks. "Is he here in the city?"

"Jonathan, and yes, his parents live here, thank God. I couldn't imagine not being able to support them through this."

"Is Jonathan allowed to have visitors?"

"Yes, as long as he hasn't just had chemo," she says.

Caden grabs a napkin and writes down a number, handing it to the woman. "This is Melanie's number, she's my assistant. Please call her tomorrow and work out with her when I can go see him. I'll bring him a signed ball and a few other things if that's okay."

The woman covers her mouth in a sob. "You would do that?"

"I'd be happy to."

She reaches out and touches Caden's hand. "Bless you, Mr. Kessler. You have no idea what this means to me."

"I'll see you in a few days, then, Mrs. …"

"Murphy. Donna Murphy. Thank you again. I hope you have a wonderful dinner with your beautiful companion."

The lady walks away and Caden turns to stare at me. He doesn't have to say it. All the coincidences. Are they just coincidences? Or is it fate?

The waiter brings our dessert, but I can barely get a bite or two down after the spread we've eaten. "I'm stuffed," I say. "If I eat any more, my dress will split in two."

Caden laughs, pushing the dessert plate to the other side of the table. "While I wouldn't mind your dress coming off, I'd rather it be me who removes it."

I blush under his heated perusal. The sexual tension between us has been off the charts. We've been a couple for almost a week, yet we've not been able to be alone together because my mother has been around. And I've been able to think of nothing else but what will happen when we finally are.

He squeezes my hand. "I love your mom and all, but I have to say I'm glad she's not crashing at your place anymore."

"My mom is better in small doses," I say. "Especially now that she's got it bad for your father. God, Caden, I never heard the end of it."

"I'm pretty sure they had lunch together yesterday," he says.

"And today," I tell him. "Your dad drove her to the airport."

He looks surprised. "I thought he and Scott left early this morning."

"He changed their flight, Caden. Postponed it to coincide with *her* departure time."

He laughs, shaking his head.

"What?" I ask. "This is seriously twisted, don't you think?"

"You want your mom to be happy, don't you?"

"Absolutely. She deserves to be happy after all these years."

He caresses my knuckles. "Are you happy, Murphy?"

I glance outside at the view. Then I look at him, remembering the conversation we had under the stars. I trace the angles of his face with my eyes. I think about everything that has happened to me since moving to New York. "Happy isn't a strong enough word."

A slow smile turns up the corners of his mouth. Then he bites his lip and groans. "I need to get you home. Right now."

I smile back at him and lean close to his ear. "Everything *under* the dress is blue, too. Well, what there is of them."

"Shit, Murph. Now I won't be able to stand up."

He motions for the check as I take the last few sips of my wine. Then while he pays the bill, I pour what's left of the bottle into my glass and drink that, too. Because I think I'm about to make love with New York's hottest sports star.

And suddenly I'm scared to death.

Chapter Forty-one

Caden

I can't get her clothes off fast enough. But this dress—it has about a thousand buttons down the back. "You're really making me work for this, aren't you?"

She laughs. "Blame yourself, Kessler. You're the one who said it had to be this exact color. Well, this is what you get."

I turn her around and look at the deep V between her breasts. "Oh, I'm not complaining. In fact, I think the anticipation is half the fun."

I've anticipated this moment for days. Hell, months if I'm being honest. And the cab ride home was torture. All I could think about was what she would look like in small scraps of blue beneath the dress that matches her eyes. We both teased each other in the back seat, our hands wandering up arms, down legs and between thighs. We pushed it as far as we could without becoming indecent.

But now that we are safely in my apartment, indecent is exactly what we are going to be.

I finish with the buttons and her dress falls to the floor. She steps out of it, still in her heels, and I have a hard time controlling my deep, carnal groan. Holy God, she's incredible. I've seen her before in a bra and panties, but this—with her standing up before me—I can't believe she's not gracing the cover of every major magazine in the world. She's perfect in every way.

And she's mine.

My dick is becoming painfully hard as my eyes trace every curve of her.

I see her shiver and it concerns me. "Are you cold?"

She shakes her head.

"Are you nervous?"

She nods.

"Babe, you have nothing to be nervous about. I told you. We can wait as long as you want."

"It's not that." She shuffles her feet anxiously. "It's just … Caden, why me?"

I blow out a breath in frustration. "You're kidding me, right?"

"This isn't about beauty or self-confidence. I really want to know. Girls throw themselves at you. You could have your pick of anyone. Why break your rules for *me?*"

I nod because it's a valid question. So, I try to give her an honest answer. "For one, because you *don't* throw yourself at me. Sometimes I get the feeling you couldn't care less that I play baseball. It's a huge turn on, Murph. But I think the biggest reason is how tough and resilient you are." I walk up to her and run my finger across her scar. "So many women would have been crushed by what happened to you. But you never once felt sorry for yourself. You never once asked *'why me'*." I shake my head and laugh. "Okay, until now, but that doesn't count. You take everything in stride and don't wallow in self-pity. You made buckets of lemonade out of lemons. I'm in awe of you. Don't you know that?"

A smile creeps up her face. "What are you waiting for then?" she says, looking up at me through her lashes. "Take me to bed, Caden Kessler."

I sweep her into my arms. "Nothing would give me more pleasure, Murphy Cavenaugh. And believe me, we're in for a mountain of pleasure."

She giggles into my neck as I carry her back to my room.

After I place her on my bed, I realize I have far too many clothes on. I remedy the situation by stripping off my jacket and tie. Her eyes follow my every move, and then she crooks her finger, beckoning me closer.

"I want to unbutton you like you did me," she says.

Then she slowly, almost painfully, undoes each button, tracing her fingertips down my abs as she goes. When she reaches the bottom, she pulls my shirttails out and pushes my shirt off my shoulders so it falls to the floor. It's the most seductive removal of a shirt I've ever experienced.

When she focuses her attention on the fly of my pants, *I'm* the one who starts to shiver. Not because I'm cold. Not because I'm nervous. But because every time this woman touches me, she sends bolts of electricity down my spine. Right to my balls. To my toes. To my goddamn heart.

When my pants fall down around my ankles, I hastily remove my boxer briefs right along with them, leaving me standing naked before her. She's getting her first look at every part of me.

I can almost see her heartbeat through the wall of her chest. She stares at my cock as it jumps under her heated perusal. And when she reaches out to touch me, I think every fantasy I've ever had about being with the most gorgeous woman in the world is coming true.

"Jesus, Murph," I groan as her hand strokes me just so, as if she can read my mind and knows precisely how I like it.

She's had her hand on me for two seconds and I'm about to blow. I reach out and lower the cups of her bra, trussing her up so I can fondle her as she is me. I caress her gently. I knead her soft, voluptuous mounds. I pinch her stiff nipples. She throws her head back and strokes me faster, every tug of her hand bringing me closer and closer to where I need to be.

Her other hand reaches down and cups my balls, just as they start to tighten. Waves of painful pleasure coil my insides as I build up higher and then explode as I call out her name in guttural shouts.

Holy shit.

I sit on the bed beside her and catch my breath. "And that's number three," I say.

"Number three?" She looks at me, confused.

"The third answer to your *'why me'* question."

"Oh." She pinks up as she giggles.

Once I gain my composure, I lean her back, climb on top of her, and cage her to the bed. "My turn," I say, looking deep into her eyes before I kiss her.

I kiss her until her hips buck under me. Until she squirms so hard it's like she's begging for more. Then I run my lips and tongue down her neck, stopping to suck on the skin covering her throbbing pulse. When I travel south, taking a nipple into my mouth, she calls out my name.

I smile against her skin as my fingers wander down her stomach and under her thin scrap of panties. When I feel how wet she is, I start getting hard again. I rub her wetness around with my fingers, coating her tiny nub and working it around in circles. I slip a finger inside her, then two. She arches her back into my hand and moans in pleasure.

She's very responsive and it's a huge turn on. But I don't want her to come this way. I want to send her over the edge with my tongue. So I crawl down her body and remove her panties, inch by slow inch, torturing her with my light touch as my fingers graze every erogenous zone from hip to foot.

Then I slowly climb back up, holding her eyes with mine as I make it clear what I'm about to do. When I smell her, I'm grateful I just came myself, otherwise it would be my undoing. I spread her silky folds and put my tongue on her, feasting on her as she looks down on me from propped-up elbows. It's damn sexy the way she's watching me pleasure her.

When I add my fingers to the mix, sliding them up her slick channel, her head falls back onto my pillow and her hands grab my hair, pulling it hard as she pins my head against her and comes apart beneath me.

I tongue her until she stops shuddering and pushes me away because she's too sensitive.

"Wow," she says to the ceiling, looking satiated.

I hover over her and smile. "If you liked that, wait until you see the second act."

"Don't get cocky, Kessler." She reaches around and pinches my ass.

I laugh. "Not cocky. Just confident," I say.

I lean down and kiss her neck, her shoulders, her temples, her lips. When I pull away, I look into beautiful blue eyes that are burning with carnal desire. "I want to make love to you so badly, Murph."

"I want that, too," she says, running her fingers in a trail down my spine.

"Are you sure?"

She nods. "I've never been more certain of anything."

I reach over into my nightstand and pull out a box of condoms. When she eyes them, I feel the need to explain. "You are the only girl I've ever had in this bed, Murphy."

She grabs the box from me, opening it. "Caden, I know you weren't a monk before me. And as long as you don't use these with anyone else, we're good."

"You can bet on it," I tell her.

She puts the box aside and hands me two square wrappers.

I take them, tossing one to the floor. "One will do."

"But—"

I put my finger on her lips to shut her up. "But nothing. I told you you're different. *Everything* is different with you."

"Everything is different with you, too."

She watches as I roll on the condom. I like the way she studies every move I make. I like the way her hands need to be touching my flesh at every moment. I like the way she makes me a better, stronger man than I am.

I more than like it.

I more than like *her.*

Damn.

I hover over her, waiting for her to give me the final okay before I enter her. I hover over her, wanting to tell her what just hit me like a ton of fucking bricks. I hover over her, needing to be with this woman as badly as I need air to breathe.

She grips the globes of my ass and raises her hips in invitation. I don't even hesitate a second before savoring the feeling of slipping inside her. She's snug and the friction is amazing. I take it slow at first, enjoying every small movement as I glide in and out. I watch every nuance of her face, figuring out how she likes it best.

I put my weight on an elbow and reach up to fondle her nipples. The sounds that come from her implore me to increase the pace of my thrusts. I know she's close. I've made her come twice now and if I know anything about her, I know she bites down on her bottom lip right before she comes.

I move my hand lower so it's right between us. I circle her pulsating clit as we pound our bodies together, each needing something from the other. Each giving as much as we take.

She screams out my name, spiraling me into my own orgasm as my husky voice echoes off the walls.

I collapse down onto her, my body languid and raw. My mind overwhelmed with feeling.

When I can finally rise up, I push her hair out of her face and smile down at her. "I think I just found my new pre-game ritual."

She laughs.

She has no idea what I really wanted to say.

She pulls my face down to hers and kisses me with as much passion as I've ever known.

Then again, maybe she did.

Chapter Forty-two

Murphy

"Tell me about it," I say, settling my head onto his chest as he wraps an arm around me and holds me close. "Your pre-game ritual. I've often wondered what it is you do."

"It's no big deal. And not nearly as interesting—or as illegal—as some people I know."

"Illegal? Really?"

He shrugs. "People do strange things if they think it will help them succeed."

"But yours isn't strange?" I ask.

"I listen to music."

I find it hard not to laugh. I had pictured him putting on his lucky underwear and meditating. Or maybe doing some weird handshake with the guys. Perhaps eating the same thing for breakfast. But music? It's so … benign.

"What?" he says, feeling my silent giggle.

"It's just so normal," I say. "Everyone listens to music when they are stressed."

"Yeah, well, everyone doesn't listen the way I do."

He has my attention now and I turn my body, perching my chin up on his chest. "Oh?"

"I listen to the same music before every game."

"That doesn't seem all that unusual. Do you have a pre-game playlist?"

"Yeah."

"What's on it?"

He sighs. "The entire Beatles White Album."

My jaw drops. "You listen to the entire Beatles White Album before every game?"

He nods. "All ninety-three minutes of it."

"How do you have time for that? Don't you guys have to warm up or something?"

"We do warm up. I do it with earbuds in."

"And they let you do that?"

He laughs. "Murph, if they think that we think something will make us perform better, they will bend over backwards to make it happen. Especially when we're on the road."

I lay my head back down on his chest, not wanting to think about him being on the road.

"What is it?" he asks. "I just felt you tense up."

I shrug into him. "I guess I'm just not sure what comes next," I say. "What are we going to do when you have to travel all the time? We'll never see each other."

He kisses the top of my head. "We have over two months to figure that out, babe."

"Two? I thought baseball season didn't start until April. That's four months away."

"It doesn't, but spring training starts around the third week of February."

"Oh, well, how bad can it be? It's just a bunch of practices, right? We'll still get to see each other. That is unless they have a no-girlfriends rule or something." I suddenly get a bad feeling in the pit of my stomach. I look up at him. "There isn't a rule, is there?"

He chuckles, his chest bouncing under me. "No, there's no rule."

"But what about you?" I ask. "I remember you once telling me you didn't want a girlfriend because you didn't want distractions. What if I'm a distraction, Caden?"

His hand rubs up and down my arm. "You are anything but a distraction. You're my good luck charm, remember? But, Murph, spring training isn't here in New York. It's in Florida."

I sit up and pull the sheet around me. "Florida?"

He runs a hand through his hair and then sits up against his headboard. "Yeah. We'll be down there for about six weeks."

I sigh. "I guess six weeks isn't so bad."

He pulls me to him, settling me between his legs so my back is resting on his chest. "You could go with me."

I glance back at him, giving him a look. "I have a job, Caden. One I like very much."

"I know," he says. "How about I fly you down every weekend then? I'm in tight with one of your bosses, so maybe he'll agree to let you fit your hours into four days or something."

I shrug. "We'll see. We have some time. We're not even sure where this is going yet."

"This? You mean *us?"* He surprises me by turning me around and pinning me down onto the bed. "This is going all the way. All nine innings."

I smile. "You say that like you know we'll be together. But we've just gotten started. How can you be so sure?"

He leans down to kiss me. He starts out softly, kissing each side of my mouth and then my top lip, followed by my bottom. He kisses my cheeks, taking extra time over my imperfections. When his lips move back to mine, he devours my mouth with his tongue, exploring, tasting, savoring.

When he's kissed me breathless and is growing hard on top of me, he pulls away, running a finger across my scar. "Don't you know by now that you're my perfect game?"

I've known him long enough to understand what saying that means to a guy like Caden. A guy whose whole life has been dedicated to one thing. I look into his eyes and see how much he means it.

A knot forms in my throat as I feel emotion pass between us. My eyes pool with tears. "Getting hit by your ball was the best thing that ever happened to me."

He nods and I can tell he's trying to keep his emotions in check. "I … I'm not good at this romance stuff, Murph. I never *wanted* to be good at it. You've changed everything for me. I know I freaked you out last week when I told you like wasn't a strong enough word. After that, I promised myself I wouldn't move too fast and risk scaring you. But if I've only got two months to convince you this is real—that you're it for me, then I'm not holding back. Because I'm pretty sure I love you, Murphy Brown. And I don't know if me saying that is going to make you run out that door or not. But if you do, I'll chase you. I'll always chase you. And I'll make you realize you need to be with me. I'm never going to be happy that I hit you with my ball, but now I know it was fate. The beautiful scar on your face brought us together. And every time I look at you, all I see is a reminder. A reminder that you belong to me."

I can't even see him clearly anymore with the steady stream of tears escaping my eyes. I gently push him off me and get out of bed.

"Shit, Murphy, I'm sorry."

I pick up the unused condom he threw on the floor and climb back into bed, right on top of him, smiling. "Whoever told you you're not good at the romance stuff is wrong. Is there *anything* you don't excel at?"

He laughs. "Damn, woman. You scared me for a second." His eyes fall to my breasts that are dangerously close to his face now. "You're not mad?"

"Mad?" I lean down and feather kisses along his jaw. "How could I be mad when I feel the same way?"

His breath catches and he cups my face in his hands, forcing me to look at him. "I'm going to need to hear you say it."

More tears threaten to fall. "I love you, Caden."

His eyes close briefly and he sighs. "Again."

"I love you, Caden Kessler."

"I never thought I'd want to hear those words," he says, brushing some hair out of my face and tucking it behind my ear. "And now, I hope I never have to go a day without you saying them."

"This is going to work, isn't it?" I ask hesitantly. "We'll be apart a lot of the time, but we can make it work, can't we?"

"We have to make it work," he says. "Us not working is not an option."

I hold out the condom. "Then we better get started, because I plan on showing you over and over what you'll be missing when we're apart."

He takes the square package from me, leaning up to give me one more kiss. "We may not always be in the same city, Sweet Caroline. But we'll *never* be apart."

We stop talking. But we don't stop telling each other everything we need to hear.

Chapter Forty-three

Caden

My eyes scan the arrivals terminal as people make their way to the luggage carousels. Every time I see a head of blonde hair, my heart jumps. And maybe another part of my anatomy as well.

It's been three weeks since we've seen each other. We just haven't been able to get our schedules to mesh. Taking on more responsibility at the gym means it's harder for her to get away. But now she's on vacation and I get her for an entire week.

I used to love spring training. Being down in Tampa for six weeks when it's bitter cold up north was just another perk of the job. But this year is different. This year I have someone to go home to. Someone who is waiting for me.

A smile splits my face when I see her. When she notices me standing here, her steps quicken and she walks as fast as she can without running. Our eyes are locked together. Hundreds of people surround us, yet we only see each other. I want to go to her but security would probably apprehend me.

I start laughing when I realize what she's wearing. Shorts. A halter top. Flip flops. Appropriate attire for Florida, but not for New York City the first week of March. She must have frozen her butt off in her excitement to get here.

She passes security and jumps into my waiting arms, wrapping her legs around me. Cameras come out and photograph us, but I don't care. In the past four months, we've graced the covers of so many tabloids it doesn't even bother her anymore. Just like everything else in her life, she's taking this in stride.

We kiss like we've been apart for three decades, not three weeks.

This, right here, makes everything worth it.

When we finally pull apart and I return her to her feet, she tries to compose herself. "Well, that ought to give them something to write about," she says, nodding at the paparazzi who caught wind of us.

Several photographers follow us as we retrieve her suitcase and walk out to my rental car.

"Caden, is there a wedding in the future?" one shouts.

"Miss Cavenaugh, does it bother you that he's down here bar-hopping?" another asks.

Having heard enough, I turn to them. "I haven't seen my girl in weeks. We'll be happy to pose for a photo if you'll then give us our privacy."

Murphy pastes on her best model smile as the cameras snap repeatedly. Then, just as asked, they leave us alone. Sometimes I find it easier to give them what they want rather than try to fend them off.

I open the door for her and she gets in the car. "It's not true, you know. I don't go bar-hopping. I mean, I've been to a few bars, but I'm not out trolling or anything."

"Caden, I don't expect you to sit in your hotel room twiddling your thumbs while you're down here. I hope you're going out with your friends. You deserve to have a little fun after working so hard."

I stick my head in the car and lay a kiss on her. "Are you for real?"

"I'm for real in love with you, Kessler."

I smile, knowing she'd find some way to tell me she loves me. She does every day. "Right backatcha, Murphy Brown."

I walk around the car and get in, starting it up and backing out.

"Where are we going first?" she asks in excitement.

I stare at her. I sure as hell don't need words to tell her what I have planned.

She wiggles out of her flip flops. "Okay then, I guess the beach will have to wait."

"I have big plans for us and the beach," I say. "But not today. I don't have the tent with me."

"You have a tent? Why do you have a tent?"

"You don't expect me to make love to my girl out in the open do you? That shit would end up on YouTube."

I glance over to see her swallow. Hard. "We're going to make love on the beach?"

"It's one of your fantasies, isn't it?"

"Well … yes, but—"

"But nothing. It's happening. I even got a tent that opens at the top for star-gazing."

"It sounds like you thought of everything," she says, smiling.

"I did. Wait until you see the hotel suite. We could hole up in there all week and never leave. I've stocked it with all your favorite snacks and drinks. And with room service … hell, we won't even have to get out of bed until Monday."

She reaches over to grab my hand. "Sounds like the perfect vacation."

I laugh, settling our entwined hands on her bare leg. "Don't worry, babe. I'll get you to the beach. Maybe you can hang out there when I'm at practice."

"That might be okay for a day or two, but I'd also like to watch a few practices if that's allowed."

"Of course. Anything you want."

Her phone chirps with a text. When she looks at it, she seems upset.

"What is it?" I ask.

She shakes her head. "It's Tony. He says he wants to talk to me."

"Give it to me," I say, reaching over to get her phone. "I'll text him. I'll tell him where he can shove his misguided attempts at extortion."

She holds the phone out of my reach. "You are not going to text him, Caden. I don't care what he wants, I'm not even going to answer him. Plus, you're driving."

"I wasn't going to text him this second," I scoff at her. "I'm not stupid, you know."

She taps around on her phone. "Problem solved," she says. "I blocked his number."

"How does that solve the problem, Murph? It's not like he's some random caller. He has your number. He can call it from anyone's phone."

"Well, it solves the problem for now," she says. "And if he keeps texting from another phone, I'll turn the thing off. He's not going to ruin my vacation."

A few months ago, the snake contacted her, threatening to sue her for throwing his home run ball out the window. He said he could have gotten money for it so she should pay him to compensate. Asked her for a few thousand dollars. It was ridiculous. I hadn't even signed it. I wonder what other scheme he's come up with now.

I've considered filing a restraining order against him, but Ethan said if he hasn't physically threatened her, they won't issue one. So, the prick continues to be a thorn in my side.

We pull up to the valet parking at the hotel. I pop the trunk and leave her suitcase for the bellhop so I can quickly get us through the swarm of the dozen-or-so girls who have decided to camp out in front of the hotel this afternoon.

I get no less than two marriage proposals on our way by. But it's not those that bother me. It's the remarks about Murphy. Girls asking why I'm with her when they can offer me a perfect face. It takes a lot of willpower not to stop and tell them off. But I learned a long time ago, that won't accomplish anything.

Once we're safely inside, Murphy asks, "Do you have to deal with that every day?"

"Pretty much."

"That's awful. Can't the hotel do anything about it?"

"If the fans get unruly, they will ask them to leave. But they always come back. The hotel does a good job of keeping them out of the lobby, but sometimes an overzealous fan will slip by them, going to great lengths to pretend to be a guest."

Murphy gives me an incredulous look. "What's wrong with people?"

I grab her hand and lead her into the elevator. "You know as well as I do, everyone wants a slice of the pie."

"People suck," she says.

I cage her into the corner of the elevator, not wanting to wait another minute to kiss her again. "*You* don't suck," I say, looking down on her.

"You don't suck, either," she says, pulling my head closer to hers.

When my lips are about to touch hers, I say, "Now that we've cleared that up, what are we going to do with each other?"

"Anything," she says, longingly. "Everything."

I kiss her until the door opens on my floor. Then I sweep her into my arms and carry her to my suite, having every intention of holding her to her unspoken promise.

Chapter Forty-four

Murphy

There is a knock on the door to our suite. Caden's still in the bathroom getting ready for practice, so I throw on a robe to go collect our breakfast.

When I open the door, however, there isn't a tray of food. There's a girl leaning against the opposite wall with her blouse practically unbuttoned to her navel. Her boobs are spilling out of her push-up bra so much I can almost see her nipples.

I raise my eyebrows at her.

"Oh." She barely has the decency to look embarrassed. "Is Caden here?"

"Yes," I say dryly, without making any indication that I'm going to fetch him.

"Well, do you know when you might be done with him?"

My jaw drops at her audacity. "Yeah." I look at my wrist as if there's a watch on it. "In about seventy-five years."

The girl doesn't look amused, but Caden does as he walks up next to me and plants a kiss on my forehead.

His smile turns into a scowl when he addresses the girl. "How did you get my room number?"

She stands up straighter and squeezes her arms together to give her boobs a lift. "How do you think?"

"Leave now," Caden says. "Or I'm calling security."

The girl pulls her blouse together. "Fine. Jeez. I'll just go find someone else. I hear Brady Taylor is a good lay. But you don't know what you're missing."

Caden eyes her up and down. "From the looks of it, a shot of penicillin."

She walks off in a huff and Caden slams the door as I laugh at his epic joke. Then he picks me up and carries me over to the couch. Picking me up is becoming a habit of his. One I hope he never breaks.

He sits down with me on his lap. "Seventy-five years, huh?"

I shrug a provocative shoulder.

He leans in to kiss my neck. "Won't be long enough," he says against my skin.

I glance up at the clock. "Caden, while I'd love to go for round three, I'm not planning on being the reason you're late to practice. And you haven't eaten yet."

A knock on the door has us laughing at the timing. "I'll get this one," he says.

After our breakfast gets delivered, Caden pulls me back onto his lap and feeds me. "Do you know what I find extremely sexy?" he asks.

"Other than the black negligee I wore last night?" I shimmy myself around on his lap.

I feel him harden beneath me. "Stop it or I'll never leave," he says, forking a bite of eggs into my mouth. "What I was going to say is that it's a huge turn on that you don't get jealous, Murph.

Most girls would have seen that tramp in the hallway and immediately assumed their boyfriend would invite her in."

I don't think for a minute that he would have invited her in. I trust Caden completely. But that doesn't mean I don't see green from time to time. Every beautiful woman who throws herself at him makes me want to gouge her eyes out. Every girl who sends him love notes has me wanting to brand him publicly as mine. Every person who puts me down because they think they are better than me puts a small chink in my self-confidence. But I work hard not to show him any of that. He has enough to deal with because of his celebrity status. He doesn't need a jealous girlfriend breathing down his neck.

"What good would that do?" I ask. "If you want someone else, nothing I say is going to stop you. And if it comes to the point where I'm not enough for you—"

"That will never happen." He situates me so I'm straddling him on the dining room chair. "I'm going to marry you one day, Murphy Brown. And you're going to have all my babies. And we're going to live happily ever after for every one of those seventy-five years."

He pulls my face to his and kisses me. He kisses me senseless and then he stands up with me in his arms, depositing me back on the chair before he grabs his bag and walks to the door. "Don't get too sunburned today," he says. "I have big plans for that body later."

Then he walks out of the suite leaving me a hot, speechless mess.

~ ~ ~

Caden winks at me from the practice field. I love watching him play. And the man finally got his wish. I am, in fact, now a bona fide baseball lover. He taught me a lot during the off-season and I can't wait to go to his games, knowing I'll be able to fully understand everything that's happening.

My phone chirps and I look to see Kirsten has sent me a text.

Kirsten: Did you block Tony?

Me: Yes. I don't have anything to say to him.

Kirsten: But he needs to talk to you.

Me: Every time he's needed to talk to me in the past six months it was to ask me for money.

Kirsten: You really should talk to him.

Me: You haven't contacted me since the day I moved out, Kirsten. If Tony is just getting you to do his dirty work, I'm going to block you, too.

Kirsten: I wouldn't do that if I were you.

I don't even acknowledge that with a reply. I just block her number. Jamie is the only one of my old roommates who I've talked to since I left. She told me that Kirsten hasn't been able to land much work lately, but that Tony stays with her because he can't get anyone else. Even Tori and Pauline stopped sleeping with the bastard. Does that mean they developed a conscience, or that he's just gotten to be *that* bad?

It makes me feel dirty that he was able to 'get' me. How could I have been so gullible?

I pull out my sunscreen and lather it on. I don't want to get red like I did at the beach yesterday. Caden wasn't happy that he had to handle me with care last night. But then again, he didn't mind it when I asked him to rub aloe on me. And boy did he give me a good rub down.

I hear some girls laughing a few rows over. The stands are fairly empty in this minor-league stadium, but there are a few pockets of girls, and even guys, who have come to watch the Nighthawks pre-season workouts.

I shake my head in irritation when I overhear one of the girls bragging about how many of the players she's slept with. I'm not surprised to hear the names of both Brady Taylor and Sawyer Mills. Those boys better be careful or they will end up getting someone pregnant. I know Caden has told me they claim to be as careful as he was, but still—if you throw enough darts, one of them is bound to stick.

My back stiffens when I hear one of them mention trying to get with Caden. I smile when she calls him an arrogant prick for ignoring her advances.

When Caden gets a break and jogs over in my direction, the girls next to me start squealing, thinking he's coming over for them. When he walks past them and over to me, they all look at me with pure hatred. I think they finally realize who I am. Our relationship is no secret. Caden and I were interviewed by a popular nightly news show last month. Anyone who follows baseball has heard about the love story of the Hawks player and the girl he hit with his home run ball.

I stand up and walk down the bleachers to meet him, fully aware of a dozen eyes burning into the back of my head. Then one of them yells out, "Caden, you don't have to hit me with a ball to get me to fuck you."

He looks at her and laughs. "Yeah, because your incredible charm would win me over."

The girls scoff at him.

"I told you he was an arrogant prick," another girl says.

I lean over the bulkhead and wrap my arms around him. "I love you, you arrogant prick," I say.

He pulls me over the wall and into his arms. "I don't know what I'm going to do when you leave, Murph. It's great having you here."

"You're going to focus on being the best ball player you can be, that's what."

"I predict this will be my best year ever because I'll have my lucky girl with me."

I roll my eyes at him. "We've gone over this, Caden. There is no way I can go to every game."

"How about just the home games?"

"That's still a lot."

"Okay, four games a week," he says.

"Are you negotiating with me, Kessler?"

He laughs.

"One," I say. "I promise to go to one game a week."

"Three," he says, leaning down to nibble on my ear.

"You're incorrigible," I say, laughing. "Fine. Two. Two games per week and that's my final offer."

Someone calls him back over to practice, so he lifts me up over the half-wall and gives me a kiss. "I would have settled for one," he says, walking away. "I'll take you any way I can get you."

I blow him a kiss. "I almost caved at three."

He shakes his head, laughing as he jogs back to the others. Before he gets there, he turns around and gives me a big smile. A smile that says it all. A smile that says he's mine.

Yeah – happy is definitely not a strong enough word.

Chapter Forty-five

Caden

Opening day. There is nothing like it. Looking up into the stands and seeing forty thousand fans is surreal. Some days I still can't believe I get to play ball for a living. I stick my head out of the dugout and take a long look around. Just as the last Beatles song is finishing up in my ears, my eyes land on Murphy. She's gorgeous in her Hawks shirt.

I wonder what hat she's wearing today. She has quite the collection of hats in her apartment now. And often when we're together, she'll wear one and I'll take it off her to see which date is inside. Then we'll reminisce about how she came to have the hat.

I try to guess which one sits on her head right now. The one I gave her on our first Christmas? Or maybe the one I gave her the day we met in the hospital. Or better yet, it could be the one I gave her in the tent on the beach when she came down to Tampa. Each one holds a special meaning. And I find myself hoping she never stops wearing them.

I take my earbuds out and stash them in my bag. When I do, something falls out and Sawyer reaches down to grab it. He opens the small velvet box to reveal a diamond ring.

"Shit, Kess. Really?"

I shrug my shoulders. "What can I say, man? She's the one."

I bought the ring in Florida a few weeks ago. I've been carrying it around with me because I'm waiting for the perfect time to propose. I still haven't figured out if I'm going to plan out an extravagant proposal or let it be a spur of the moment sort of thing. All I know is that I'll know when the moment is right.

Sawyer takes the ring out of the box and examines it. "Damn fine ring," he says.

"Damn fine girl," I tell him, taking it back.

"We love you, Caden!" some girls scream next to the dugout.

I quickly throw the box into my bag and slip the ring in my back pocket to keep anyone else from seeing it. I don't need some teenage fan-girl ruining the surprise by tweeting about me showing off an engagement ring to my buddies.

"Gear up," our coach says.

Adrenaline flows through me like hot lava. I can't wait to get back out on that field.

God, I love baseball.

~ ~ ~

My teammates pat me on the back on the way to the clubhouse. Today was an epic day by anyone's standards, but a personal best for me. Not only did I have a two-run homer, but a total of four RBIs, and three double plays.

Lady luck was surely on my side. As I undress, the ring falls out of my back pocket. I forgot it was even there. I study it for a minute, thinking of the game I just had. I smile as I put it back into the black velvet box. It's Murphy. *She's* my lady luck.

I see an envelope taped to my locker. It has a sticky note on it from Melanie that says she was told the message was urgent. I rip it open and pull out a letter.

> Since Murphy will no longer take my calls, and she walks into the back office when I try to confront her at the gym, I have no choice but to come to you.
>
> I have something you want.
>
> If you want to protect your girl, I suggest you meet me in the tunnel to parking lot B, right outside the locker room.
>
> Now.
>
> Otherwise, I can't guarantee she won't get hurt.

There's no signature, but it doesn't need one. It's from Tony Fields. My blood boils. My jaw tightens. My temples pound. I want to tear up the letter, but I don't. It could be evidence. He wants to *hurt* her?

Before I'm even fully out of uniform, I pull my pants back on, grab the letter and my phone and go out the back entrance of the clubhouse.

I text the head of security along the way.

Me: Meet me behind the clubhouse in the parking lot B tunnel. Now.

Drew: I'll be there in 5.

I spot Tony immediately. I'm not sure how he got access. This tunnel is off limits to fans. It only gets used by players and stadium workers.

"You threatening her?" I yell at him on my approach.

"Well, if it isn't the famous Caden Kessler," he says, mocking me. "Can I have an autograph?"

"Are. You. Threatening. Her?" I say, slow enough for his pea-sized brain to understand as I press him hard against the wall.

He has the gall to laugh. "That depends on what you mean by threaten," he says, trying to break free. "I'm not going to hurt her physically, if that's what you mean. I'm not like that, man. I've never hit a girl in my life and I won't start now."

"And yet that fact still hasn't kept you from being a complete asshole."

"You might want to choose your words carefully," he says. "Otherwise I might not play nice."

"What the hell do you want, Fields?"

"I'll tell you as soon as you take your hands off me."

I take a step back, but still stay in his face. "Spill it."

"What do you think I want?"

I shake my head. "Same thing as every scammer. Money."

"Ahh, yes, it's true," he says. "Except for one thing. I'm not a scammer, big man. I'm merely an enterprising businessman. I have something you want and you are going to pay me for it."

"Blackmail? Nice try. There is nothing you have that I could ever want." I turn to walk away.

"I beg to differ. And I'll bet Murphy would, too. But I guess it's up to you if you want your girlfriend's naked body all over the internet."

Fuck.

I know he's probably lying. I mean, this is Murphy we're talking about. No way in hell would she have given him a naked picture of herself. But I need to be sure. I turn around. "If you have a naked picture of her, prove it. I want to see it right now."

"Well, it's not a naked picture exactly," he says, chewing the inside of his cheek.

There. That's it. He's lying. Murphy said he chews his cheek when he lies. Or was it that he bites his nails? *Shit.*

"What do you mean it's not exactly a naked picture? Either you have one or you don't."

"Oh, it's a lot better than a naked picture, man. I've got full-blown video."

"You're lying," I say.

He shrugs. "I guess I could be. But then again, are you willing to risk a million people watching your girlfriend come as she rides me?"

I pin him to the wall by his neck. "You stupid prick. If you really had a video, you'd show it to me."

Drew walks up behind me. "Is there a problem here?"

I drop my hands away from Tony. "This shithead is trespassing," I say. "Please make sure he gets to his car."

Drew takes Tony by the elbow. "Sure thing, Mr. Kessler."

Tony yells back over his shoulder. "I'll give you a week, *Mr. Kessler.* If you can't come up with a cool mil by then, I'll make good on my word."

I walk back into the clubhouse and take a quick shower. I know Murphy is waiting for me and I don't want her to worry. But the whole time, I wonder. I wonder that despite the little prick biting his cheek, could it be true?

I can't tell her about this. She'd be mortified. It's most likely bogus anyway. He's going to have to offer me proof. Proof he doesn't have.

When I walk out the door, fans are screaming. I stop to sign some autographs and pose for a few pictures. Then I see her coming towards me. She's still wearing my hat and one hell of a smile. I catch her when she flings herself into my arms.

"You were great, Kessler," Murphy says, planting kisses on me.

I want to be happy. I want to celebrate with her. But I can't. All I hear are Tony's words about a million people watching her ride him. "Hey, what do you say we celebrate?"

"Definitely," she says. "What did you have in mind?"

I lean in close to her ear. "Let's get crazy and video ourselves making love."

She pulls back, looking horrified as she studies me with a slack jaw. "Kessler, you *are* crazy if you think I'd ever do anything like that. Have you completely lost your mind?"

I can't help it when my lungs deflate and I blow out a huge sigh of relief. I knew the asshole was lying. "Sorry," I say, flashing her an innocent look. "I guess the adrenaline of tonight just got to me. I was only joking, Murph."

She rolls her eyes, laughing. Then she leans up and whispers back to me. "But I'm not opposed to watching you make love to me," she says, her hot breath flowing over my ear. "You do have a floor-to-ceiling mirror in your bathroom."

And suddenly, I've forgotten all about the asshole scammer. Hell, I'm not even sure I can remember my own name. Because all

I can think about is what I'm going to do to my girl when I get her home.

Chapter Forty-six

Murphy

Having Caden back home this past month has been both wonderful and eye-opening. He wasn't lying when he said baseball owns his life during the season. Between his job and mine, we're lucky if we get to see each other twice a week. And that's when he's *not* traveling.

He's asked me to move in with him. In fact, he asks me whenever we're together. He says he wants to wake up with me every day. I want that, too. But I keep making up excuses. What he doesn't know, however, is that as soon as Trick finds a new roommate, I'm going to take him up on his offer.

Today is Saturday so the stands are jam-packed at the game we're attending. I love the energy in the stadium—it's like a drug. I can see why Caden embraces it.

Lexi and I make our way to our seats to find Scott and her dad already there. She hugs her dad and little brother. Since Shane and Scott moved to the city a few months ago, they have become a close-knit family. Caden and his dad are more than family now, they are friends. And I couldn't be happier. And with Shane and my mom dating, she flies in from Iowa a lot so I get to see much more of her these days.

I look around and wonder how I got so lucky. How did I end up here … with this man, in this life? Sometimes it seems too good to be true and I wonder when the other shoe is going to drop. Will Caden's life ever become too much for one of us to handle?

Then we make eye contact when he looks up at me from the dugout, and all my fears disappear. Because the way he looks at me, it's as if we aren't surrounded by forty thousand people. We might as well be the only two people on Earth.

I give him a thumbs-up and blow him a kiss. It's what I do before every game. He expects it. And he won't look away until I do it. I guess it's become another one of his rituals. *Our* rituals.

When he puts his game face on and turns around to do his job, Lexi hooks my elbow with hers. "You're good for him, you know. In more ways than one."

"I hope so," I say.

"I've never seen my brother so happy, Murphy."

I glance over at Shane and Scott. "I'm not the only one responsible for that."

"I don't know," she says. "From what I hear, you *are*. Caden told me you are the one who convinced him to give our dad a chance. So, the way I see it, you brought our family back together. And Caden has never performed better on the field. He was great before, but now he's on a whole other level."

"That has nothing to do with me, Lexi. It's all him."

I look down at the dugout to see Caden and his team taking the field. He won't look up at me again until after the game. He never does. Not unless he has a home run. Whenever he hits a home run, he will find me in the crowd, pound his heart and point to me right before he steps on home plate. Even if I'm not at the game, he will still do it—he will look over to where I usually sit behind the net by the first-base dugout and go through the motions. It's become a thing. And it hasn't gone unnoticed. Even the ESPN announcers have picked up on it.

She laughs. "If he *thinks* it's you, then it's you, Murphy. You've been with him long enough to know that."

In the sixth inning, I take Scott to get a hot dog and a Coke. Scott is a good kid. It must have been hard leaving the place where he grew up for almost thirteen years to move here. He seems to have fit right in however, and has become a celebrity in his own right at his school for being a carbon copy of his older brother. He's even following in his brother's footsteps and is a top player on a local Little League team. Lexi, Shane and I have skipped out on a few Hawks games this spring to watch Scott play.

"You're Caden Kessler's girlfriend, aren't you?" a young lady asks on our way to the concession stand. "Can I have your autograph?"

I look at Scott. "You don't want *my* autograph," I tell her. "I'm not even related to Caden. But this is his brother. You should get *his* autograph."

The girl squeals in delight and then gushes over Scott, realizing how much he looks like Caden. I smile, watching Scott get fawned over by an excited co-ed. He poses for a picture with her and signs her program. The grin on his face is priceless.

We make our way back to our seats, our hands filled with junk food. But before we get there, Scott stops walking. "You're pretty cool, Murphy," he says.

"You're pretty cool yourself," I tell him.

He nods to the field. "I'm going to be out there one day."

"I don't doubt it. You're a great player, Scott."

"Will you come to my games, too?"

I can't help the smile that overtakes my face. Scott, like his older brother, believes I'll still be around ten years from now. He's accepted me as family. And I love him like a brother. "You can bet on it."

"What'd we miss?" I ask Lexi when I settle back into my seat.

"Nothing much. It's still three to two. Caden didn't let anything get by him."

I look up at the scoreboard. "I love close games," I tell them. "I mean, what's the fun if every game is a blowout?"

"You like living on the edge, huh?" Shane asks.

I shrug. "I don't know. I just think if things come easily to you, they aren't worth having. It's the hard wins that are most important. Those build character."

The players all leave the field for the seventh-inning stretch. The JumboTron starts zooming in on people which means they are supposed to kiss. The crowd cheers as couples happily oblige.

Then the screen goes blank and people boo and hiss at the malfunction. I take the opportunity to check my phone for messages.

Suddenly, Lexi grabs my arm. I look at her face to see her wide eyes. I follow her gaze back to the screen and see myself up on it. Picture after picture of Caden and me flash up on the screen. Good pictures—like the ones taken for interviews. Candid pictures—like the ones from tabloid magazines when we were caught kissing in public.

I'm confused. Why are pictures of us on the JumboTron? "What's going on?" I ask no one.

Lexi tightens her grip on me and squeals. "Oh my God, Murphy. Do you think my brother is going to propose?"

My heart pounds almost painfully in my chest when her words sink in. I look down to the dugout, but don't see any trace of Caden. I look over at the nearest tunnel, expecting him to appear. I look at the field wall a few rows in front of us and think maybe he'll pop out from behind it. But none of those things happen.

Then I hear collective gasps of shock from the crowd.

I look back up at the massive screen and see what appears to be a pornographic movie playing. My jaw drops. *What on Earth?*

Everyone in the stadium is watching. It's like the train wreck you can't peel your eyes away from. Parents are covering the eyes of their children. Women start screaming in horror. But most people can't tear their eyes away. Including me.

Lexi cries, "Oh, my God, Murphy!"

And all at once, my perfect world collapses. My happy life crumbles. Because I realize that forty thousand people are looking at *me*. It's me up on that screen having sex. It's me straddling a man, riding him like he's a wild horse. It's my breasts bouncing around as my face contorts in pleasure. It's me having sex with my bastard of an ex who obviously taped me without my consent.

Hot tears stream down my face as the video finally gets cut off and the JumboTron displays a message of technical difficulty. The stadium is in an uproar as everyone is trying to deal with what they just saw. Lexi and Shane are looking at me in disbelief. Shane uncovers Scott's eyes and bile rises in my throat when I wonder if Caden's thirteen-year-old brother just witnessed the most horrific moment of my life.

I look down at the dugout to see Caden running out of it. He looks up at me and we stare at each other helplessly. So many things bleed from his eyes. Empathy. Horror. Sorrow.

My stomach churns and I know I'm about to lose my lunch. I turn and plow through the crowd, running to the nearest bathroom and barely making it before I wretch into the toilet of the first stall.

Lexi runs in after me. She holds back my hair. There's some commotion behind us and I hear Caden's voice asking women to give us some privacy. I stand up and go to the sink, splashing water on my face.

"Lexi, can you make sure nobody comes in?" he asks.

"I'm on it," she says, rounding the corner to guard the entrance.

Caden runs his hand over my back trying to comfort me in a moment when I can't be comforted. I don't even want him to look at me. What must he be thinking? Why is he even in here?

"Caden, the game." I finally lock eyes with him in the mirror.

"Fuck the game, Murphy."

I shake my head as more tears roll down my cheek. "I didn't know he taped us. I swear I didn't," I tell him, hoping he will believe me. "I would never do that, Caden. You must know that. I could never …"

Then something occurs to me and I feel sick again. I turn around and look directly at him. "A few weeks ago, you asked me to do it." I cover the sob begging to break free. "You joked about making a sex tape. Why did you ask me that, Caden?"

I take a step away from him, already fearing his answer. His hands run through his hair and he glances up at the ceiling before looking back at me. When he does, guilt is written all over his face. "I thought he was lying about having the video, Murph. He did that thing where he chews on his cheek. You said yourself that's his tell. He tried to blackmail me. Asked me for a lot of money. I thought he was lying like all the other times. I'm so sorry, Murphy. I'm so sorry."

I back up and lean against the sink. "Tony contacted you? You *knew* about the tape. And you didn't tell me?"

He scrubs a hand across his jaw. "I'm sorry. I didn't want you to worry. You have enough to worry about with your job and me being gone half the time. If you thought there was a tape out there, you'd have freaked. And I knew you wouldn't let me pay him off. But I would have, Murphy. I swear if he'd shown me the tape I would have paid him. I wouldn't have thought twice about it. But he didn't show me anything. And he bit his damn cheek."

He takes some steps towards me to close the gap, but I move away, disgusted. "You didn't want to *worry* me?" I yell at him. "It's *my* life, Caden. What right do you have to make decisions for me?"

"It's not like that. I thought he was lying, Murph."

"But he wasn't, Caden. He wasn't lying. And now I've been humiliated. How can I ever show my face again? Your dad saw it. Your thirteen-year-old brother saw it. Half of New York City saw me naked and having sex. And I'm sure it's all over the internet by now as well. This can never be undone, Caden. How could you do this to me?"

"Babe, I didn't do anything. Tony did. I was trying to protect you."

"By taking away my choices?"

"That wasn't my intention," he says, reaching for me.

He tries to hold my hand, but I pull away. "Don't touch me!"

"Murphy, I will fix this. I swear."

Tears pool in his eyes. But I can't think about *him* now … him and his lies. All I can think about is getting away. Leaving this place. Escaping this nightmare.

"This is one thing your money can't fix." I start walking out of the bathroom, but he grabs my arm. I rip it out of his grip. "I said don't touch me, Caden, and I meant it."

He holds up his hands in surrender, the pain on his face almost mirroring the pain in my heart. Almost.

I walk around the corner to see a large crowd gathering outside the bathroom, and Lexi, Shane, and some men in security shirts are keeping everyone at a distance. Cameras come out and flash and film as I come into view.

I pull Lexi aside. "If you care anything about me, please do not let Caden follow me. I need some space, Lexi. Please. I beg you."

She nods. "Okay."

I ask one of the security guards to escort me out of the park as Caden calls out behind me. I turn briefly to see Lexi holding him back. She says something to him and he stops fighting her. He looks at me as I walk away. He looks broken. He might even look as broken as I feel.

Another security guard runs up alongside us. I recognize him from before. He's the one who gets to peel screaming girls off players outside the clubhouse after games. "I'm Drew," he says. "Caden wanted me to make sure you were okay, Miss Cavenaugh."

"Thanks, Drew. But I'm not sure I'll ever be okay after that."

"I'm sorry," he says. "Is there anything I can do for you?"

We reach the front of the stadium and the guards stand with me while I hail a cab. I pull my phone out of my pocket. The phone that is already blowing up with calls and texts. I hand it to Drew. "There is one thing you can do for me. You can return his phone to him."

He takes it from me. "I'll make sure he gets it."

Then I take my hat off and look at the date inside. It's from the first day we made love. I hand it to Drew as well. "You can give him his hat back, too."

Drew eyes it curiously. "I'm sure he doesn't need it. He has plenty."

"I know he does. But I don't want it anymore. Please return it to him."

A cab pulls up and I slip inside. "Where to, Miss?"

I look up at the stadium, knowing it will be the last time I see it. "J.F.K," I tell him. "I'm going home."

Chapter Forty-seven

Caden

I don't bother going back on the field or even into the dugout. No way could I play right now. And I realize this has never happened before. Never in my life have I been too distracted to play ball. Hell, I even played in a game the day my mother died back in college.

After I cuss out my locker and throw a few things around the clubhouse, I pocket my phone and go up to the communications booth, pushing past reporters to get through the door. "What the fuck happened?" I yell to the boisterous room.

All eyes turn to me. The owner of the team looks more than a little pissed off, but not at me. He wants answers same as I do. "We're working with our technology team and the police to figure that out right now."

I write down a name and Murphy's old address and show it to one of the officers. "The guy's name is Tony Fields. I don't know his address, but that's where he hangs out a lot. He's my girlfriend's ex and I can tell you with one-hundred-percent certainty she had no knowledge of that video. It was taken without her consent. He tried to blackmail me a few weeks ago, but I thought he was lying about the tape." I pick out the police officer who looks like he might be in charge. "I want to press charges. As many of them as I can. That asshole is going down."

The officer looks at me in sympathy. "I understand your frustration, Mr. Kessler. But there is an order to things that we must follow before any arrest can be made; if it even comes to that."

"If?" I say incredulously. I look to see a ring on his finger. Then I read his nametag. "I'm not sure you *do* understand, Officer Carson. Because if what happened out there had happened to your wife, you know as well as I do you'd already have the guy in cuffs. And I'll bet his face would be beaten to a bloody pulp, too. Am I wrong?"

The guy's jaw twitches and I know every word I said is true.

"Still, Mr. Kessler, we have men working to find out how the stadium's video feed was commandeered. And we'll need to interview your girlfriend. If she was the woman in the video, she'll be the one to press unlawful surveillance charges, not you. Even without her we should be able to pin him with a slew of charges, which may include extortion, computer trespass, unauthorized use of a computer, not to mention dissemination of lewd and lascivious material contributing to the delinquency of about five thousand minors. But that's the prosecutor's job, not mine. Best guess, if everything you told me is true, I'd say he will have one hell of a case against him and a nice stay in one of New York's finest prisons."

I see Drew slip in the door and nod his head to me—his sign that Murphy is okay and she got out of the park without incident.

I give Murphy's information to Officer Carson and then I call her so I can give her a head's up.

Drew eyes me in confusion. He pulls a phone out of his pocket, looking between me and it. He walks over to me with the ringing phone and shows it to me.

My goddamn picture is displayed on the phone he's holding. *I'm* calling that phone. Murphy's phone.

"What the hell?" I ask Drew.

He hands me the phone. "She told me to give it to you. Said it was yours." He pulls a hat out of his back pocket. "And she wanted you to have this, too."

My eyes close briefly before I look inside the hat to see which one it is. My fingers pinch the bridge of my nose as I absorb the gravity of the situation. She gave me back the phone I bought her. She doesn't want the hat.

She doesn't want *me.*

There is a little voice in the back of my head saying, *'Three strikes – you're out.'*

"Where did she go?" I ask Drew.

"I put her in a cab by herself. I don't know where it took her." He shakes his head. "Sorry, Mr. Kessler."

I get the attention of the owner. "Jason, I'd like to call a press conference."

He nods. "I think that would be a good idea. I'll do it with you. I'll apologize to the fans for the video and tell them we're doing everything we can to apprehend those responsible. Then I'll give you the floor and you can do what you need to do. I'll get the ball rolling and text you with the details. With the press already here, we should be able to set it up within the hour."

"Thank you. I'll go get a shower and see what I can find out before then."

Drew walks with me back to the clubhouse, keeping eager reporters from getting too close. They are itching to scoop the story. But I'm hoping to keep the damage to a minimum with the press conference.

I pull out my phone to call Ethan, finally taking time to glance at the unread text messages on my screen. One of them catches my eye.

> **Unknown: Time's up. Last chance. Before game time today.**

Shit.

I never check my phone on game days once I put it in my locker. I can't have the distraction. Between my pre-game workout and my music, he could have sent it hours before we took the field. I momentarily wonder how he got my private number. Then again, the guy just hacked into Hawks Stadium, so finding an unpublished number probably wasn't that hard for him.

I place a call to Ethan and tell him to do everything he can to keep the video off the internet. I tell him I don't care how much it costs, I want people on it around the clock until every last one is taken down.

Even though the video was only playing for a minute or two, I'm sure hundreds if not thousands of fans captured it with their phones. And Tony threatened to release it on the internet, so as far as I know, the entire video is already out there.

By the time I end the call, the game is over and my team trickles into the clubhouse. Most of them avoid me like the plague, not knowing what to say or how to say it. Some guys come over and give me a supportive pat on the back. Brady and Sawyer pull up chairs and sit down next to me.

"Where is she?" Sawyer asks.

"That's the million-dollar question," I say. I hold out her phone. "She left her phone. I can't even call her."

I explain to them how Tony came to me a few weeks ago and I discounted his threats.

"I would have done the same thing, Kess," Brady says. "You did nothing wrong."

I shake my head. "Oh, but I did. I fucked up. She thinks I lied to her and" —I scrub a hand across my jaw— "and I think she's done with me."

Our manager enters the clubhouse, slamming the door on his way in. He hands me a piece of paper that has a fine on it along with a seven-game suspension.

"Are you kidding me?" I yell after him as he walks away. "You're suspending me?"

Rick turns around. "It's the usual penalty for walking out of a game."

"The *usual* penalty?" I ask, dumbfounded. "Rick, there was nothing usual about what happened. The girl in that video is my girlfriend. The fucking love of my life. She's someone's daughter for Christ sake. What if that were *your* daughter up there?"

"My hands are tied, Caden."

Brady stands up. "If Kessler is suspended, consider me suspended as well."

Sawyer stands up too. "And me."

One by one, all my teammates stand up and cross their arms, putting up a front of solidarity. These guys are not just my teammates, they are family.

Just then, Jason walks in and looks around at everyone standing up in the room that is so silent you could hear a pin drop. "What's going on here?"

Brady takes the letter out of my hand and walks it over to the team owner.

Jason reads it and looks at Rick. "This is bullshit," he says, tearing the paper in half. "There will be no such injunction imposed against him. Understood?"

Rick doesn't look pleased to have been contradicted in front of the team, but he takes his lumps and leaves the room.

"Can you be ready in thirty minutes?" Jason asks. "The press is setting up now."

"I'll be there."

After my shower, I call everyone I know, including Murphy's mother, to see if I can find her. But no one has seen or heard from her.

No one.

~ ~ ~

Reporters are going wild with questions. They've been asked to back off more than once after Jason explained that someone hacked into the system but that we have no other information.

"Who was the man in the video?" a reporter asks.

I look over at Officer Carson and then our PR rep. Both told me that while I could ultimately be liable for what I say, there is hardly any question as to who is behind this.

"The man's name is Tony Fields," I say. "He is Murphy's ex-boyfriend. For six months, he's been trying to extort money from me in one way or another. When he came to me a few weeks ago, trying to blackmail me with a supposed sex tape, I thought he was lying. He had lied before and I had no reason to believe such a tape existed."

"Mr. Kessler, if you had known the tape was real, would you have paid Mr. Fields off?" a reporter asks.

I nod my head. "I like to think I wouldn't. I like to think I might have gone to the police and let them handle it. But that woman is my life." I look the older male reporter in the eye. "What would *you* have done?"

"Where is Miss Cavenaugh now?" another reporter asks.

"Where do you think she is?" I say. "She's been publicly humiliated in the worst way." I look directly into one of the cameras. "Murphy, if you are watching this, please reach out to me. I know you're hurting. I know you're mad at me for not telling you about his threats. I did what I did to protect you."

The room is abuzz. "You don't know where she is?" someone asks, shouting over the loud murmurs.

I shake my head. "I screwed up. I should have told her about Tony's threats, but I didn't. She has every right to be upset with me. Right now, she must feel like she can't trust anyone. Men especially." I look back into the camera. "Please, anyone who is listening, if you see her, don't laugh. Don't point. Don't make a spectacle out of her more than Fields already has. Murphy is strong, but this … this is enough to break anyone."

I take a few more questions and then Jason ends the press conference.

The police question me for another hour. Then Drew hands me his phone. "You should see this."

I press play and there is a video of women who have gathered outside the stadium. They are holding signs supporting Murphy and denouncing Tony and any man who violates a woman's right to privacy.

I wish she could see this. I want her to know that not everyone out there is going to ridicule her. That it could have happened to anyone. That she shouldn't be ashamed to show her face.

But I can't tell her any of that. Because she left.

I just hope to God she comes back. I hope she just needed some time to cool off and realize that I was only trying to do what I thought was right. I look around the stadium and let out a sigh. If I lose her, none of this will mean anything.

Baseball used to be my life. My one true love. The thing I couldn't live without.

What a difference that one person can make.

Chapter Forty-eight

Murphy

Mom comes up behind me, draping her arms over my shoulders when she kisses the top of my head. "You're going to have to talk to him sometime, honey. He's been calling and texting my phone for two days straight."

"Why?" I ask. "Why do I have to talk to him after what he did to me?"

She pulls up a kitchen chair and sits next to me. "I've talked to him, Murphy. And I understand what he did. He wants to keep you safe. He didn't want you to worry about it. He was taking care of you."

I try to rub the tension from my neck. "Is it possible to love and hate someone at the same time?"

"Absolutely," she says, taking my hand in hers. "For years after he died, I hated your father. I hated him for leaving us. I know it wasn't his fault, but when you're grieving, you need someone to blame. You are grieving, Murph. What happened to you was horrible. But we tend to blame those who are closest to us.

Tony is not around for you to hate, so maybe you've projected that hate onto Caden—the very man who would do anything for you."

"But he lied to me, Mom. And it's not the first time."

She shakes her head. "You've told me all about his so-called lies and to be honest, honey, I don't see any wrong-doing on his part."

"Mo-om," I pout.

"I'm on your side, Murph. I'm always on your side. That's why I am pushing for this. Caden makes you happy. I would give anything to have one more day with your father. You have the chance at a lifetime of days with the man you love. I don't want to see you throw that away."

I stand up and grab my jacket. "I'm going for a walk."

She follows me out the front door. "Don't forget the flowers," she says, nodding to the roses in her garden.

I look back and nod sadly at her before she retreats into the house. She knows where I'm going. She always knows where I'm going when I take a walk. I crouch down and break off a few stems at the base, careful not to prick myself. Then I make my way down the road to the cemetery.

"Murphy Cavenaugh, is that you?" I hear when I turn the corner.

I look over to see a familiar face from high school. "Hi, Matt."

Matthew Jenner was the star quarterback. The homecoming king. The most popular kid in school. Right up until he broke his leg in three places, ruining his chances at a college scholarship and landing him a management position at The Pit Stop—the local high school hangout.

"I didn't know you were back in town," he says, blatantly staring at the scar on my face. "Are you here for good?"

I shrug, not wanting to get into it if he hasn't seen my predicament pasted all over the news and social media. "I haven't decided yet."

"Where's your phone?" he asks. "I'll give you my number so you can hit me up while you're back. We can hang out like old times."

I nod at a friend of my mother's who walks into a coffee shop. Then I stare at Matt and wonder if he's lost his mind. "Matt, there were no 'old times.' In case you've forgotten, you wouldn't give me or my friends the time of day back in high school. Or even last year."

"That's not true," he lies. "Hey, why don't you and, what's your hot friend's name—Kelly? She still lives here, doesn't she? Why don't you and Kelly come over to my place this week? I'll get Davis to join us. You remember Davis? We can party."

Davis is another has-been football player who couldn't make it out of Okoboji.

"You're kidding, right? You want me to bring my dead friend to your house so we can party?"

He cringes. "Oh, shit. Was she the one who died in the bee attack?"

I shake my head and start walking away. "It wasn't a bee *attack*, it was one bee. She was allergic. And how did you not remember that—there's only eight hundred people in this town?"

Because apparently, even diner managers can be narcissistic pigs.

"Well, you can still come over yourself," he calls after me.

I wave my hand backwards, ending the conversation.

"You sure looked like a girl who likes to party when you were riding that dude's cock!" he yells.

My throat tightens as I look around to see who might have heard. A few ladies look at me in sympathy. Some teenagers don't even try to hide their laughter. Then Matt falls to the pavement after being punched in the face.

"Leave her the hell alone," Austin Helmsley says to him. "And go back to your grease pit."

"Douchebag," Matt says, rubbing his jaw as he walks away.

"Are you okay?" I ask Austin, looking at his injured hand.

"I should be asking you that, Murphy."

"I'm fine. Uh, thanks for that, I guess. But I can take care of myself."

I stare at him, trying to reconcile the person before me with the scrawny band geek I sometimes hung out with in high school. I haven't seen the guy in five years. He's almost unrecognizable now with his longer hair, his straight teeth and his … wow, all his muscles.

"I'm sure you can, but he was out of line." He laughs. "Plus, I've wanted to do that since middle school when he stuck my head in the toilet. So, I guess you could say that punch was as much for me as it was for you."

"Okay, well, I'd better go. I have somewhere to be."

"Murphy?" he calls after me.

I turn around and raise my eyebrows.

He nods to the coffee shop on the corner. "Can we get coffee one day this week? I'm only here until Friday and I'd love to catch up."

I think about the last few days being holed up in my mom's house. Then I look at the coffee shop and my mouth waters thinking about the epic pastries they make there. I glance down the street of this sleepy little town before looking back at Austin.

Coffee, Austin, Okoboji—they all seem so … wonderfully normal.

"Sure," I tell him. "Coffee would be nice. How about tomorrow morning at ten?"

He smiles. "I'll be here. Nice to see you again, Murphy."

~ ~ ~

"Hi, Daddy," I say, placing a rose into the vase attached to his headstone. I sit on the cold earth over his grave. "I've made a mess of things, haven't I?

"I know what you would tell me. You would remind me of the time I was in eighth grade and I tried out for the cheerleading squad. I thought anyone could be a cheerleader. I could do a cartwheel, so why not? I think you and Mom knew what I was in for, but you still didn't stand in my way. And then at try-outs, when I couldn't even do the splits or a jump-kick, I became the laughing-stock of the school. Girls mocked me for weeks. Every time I passed one of them in the hallway, they would mimic the kick I tried to do and everyone would laugh. They told me I was developmentally challenged and that I should be in a special class."

I pick at the grass that is just now starting to turn green. "You told me it was character-building. You said I could let it break me or make me stronger." I sigh, looking up at the cloudless sky. "But this is different, Daddy. Back then, I only had to deal with a few dozen middle-school students. *Everyone* has seen this." I shake my head and look back towards town. "Even people here know about it. *Here*, in nowhere, Iowa, where I was sure I'd be able to hide from it. The whole world knows about it, Daddy.

"Okay, fine. I know you would tell me that when I was thirteen, this town *was* my world and what happened to me back then seemed as horrible to me as this does now."

I look over at an older woman visiting her late-husband's grave. "Mom misses you," I tell him. "She told me this morning that she'd do anything for one more day with you." I rub my hand across the base of his headstone. "Would you be mad if she found someone else? I don't think you should be mad. The guy she's been seeing is nice, Daddy. But maybe you already know that. Do you know that? Do you know everything? Do you know what's going to happen to me?"

I kiss my fingers and touch them to his grave. Then I stand up and brush off the seat of my pants. "Bye, Daddy. I'll come back soon."

I walk to the other side of the cemetery and put my other rose into another headstone vase. "I could really use you right now, Kel. I need my best friend."

He's *your best friend, Cavenaugh*. Tears trickle down my cheek when I hear Kelly's words in my head.

"Is he?" I ask her. "Wouldn't a best friend have told me everything? Wouldn't a best friend have given me the choice of how to handle things?"

Johnny Davidson, I hear in my head.

"What? No, that's different. Johnny was a short little turd who dug your stained underwear out of the trash at school that day you got your first period. He was going to humiliate you, Kel. I couldn't let that happen. So, I offered to give him my lunch money for a month if he'd give them to me. *So* not the same thing. Wait—did you even know about that? I don't think I ever told you. I didn't even want you to *think* about what could have happened if he'd shown the entire school."

I look at her headstone and roll my eyes.

"Oh, shut up."

I spend the next half hour telling her about my run-in with Matt and Austin. I tell her about my job—the one I'm not sure I'm going back to. I tell her about my mom's new boyfriend. I tell her about everything except the one thing I really want to talk to her about. Caden.

Because I can't talk about him. I can't think about him. Not without hating him as much as I love him.

Chapter Forty-nine

Caden

Brady calls time and motions for me to come to the mound. "You might as well have been suspended, because you're not even in this damn game. Get it together, Kess."

I berate myself as I look down at the dirt. He's right. For days now, I haven't been able to concentrate. My mind has been anywhere but on this field. It's been at the police station, wondering how much progress they are making in the case against Tony. It's been at Ethan's agency, hoping they've tracked down every single video that made it to the internet. It's been in Okoboji, Iowa, praying the woman I love is finding what she needs so she can come back to me.

"You want me to pull myself out of the game?" I ask.

"No, Caden. I don't. But I do want you to get over your shit and help me out. You're making me look bad up here. It's not all about *you*. You're like my brother, man, but when you're out here, make it about *us*, not everything else going on in your life. This is your team. Your family. We're counting on you."

"You're right. I'm sorry, I know I've been distracted. I'll do better."

On my way back behind the plate, I find myself once again glancing up at the stands. I look behind the net over by the dugout to where she usually sits. Then I promise myself I'm not going to look over there for the rest of the game. If I already fucked up one part of my life, I sure as hell better not fuck up the other.

~ ~ ~

"I'm glad we were able to pull that one out," Brady says, patting me on the back after the game.

"Yeah, no thanks to me." I throw my batting helmet into my locker.

"You need a drink. Let's go out. Mills, you up for it?"

"Not tonight. I've got this thing with my cousin," Sawyer says.

"Another setup?" I ask.

He shrugs. "What can I say? He's good at finding chicks who don't care to be called the next day."

"I think they're called hookers," I joke.

Sawyer throws his shirt at me as those around us get a good laugh. "You two love-birds go have your drink. I'll have some girl shouting out my name by midnight."

"Don't forget your penicillin," I say, handing him back his shirt.

"Dude, I double wrap just like you do."

Then I frown, not able to come back with another joke because I'm thinking about *her* again. The woman I don't need to double-wrap for. The one woman who I wouldn't mind getting pregnant. Hell, I even wish she already was, that way she'd be more likely to come back to me.

Damn—that makes me a hypocritical douchebag, wanting to trap a woman that way.

"Hurry up, Taylor," I say on my way to the shower. "I really need that drink."

~ ~ ~

"Does it hurt?" Brady asks, slurring his words after five shots.

Even half-wasted, I know what he's asking. "Like hell," I tell him.

"That's nothing," he says, downing another shot. "The pain you feel right now? It's nothing compared to how you'd feel if you went after her, found her, married her, maybe had a couple of kids and then it all gets ripped to shreds. Because one minute you're happy and you're planning things like Easter egg hunts and costumes for the spring play and then in the blink of an eye it's all gone. All the planning, all your hopes and dreams for the future. Gone. Gone because of something you did. Something so fucking trivial …"

He takes another shot, his eyes glazing over, and I'm not even sure he's aware of what he's telling me.

He points at me. "So, get out, bro. Get out now before you're in so deep you can't come up for air."

"I can't get out, Brady. She *is* my fucking air."

I make a split-second decision and pick up my phone to make a call. "Melanie, I know it's late, but I need a huge favor. I need to get to Okoboji, Iowa in the morning. Get me the first flight out, I don't care how early. In and out the same day. Back by game time. I don't care what it costs. Can you do that?"

A half-hour and two shots later, Melanie texts me the details of my flights.

When curiosity gets the best of me and I can't stand it anymore, I finally ask the question that's been burning my brain. "Brady, do you have kids, man?"

"Kid," he clarifies. "As in one. And not *do. Did.*" He throws back another shot and slams the glass on the table. "I don't talk about it, Kessler. Not ever."

Damn. How did I never know this? He has a kid? *Had* a kid? What does that mean? Is the kid dead or just not in his life? So many more questions churn in my head, but with the way he's looking at me, I know better than to ask. He's already said more than he wanted to. More than he's ever said in the three years I've known him.

I get up to leave. "Can you find your way home? I have an early flight to catch."

~ ~ ~

I make my way to the gate and see Brady standing there with a smirk on his face.

"Why are you here and how did you get past security?"

He holds out his ticket for me to see. "I'm going with you. But I upgraded us to first class, screw that coach shit. You're paying, by the way. Your girl—your dime."

I smile, knowing that even if he disagrees with me, he's still got my back. But I have to know anyway. "Why the change of heart?"

He gives me a sad nod. "When I sobered up, I realized that you're already as wrecked as I am, so what could it hurt? Plus, you suck playing ball. And just so you know, we owe Melanie big time for keeping her up all night."

"I'll take care of it," I tell him. "Thanks for coming, Brady. I don't know what's waiting for me when I get to Iowa, but I sure do appreciate the support."

They call our flight and he nods his head towards the gate door. "Come on, let's go get your girl."

Chapter Fifty

Murphy

I walk into the coffee shop and see Austin sitting at a table in the front by the window.

He stands up and greets me. "Murphy, glad you could make it. Can I get you a coffee?"

"I'm getting coffee *and* a danish. They are so good here. But you're not buying."

"Right. Because you can take care of yourself," he says, jokingly, reiterating what I told him yesterday.

I laugh. "Something like that."

When we go back to his table, he takes the seat across from me. "You look great, Murphy. The past five years have been good to you."

"Thanks," I say, absently touching my scar. "You look good, too. I can't believe how much you've changed since high school."

He laughs. "I don't think I hit my growth spurt until I went away to college."

"Where did you end up going? I remember you saying you wanted to go out west."

"I did go out west. UCLA. In fact, I'm still there working on my MBA. I just finished spring semester so I decided to come home for a week for a change of pace."

I crane my neck to look out the window, and I chuckle. "Yeah, I guess this is about the opposite of both L.A. *and* New York. And, wow, a master's in business, that's great. I never made it past my A.A. But I still have a good job." I wipe an invisible spot on the table. "Or I did. I kind of left in a hurry."

He gives me a sad smile. "I'm really sorry about what's happening to you, Murphy. I can't imagine what you must be going through."

I close my eyes. "Please tell me you haven't seen it."

"I haven't. I heard about it on the news. I wouldn't sink so low as to try and find it on the internet. What you do behind closed doors is private and nobody's business. I hope they hang the guy who did it to you."

"Thanks for not watching it. I hope they hang him, too. I talked to the New York City police again this morning. They keep calling me to ask me the same questions over and over. They said he's going to be charged with a bunch of stuff. Something like three felonies and over five thousand misdemeanors."

"Five thousand?" he says, his jaw dropping.

"One for every minor who was in the stadium when he played the video. They said that in reality, those charges will boil down to one charge, but hopefully the other things will send him to jail."

"So, what are you going to do? Will you go back there? You have a good job and I know you're dating Caden Kessler."

I shrug. "I'm not sure what I'm going to do. I came here to get away, but it seems everyone here knows everything about me anyway. And I'm not sure I'm dating him anymore."

"Really?" He looks confused. "He wasn't mad at you for the video, was he? I saw the press conference he held. It didn't seem like he was mad at you at all."

I sigh. "Yeah. I saw it too. But it's complicated. There's more to it than that."

He laughs. "There always is, isn't there?" He looks behind me, out to the street, surprise overtaking his face. "Uh, Murphy, if you're not dating Caden Kessler anymore, why is he here in Okoboji?"

My heart thunders as I turn to see Caden and Brady standing on the sidewalk outside the coffee shop. Caden's eyes dart between Austin and me. His jaw twitches and he runs his hands through his hair.

"Austin, I really have no right to ask this of you, but I'm not ready to talk to him. Would you mind telling him I want to be left alone for a while? Tell him I'll call him when I'm ready."

He thinks about it for a second, his mind probably racing with thoughts of what could happen if he goes out that door and is confronted by two rather large professional baseball players.

"Please?" I beg.

He nods. "Okay." He stands slowly and makes his way out the door.

I watch Caden try to keep his cool as Austin presumably tells him to back off and give me some space. I wonder if he thinks we're on a date. Caden looks at me but I look away. Then Brady gets my attention and points to himself, I suppose asking if I'll talk to *him* if not Caden. I nod my head. He has some words with Caden, who looks frustrated if not pissed, and then Brady and

Austin come into the coffee shop, leaving a brooding Caden on the sidewalk.

I turn my chair so my back is to the window. I can't sit here and watch him stare at me.

"Are you okay with this?" Austin asks.

"Yeah."

"I'll be right over there if you need anything."

"Thanks, Austin."

Brady motions to the chair Austin was sitting in. "Mind if I sit?"

"Go ahead."

"I'm not very good at this kind of thing anymore," he says. "But that man out there loves you. He wants to protect you. And no matter what you say to him, he's always going to want to protect you."

I don't miss that his voice cracks while he's talking. It cracks as if he's speaking of something personal to him.

"Brady, I understand that. But there are ways he could have protected me without lying to me. Without going behind my back. How can we build a relationship if he keeps deceiving me?"

"He didn't deceive you, Murphy. God, why are females so infuriating sometimes? He didn't lie to you either. He did what he thought was best to protect you and keep you safe. And now you want to go and ruin what you two have? I've only known him for three years, but I've never seen him so happy. And now, since you left, I've never seen him so goddamn miserable. He can't even play ball. Did you know that? Have you bothered to watch any games to see what your leaving has done to him?"

"He's a grown man, Brady. I'm not responsible for his happiness. And I'm certainly not responsible for his job performance."

"That's bullshit," he says, raising his voice so that some patrons turn our way. "You two are the best couple I know. You guys live for each other. Hell, he told me last night that you are his fucking *air*. That's some deep shit, Murphy. He loves you. Like forever love. Take it from someone who had everything and then lost it—you want to hold onto what you have for as long as life will allow you to have it."

Tears well up in my eyes. Because those aren't the words of someone whose girlfriend left him. Those are the words of someone who's been destroyed by loss. And those are the eyes of someone who knows profound pain. I put my hand on his. "I'm so sorry you lost someone."

He nods sadly. "I lost two someones," he chokes out.

I motion out the door, to the cemetery he can't see. "I've lost two someones, too. My dad and my best friend."

He nervously plays with an invisible ring on his left ring finger. Oh, God. He lost a wife. And maybe even a child. A tear spills over my lashes.

Brady shakes his head like he doesn't want my sympathy. "Listen, nobody knows that but you and Caden. It's not something I want people to know."

"Of course, Brady. I won't say a thing."

"When you took off, you left a gaping hole in his heart. He looks for you in the stands, you know. Like somehow, he expects you to show up between innings. Every time he looks up there, he does it with hope in his eyes. And every time you aren't there, I swear a piece of him dies." He laughs and straightens his back. "Look at me, I'm carrying on like a damn girl."

I glance out the window over my shoulder to see Caden's eyes burning into me. I know he must be sorry. I know he's hurting. I'm hurting just as badly. My life has been turned upside down. I don't even know what my reality is anymore. I don't know what to expect when and if I show my face in New York.

"I need some more time, Brady. Can you please ask him to give me that? I love him. I do. I just need to figure out what's best for me."

"So, you won't talk to him?"

I shake my head. "I can't. Not right now. I'm sorry you flew all the way out here for nothing."

He gets up to leave. "It's not for nothing, Murphy. He's shown you how far he'll go to get you back. That man will do anything for you."

"Will he?" I ask, wondering if *anything* means keeping more secrets from me.

"If you have to ask me that, then you don't know him half as much as I thought you did."

He walks out the door and pulls Caden away by his elbow. I can see Caden resisting, but Brady convinces him to leave. He looks at me one last time and we lock eyes. He mouths *'I love you'* before turning to walk away.

I slump down in my seat and cry.

Austin comes over to check on me. "Are you okay?"

"No. But I'm not sure there's anything anyone can do about it."

He offers me his hand. "Come on, once the coast is clear, I'll walk you home."

We walk out the front door and I look down the street the opposite way of my house. "Thanks, Austin, but there are two people I need to go talk to. It was nice seeing you again. Good luck in grad school."

We say our goodbyes and then I walk down the street, hoping I can find somewhere to stop and get two roses.

~ ~ ~

I don't have my phone, so I'm not sure how long I've been sitting here—hours maybe—when someone touches my shoulder. I look up to see Caden's dad. I had forgotten he was coming to town today. He flies out twice a month to see my mother and she travels to New York on the weekends he doesn't come here.

"Hey, kiddo," Shane says. "I heard you might be here. I hope you don't mind if I sit with you for a minute."

I motion to the ground next to me. "So, you saw him?"

"I did. We crossed paths at your mom's house before he went back to the airport." He pulls a small envelope from his pocket. "He left you this. Your mother thought you'd want to read it while you were here. She wanted to bring it to you, but I asked if I could. I thought maybe your dad and I should be properly introduced."

I look at Shane, studying him for a minute as he stares at my father's grave.

"You love her, don't you?"

He gives me a sad smile. "Would it be okay if I did?"

I look at the headstone and then back at Shane. I think my dad would approve. And I know he'd want her to be happy. I nod my head.

"Well then, I don't mind telling you that I'm a very lucky man," he says. "I've been fortunate enough to have the love of several incredible women in my life. But Murphy, that kind of love doesn't happen often. The kind of love you and my son share. I know he hurt you. But it's a fact of life that lovers will hurt each other eventually. It's how you deal with that hurt that matters. Life isn't always fair. People aren't always perfect."

He stands up and touches my father's grave almost as if he's shaking my dad's hand. He starts to walk away, but hesitates. "You told me not so long ago that if things come easily, they aren't worth having. You said it's the hard wins that are the most important." He nods back towards my dad's grave. "That man raised one hell of a daughter."

Long after he's gone, I sit and stare at the small envelope in my hands. My legs have gone numb by the time I finally open it.

Murphy,

I've only ever loved two things in my life. Baseball and you. I never thought anything would be more important to me than being out on that field. But here's the thing, and some days I can't even wrap my mind around it—I love you more. I love you more than baseball. And I would give it up in a second if it's the only way to have you. If being in New York, being in the spotlight because of my career, is too hard after what happened, we'll move. We'll move to Okoboji if you want. Or to some island where we can live away from TV and internet.

Nothing else matters if I can't be with you, Murph. Just say the word and we're gone.

I'm done apologizing. And the truth is, if it happened again, I can't say I wouldn't do the same thing. Because I will go to the ends of the Earth to protect what's mine.

Please say you're mine.

Because I'm sure as hell yours. Every damn piece of me. You own me, Sweet Caroline.

Come back to me.

Caden

Hot tears stream down my cheeks. *He's willing to give up his dream for me?*

My father's words of advice echo through my head as I can barely see his headstone through my blurred vision. Even from the grave, he's taking care of me. "Thanks, Daddy," I say, wiping my tears. "I have to go now. I have a baseball game to get to."

Chapter Fifty-one

Caden

I sit on my chair, looking at the black velvet box in my locker, debating just leaving the ring here. Why bother putting it in my pocket if the girl it's meant for will never wear it? Maybe it's not good luck after all.

She didn't call me today. I thought for sure she'd call me after she read the letter. I don't know what else I can do. I poured my heart out to her. I crossed the country for her. If I thought it would help, I'd fly back there tonight. But she made it clear she didn't want to see me.

It took all my strength to stand outside that coffee shop window when Brady was with her. I had to muster every bit of willpower to walk away when she was sitting just ten feet from me. It almost killed me to get back on that plane without her.

I open the box and take out the ring. I put it on the tip of my pinky finger and study it. I didn't get a large, ostentatious ring like some players might. I knew Murphy wouldn't want that. But I did make sure it was a perfect, flawless diamond. Because despite the scars she has—the ones I don't even see—*she* is perfect and flawless.

Sawyer pats me on the back. "She'll come around, Kess."

"You good?" Brady asks.

I know he's not asking if my heart is okay. He wants to make sure my *head* is. That I can keep my private business off the field, or at the very least, use my grief for the greater good of the team.

"I got your back, Taylor. Don't worry."

He looks at the ring I'm holding and I'm pretty sure he thinks I'm full of shit. Maybe I am. But then I remember what Brady has lost. I still don't know the details because he hasn't expanded upon what he told me last night. Whatever happened to him was obviously horrific, however, and it makes me feel like a dick thinking he got through it and can still be at the top of his game but I'm acting like a whiny little girl.

"Bring it in!" our coach yells from the center of the room.

I throw the box into my locker and stick the ring in my back pocket. Who did I think I was kidding? I knew I would. I'm having an incredible season. My best one yet, the past three games notwithstanding.

When I take the field with my team, I can't help myself. As I walk behind the plate, I look up in the stands. Girls scream my name when my eyes scan the section Murphy normally sits in. I see Scott, who is staying with Lexi while my dad is in Iowa. I nod at them and Lexi gives me a sad smile. She knows it's not them I was hoping to see.

Brady comes up behind me on his way to the mound. "Let's do this," he says, holding his glove out.

I tap his glove with mine. "Let's do this."

When we get to the top of the sixth and we're up by three, I feel like maybe I've gotten my mojo back as we take the field. I can do this. I can make baseball the most important thing again.

I don't even realize it when I glance up at the stands once more. But then I blink, because I'm sure I'm seeing things.

She's here.

I can't even help it when I stop and stare. Our eyes lock together and I watch it happen. I watch as a brilliant smile curves her lips. And as the smile gets bigger, my heart gets lighter. She came back. And she's *here.* I never thought she'd set foot in this stadium again. How could she after what happened to her?

Then I want to kick myself when it dawns on me that everyone in the stadium is looking to see what I'm staring at. My eyes shoot to the JumboTron to see the cameras focused on her. But she's not looking at the massive screen. She's looking at me. She gives me her usual thumbs up and blows me a kiss, and just like that, I know everything will be okay.

And then, while the stadium has quieted down, someone yells, "Stay strong, Murphy!"

The umpire taps me on the shoulder, reminding me I still have a job to do. I step behind the plate, unsure if I've ever played ball with a bigger smile on my face. Brady nods at me even before I give him the sign. He nods because he knows my prayers have been answered.

I give him the sign for a breaking ball. I need this game to be over and his breaking ball is the fastest way I know to get that done.

After three up and three down, Spencer gets up to bat and hits a hard ground ball to left field for a double. Then it's my turn.

I don't look at her as I take my up. I can't have the distraction. Just knowing she's here is enough. I rub my tattoo as I step up to the plate. I foul off four balls to the left. Then, on the fifth pitch, he throws me a fastball. My favorite pitch. I hear the sound. I feel it in my hands. I close my eyes briefly as I fling the bat behind me and jog my way around the bases.

When I round third base and I'm heading for home, I find her in the crowd. Just before I reach home plate, I pound on my chest, right over my heart, and then I point to her. I think she's crying. But I can't be sure, because, damn it, I just might be crying, too.

~ ~ ~

I take the quickest shower in history in my haste to get to her. When I emerge from the clubhouse, camera flashes blind me. Reporters fire questions at me as I make my way over to where Murphy is waiting with Lexi and Scott.

Thankfully, I see that Drew is already on top of things, keeping reporters away from her. Everyone wants a piece of her. People want to know how she's handling being front-page news. I can't believe she showed up here. She had to have known this would happen.

Before I get to her, a woman shouts over the crowd. "Stay strong, Murphy! Don't let that bastard ruin you. Not many people could show their face after what he did to you. You go, girl!"

Women start chanting, *"Stay strong. Stay strong."*

Murphy turns bright red. Damn, she's adorable when she blushes.

I sweep her into my arms, not caring how many people are taking pictures. I want the world to know I'm behind her one hundred percent.

I kiss her before we even say a word. Her lips taste better than I remember.

I pull away and stare into her alluring eyes.

"Hi," she says shyly.

"Hi, yourself."

Her eyes get misty. "I have so much I want to say …"

I nod. "Me too. Come home with me?"

"Yes."

A smile overtakes my face. "Drew, can you please find us some transportation?"

"Right this way," he says, motioning for us to follow him.

"Lexi, can we drop you and Scott along the way?"

She laughs. "I wouldn't dream of it, little brother. We can find our own way home."

We say our goodbyes and let Drew usher us away.

~ ~ ~

When we walk through the door to my apartment, all I want to do is take her in my arms. But we need to talk. We didn't talk in the cab. That wasn't the right place. We didn't even talk in the elevator. But she did let me hold her hand. And she did smile a lot.

"I'm sorry," we say at the same time and then laugh about it.

"You have nothing to be sorry for, Murph. What happened to you is unimaginable. You needed a minute to take a breath. And if you need longer than a minute, that's okay. Just say where you want to go and I'll take you there. I meant it when I said we could leave New York."

"You are not quitting baseball, Caden. But you offering to is why I'm here."

I motion for her to sit at the bar while I open a bottle of wine. "You might need to help me understand that," I say.

"I wish you could have met my dad. He was wonderful. He always had so many words of wisdom to offer. Words that didn't mean much to me at the time, but now I understand."

I hand her a glass and sit next to her. "I wish I could have met him, too."

"When I was little, he would warn me about boys. He would tell me that a lot of boys will say things to get you to like them, but when it came right down to it, most boys were not willing to change for a girl. He said the only way to know if a boy really loves you is if he's willing to give up his dreams for you. He said when that happened, I would know I'd found the right one." Her eyes fill with tears and she starts to choke up. "Then he told me that the way I'd know I truly loved him is that I would never let him do it."

I pull her onto my lap and wipe her tears. "Damn, I love your father."

"Me too," she says, nodding. "He's right, Caden. I love you. I love you more than I thought I could love anyone. And I would never let you give up baseball. It's what makes you *you.* It's what brought us together. And when I really thought about it, I realized I don't care what anyone else thinks. If people want to watch me and that loser have sex, they are sick and twisted and aren't worthy of me caring in the least."

"I love you too, babe. More than you could ever know. And you don't have to worry, Ethan is pretty sure we got all the videos taken off the internet."

"Really?" she asks, looking surprised. "You can do that? You *did* that?"

"We sure as hell did. Nobody gets to see my girl that way except me. And I've got a lot of people working to make sure that prick goes to prison for what he did to you."

She sighs and I can feel some of the tension leaving her body. "Thank you, Caden."

I cup her chin with my hand. "Don't you know by now that I'll do anything for you?"

"Anything?" she asks with a sultry grin.

I laugh. "Just name it."

"Take me to bed, Kessler, and I'll tell you exactly what to do."

I immediately spring to life underneath her. Then I get up, lifting her into my arms before I carry her down the hallway.

She giggles as I practically run back to my bedroom. "Don't drop me," she jokes.

"Never."

I put her down on the bed and take a minute to look at her.

"What is it?" she asks when I don't immediately climb on the bed with her.

I shake my head. "I wasn't sure I'd ever have you in my life again, let alone my bed. I'm a very fortunate man."

Her hand moves up to her face and she runs a finger across her scar. "I'm the fortunate one."

I crawl on top of her and lean down to kiss her. I kiss her scar. Her cheeks. Her neck. She's moaning beneath me before I even get to her lips. And when I do, she grabs the back of my head and holds me to her. We kiss each other breathless. We make each other understand that the words we've spoken are truer than any other words.

"Please, Caden," she begs, squirming under me.

I smile as I hastily remove my clothes and then take my sweet time removing hers. I peel her top off, kissing and licking inch by inch of her stomach as I do. I unclasp her bra and take her glorious breasts into my hands and then into my mouth. I unbutton her jeans and remove them slowly, taking care to give attention to every curve of her legs.

"I plan to take my time with you and make you come in every way possible. But right now, I need to be inside you. I need to feel you and know you're mine."

"Yes." She reaches over to my nightstand but I pull her arm back.

"Murph, I want to feel you with nothing between us. Is that okay? We've both been tested and you're still on the pill, aren't you?"

She nods, a slow smile creeping up her face. "What if I try and trap you, Kessler?"

I laugh, leaning down to devour her neck with my mouth. But before I do, I whisper in her ear. "I've never wanted anything more."

My hand wanders down her soft skin and through her fine curls to find her wet for me. I slip a finger inside her and run my thumb across her clit. Her breath catches and she moans under my ministrations. I work my fingers faster on her until I know she's on the brink. Then I climb on top of her and glide myself in, reveling in the incredible feeling of flesh on flesh.

"Jesus, Murph."

I have to control myself so I don't come too quickly. But the sensation of having nothing between us is almost too much for me to take. The sweet friction builds inside me like a tsunami, and I'm about to explode. I stop moving and reach up to grab both sides of her head. "I love you, Murphy Brown," I say, looking into her eyes as our bodies are joined in the most intimate way possible.

"The way I feel …" she chokes up as tears pool in her eyes. She reaches her hands around me to thread her fingers through my hair. "Love is not a strong enough word, Caden."

That did it. This woman owns me lock, stock, and barrel. If I had the ring with me, I'd propose to her right this very second. But I left it in my locker—the same place it's been since the first day I put it in my pocket.

"It'll always be you," I tell her. "It'll always be *us*." Then I let myself go as I reach a hand between us and make sure she is right there with me.

Our salacious cries echo off my walls as we drag every last ounce of pleasure from each other. I collapse down on top of her, thanking my lucky stars she came back to me.

When I catch my breath, I rise onto my elbows. "I hope you slept on the plane, because you aren't getting any sleep tonight."

She giggles and looks around my room. "I like it here," she says. "Mind if I stay?"

"Stay the night? Hell no, I don't mind." I wink at her. "I wasn't planning on letting you leave until I'm done with you."

She looks up at me with her gorgeous blue eyes. "Not just the night. I was thinking I might stay a little longer than that if the offer still stands."

I study her in astonishment. "You want to move in with me?"

She nods. "I was just waiting for Trick to find a new roommate and now she has. I always wanted to move in with you, Caden."

"Damn." I smile down on her and shake my head. "You sure do know how to make a guy work for it."

"I'm sorry," she says, looking guilty. "I wanted it to be a surprise. Plus, I think I needed to be sure."

"And are you?" I ask.

"I am. Thanks to my dad."

"He raised one hell of a daughter."

She cocks her head to the side. "That's what your dad said."

"My dad talked to you about your father?"

"He came to the cemetery to meet him. And to get my blessing."

My jaw drops. "Did you give it to him?"

"Yeah. My mom deserves to be happy and so does he."

"Do you think they're as happy as we are, Murph?"

"No," she says, more tears spilling from her eyes. "Because I'm one-hundred-percent sure that nobody is as happy as we are."

I kiss away her tears. "I'm going to show you just how happy I am," I tell her. "I'm going to show you all night long … and then every single day after that."

Chapter Fifty-two

Murphy

It's a relief that the Nighthawks were on the road for a full week after I came back. One: it gave me a chance to ease back into New York City without being in the spotlight; and two: I was able to move in and put my touch on Caden's place. Uh … *our* place.

He gave me carte blanche. Told me anything I desired would be okay with him. But all I really wanted to do was add something to the one bare wall of his theater room. And now, it's decorated with the hats he's given me over the past seven months—each with a date inside coinciding with a memory we won't ever want to forget. I hung each hat on a nail, that, once I have enough collected, will spell out the word LOVE. But at the moment, it looks more like LC, because I need one more hat to complete the circle of the second letter. Yes, he'll probably think it's sappy, but that's what he gets for asking a chick to move in with him.

Today, however, the Hawks are back in town and a group of us are making our way to our seats in the stadium. Even my mother is here. She no longer stays with me when she comes to town. She stays with Shane. Even Scott seems to be okay with it for which we are all grateful. He and I have had some meaningful heart-to-heart conversations about losing a parent at a young age. It's a club nobody wants to belong to. But it has taken our bond to a whole new level.

"So, they didn't fire you?" Scott asks. "You still work at the gym?"

I laugh. "No, they didn't fire me. I think they understood that I needed a few personal days. It's a great place to work."

"Do you think I could work there when I get older?" he asks.

I ruffle his hair. "You bet. When you turn sixteen, you could work in the café."

"Cool," he says. "I want to save up a bunch of money and go to a good college with a great baseball team so I can be a Hawk someday."

I can't help my smile. The kid is humble, I will say that. He doesn't want for much, especially now that he has Caden watching over him, but he expects nothing. I think he sees that with hard work and dedication, anything is possible. He has two perfect examples of that in his father and Caden.

"Are you seeing this, Murphy?" my mother asks, with wide eyes.

I look around us to see what she's talking about. Several women are wearing identical shirts. Shirts with *my* name on them. Shirts that read *'Murphy Strong'* in Hawks colors.

"Oh, my gosh!" I stop walking and watch others pass by, seeing dozens of them.

I look at my mother. "I don't understand. Why would they do this?"

She puts her arm around me. "Murphy, don't you realize you are a role model now? You took the worst experience in your life and gave it your middle finger. Less than a week after you were humiliated, you came here—to the very place that could have ruined you. You've shown women they don't have to be defined by bad experiences. That it's how you deal with those experiences that shows the world who you really are."

I look at her, confused by her uncharacteristic words of wisdom.

She shrugs and leans over to whisper in my ear. "Your father rubbed off on me, what can I say?"

Some of the t-shirt-wearing women see me and smile. Some shout out their praises to me. One even asks me to sign her shirt. I'm dumbfounded by the outpouring of support. I'm grateful that I no longer need to fear the place where I plan on spending every moment I can watching Caden follow his dream.

"Hey!" Lexi shouts to one of the women. "Where can I get one of those?"

"They are selling them by the east entrance," she tells her.

"I'll meet you at our seats," Lexi says.

"Really?" I raise my disbelieving eyebrows at her.

"So, sue me. It could be a collector's item one day. You want one, Irene?"

My mother gets out her purse and gives Lexi some money. "Get me a couple of them."

"Get me one, too, Lex!" Scott shouts after her.

I eye him skeptically.

"It's not like I'm gonna wear it or anything," he says.

Shane and my mom laugh as we continue on our way.

Once in our seats, I see the real magnitude of the situation. Women wearing the shirts are everywhere. It's not just dozens of them, or even hundreds. It's thousands.

Tears sting the backs of my eyes.

Shane puts a fatherly arm around me. "I'm proud of you, Murphy. I couldn't have hand-picked a better woman for my son."

"Thanks, Shane. That means a lot to me."

When Lexi comes back wearing one of the shirts, I roll my eyes.

"What?" she says. "Don't you think it looks good on me?"

"It looks ridiculous," I tease.

"Nonsense," my mother adds. "You've started a revolution, my girl."

Shane takes a shirt from Lexi and studies it. "Books will be written about you."

"Oh, my gosh!" Lexi squeals. "I'll bet Baylor Mitchell will write a romance novel about your love story. I mean, the way you two met and then this. And who knows what else will happen."

Lexi shares a look with my mom and Shane. Shane winks at her.

I eye all of them curiously. "What?" I ask. "You guys look like you have a secret. Oh, God—Baylor isn't really writing a book about us, is she?"

"I have no idea," Lexi says. "All I'm saying is that I would totally buy it."

When the Hawks take the field, Caden looks up at me. He usually doesn't do that. But he looks nervous today, like maybe he wasn't sure I'd be here. Which is silly, because I already blew him a kiss when he was in the dugout.

When the game starts, however, he's nothing but a machine. He makes his plays expertly. He doesn't look into the stands. He's back to being himself again. He looks so at home down on the field. So happy. It's where he belongs. I couldn't imagine him giving that up for me.

Lexi catches me wiping a tear. She looks up at the scoreboard, then back at me. "Come on, let's hit the bathroom, your mascara is running."

"I don't want to miss anything," I tell her. "I'll wait until the stretch."

"You know how busy the bathrooms get then. We should go now." She's tugging on my arm as she scoots past the others. "Come on, Murphy."

I'm not sure why she's so adamant that we go now. Maybe she really needs to pee. Or maybe my face really does need a touch-up.

When we return to our seats, the game is tied 3-3. Brady is up to bat. Caden tells me that pitchers aren't usually very good hitters, but Brady is good. He hasn't had as many home runs as Caden, but he does get on base a lot.

As I watch him at the plate, I think about what he told me at the coffee shop. That he lost two people. I wonder if that's why he is the way he is. I vow to try and get closer to him. Maybe he'd open up to a woman who is a friend. My mind goes crazy with ideas of how I can make that happen.

I guess I lost track of time, because I don't even notice when the seventh-inning-stretch starts. But what pulls me from my thoughts is when I hear a song blasting over the loudspeakers.

I turn to Lexi, who has a huge smile on her face. "I thought they didn't play this song here," I say.

"They don't," she tells me, looking like she's about to burst. "Not ever."

I look around, confused as '*Sweet Caroline*' plays in Hawks Stadium for perhaps the first time. Then I become horrified as I look at the JumboTron to see my face plastered on it. I grab Lexi's arm.

"It's okay, Murphy." She nods to the field in front of us.

When I look down, I see Caden walking over in our direction. I'm more than a little concerned that he's left the dugout during a game. I notice he's rubbing his right shoulder blade where his tattoo is. It's something he only does before he goes to bat. He motions for me to come to the wall. I shake my head. I don't know what he's doing, but he's acting very strange.

He laughs at my apprehension.

"Go," Lexi prods me.

I make my way down the four rows and lean into the net separating us. "What are you doing, Caden?"

He lifts up the net and asks a few guys to hold it. Then he reaches over the half-wall and lifts me over, pulling me onto the field. All the while, the stadium is going crazy singing the song that never gets played here.

"Have you lost your mind?" I shout as he puts me down so I'm standing in front of him.

He laughs again. "I think I have," he says. "But in a good way." He looks up at the large screen that shows me the cameras are still focused on us. "I wanted you to have a good experience here, because I hope you will be spending a lot of time in this stadium."

"Caden, I told you, I don't care what other people think. I'm going to be here for you no matter what."

He nods. "And that's just one of the reasons I love you, Murphy Brown."

He reaches into his back pocket and pulls something out. Then he drops to a knee and the stadium goes wild. My heart lodges in my throat and I lose all my breath. I look up at Lexi and my mom, who are both crying. I look down at Caden, whose eyes are locked on me as I come to grips with what is happening.

My hand covers my mouth when I see the ring in his hand. Tears stream down my face as I forget about the noise, the JumboTron, the forty thousand people watching. Nothing else matters except this man before me.

I drop down to my knees in front of him, knowing he'd have to yell otherwise.

"I've been wanting to do this for months," he says loudly, so I can hear him over the crowd. "I got this when I was in Florida. But I knew even before then that you were the one. Murphy, the day I hit you with my ball was the best day of my life." He runs a finger across my scar. "I love your scar because it's what makes you mine. I love your heart because it's what makes you compassionate. I love your mind because it's what makes you strong. I love everything about you. So, what do you say, Sweet Caroline, will you marry me?"

I have no words. All I can do is nod over and over as I stare at him with tear-blurred eyes. He slips the ring on my finger and then he stands up, pulling me with him and into his arms as he swings me around to the cheers of the crowd. He kisses me. He kisses me hard and long.

When our lips finally part, he nods to the screen. "This is one video I want the entire world to see."

He kisses me once more and then sits me back on the wall.

"I love you, Kessler," I tell him.

"I love you too, Murphy Brown." He glances over his shoulder at the dugout, where his team is watching and cheering. "But I kind of have a job to finish up here."

I laugh as he slowly backs away. But then he shakes his head and jogs back to me. "Shit, I almost forgot. I need the ring back."

I wrinkle my brow in confusion.

"I've had that ring in my back pocket all season, Murph. And it's been the best season of my life. I'm not about to screw that up now. You can have it on that pretty little finger of yours every other minute of the day—but during game time, it's mine. In case you didn't know, you're marrying a ball player. Our crazy superstitions come with the territory."

I happily remove the ring and give it to him. Then he takes his hat off and puts it on my head. "If I'm not mistaken, this one will complete the circle." He winks at me and then turns around to join his team.

Lexi and my mother pull me in for a long embrace when it dawns on me. "You knew about this, didn't you?" I ask them. I turn to my mother. "You *never* come to games."

"We knew," she admits. "And I guess I'll be coming to a lot more, now that my future son-in-law is a star catcher."

"I'd love for you to come to more games when you're in town, Mom."

She looks over at Shane and then back to me. "What if I were in town *all* the time?" she asks.

My jaw drops. "You're moving here?"

She smiles. "Would that be okay, honey?"

I pull her in for another hug. "That would be great, Mom!"

Lexi squeals in delight. "Oh, we will have so much fun planning your wedding."

I look at the woman who has become my best friend and think of how Kelly would have loved her. "I know it's kind of early, but Lexi, would you be my Matron of Honor?"

We're both crying when she wraps her arms around me. "There is no one else I'd rather have as a sister. Of course I'll stand up with you."

It's hard to concentrate on the game after what has happened. I only hope Caden isn't having the same problem. When it's his turn at bat, my body stiffens and my heartbeat shoots through the roof.

He fouls a ball to the left. Then he steps out of the batter's box and looks over at me. He pounds his chest and points at me. And for the second time today, the crowd goes wild. The stadium is as loud as I've ever heard it. The energy around me is palpable. I can barely contain my emotions as I lock elbows with both Lexi and my mother.

Then I watch my future husband step up to the plate.

Crack!

Epilogue

Murphy

Two years later …

Caden does his best to wrap his arms around me as I run my fingers across the bills of the hats displayed on our wall. The word is almost complete now and I wonder what will come next. What wonderful adventures does our future hold?

I wince and he turns me around to face him. "I felt that," he says, rubbing my belly. "Which one was it, Caroline or CayJay?"

I laugh at his nickname for Caden, Jr. "CayJay?"

"Yeah, it's a great baseball name, don't you think? CayJay Kessler."

"I thought we agreed on C.J."

He shrugs and then plants a kiss on my cheek. "Whatever you want, Kessler," he says to me. "But think about it. I bet the name will grow on you."

I lean in to give him one heck of a pre-game kiss. The twins protest when they get smashed between us, and one or both of them starts kicking again.

Caden laughs, feeling the kicks against his stomach. He kneels down in front of me and talks to my belly. "Listen up, you two. I know you are eager to come out and see what an amazing mom you have, but if you can wait one more week, I'd be most grateful."

I smile down on him and run my fingers through his hair. "Maybe next time, you shouldn't get your wife pregnant in the off-season," I say.

"Next time?" he says, looking at me hopefully.

I shrug as I flash him a playful grin.

He plants one more kiss on me before leaving for his game.

I call out after him. "Aren't you forgetting something, Kessler?" I take my engagement ring off and hold his good luck charm out to him. "You don't think you're going to win the World Series without this, do you?"

He comes back over and takes the ring. "Don't you know, Murphy Brown? I've already won."

Coming soon, Brady's story

Benching Brady

Acknowledgements

Catching Caden was a lot of fun to write. Mainly because I'm a baseball mom. For the past three years, my husband and I have spent countless hours carpooling kids, watching baseball and traveling the country with our 12-year-old son. This last year, in particular, was special because we got to go to Cooperstown, NY, so Ryan could play in a once-in-a-lifetime baseball tournament with his team. And to top it off – he hit his first home run there!

It was while watching endless hours of baseball this year that I came up with stories for Caden, Brady and Sawyer.

I couldn't have written this book without the help of baseball coach and former MLB player, Talmadge "T" Nunnari, whose expertise in all things baseball made this book believable.

I also have to thank my medical expert, Dr. Brandon Crawford, for your guidance on Murphy's injury. You were very patient with me while I made you take me through every detail of her recovery.

Thank you to my beta readers, Tammy Dixon, Laura Conley, and Joelle Yates. You all contribute greatly to making my books a better read.

Much appreciation to my hard-working editors, Ann Peters and Jeannie Hinkle, who work tirelessly to make sure my novels are in tip-top shape.

And lastly, thank you to my readers. None of this would be possible without you.

About the author

Samantha Christy's passion for writing started long before her first novel was published. Graduating from the University of Nebraska with a degree in Criminal Justice, she held the title of Computer Systems Analyst for The Supreme Court of Wisconsin and several major universities around the United States. Raised mainly in Indianapolis, she holds the Midwest and its homegrown values dear to her heart and upon the birth of her third child devoted herself to raising her family full time. While it took time to get from there to here, writing has remained her utmost passion and being a stay-at-home mom facilitated her ability to follow that dream. When she is not writing, she keeps busy cruising to every Caribbean island where ships sail. Samantha Christy currently resides in St. Augustine, Florida with her husband and four children.

You can reach Samantha Christy at any of these wonderful places:

Website: www.samanthachristy.com

Facebook: https://www.facebook.com/SamanthaChristyAuthor

Twitter: @SamLoves2Write

E-mail: samanthachristy@comcast.net